THE NINJA'S DAUGHTER

ALSO BY SUSAN SPANN

Claws of the Cat

Blade of the Samurai

Flask of the Drunken Master

THE
NINJA'S
DAUGHTER

A HIRO HATTORI NOVEL

SUSAN SPANN

SEVENTH STREET BOOKS®
AN IMPRINT OF PROMETHEUS BOOKS
59 JOHN GLENN DRIVE • AMHERST, NY 14228
www.seventhstreetbooks.com

Published 2016 by Seventh Street Books®, an imprint of Prometheus Books

Cover design by Nicole Sommer-Lecht
Cover image © Media Bakery
Cover design © Prometheus Books

Inquiries should be addressed to
Seventh Street Books
59 John Glenn Drive
Amherst, New York 14228
VOICE: 716–691–0133 • FAX: 716–691–0137
WWW.SEVENTHSTREETBOOKS.COM

20 19 18 17 16 • 5 4 3 2 1

Library of Congress Cataloging-in-Publication Data

Names: Spann, Susan, author.
Title: The ninja's daughter : a Hiro Hattori novel / Susan Spann.
Description: Amherst, NY : Seventh Street Books, 2016. | Series: A Shinobi mystery
    ; 4
Identifiers: LCCN 2016009170 (print) | LCCN 2016023062 (ebook) |
    ISBN 9781633881815 (softcover) | ISBN 9781633881822 (ebook)
Subjects: LCSH: Ninja—Fiction. | Samurai—Fiction. | Murder—Investigation—
    Fiction. | Kyoto (Japan)—History—16th century—Fiction. | BISAC:
    FICTION / Mystery & Detective / Historical. | FICTION / Mystery &
    Detective / Police Procedural. | GSAFD: Mystery fiction. | Historical fiction.
Classification: LCC PS3619.P3436 N56 2016 (print) | LCC PS3619.P3436 (ebook)
    | DDC 813/.6—dc23
LC record available at https://lccn.loc.gov/2016009170

Printed in the United States of America

For Sandra. Thank you for believing, both in Hiro and in me.

CHAPTER 1

Knocking echoed through the silent house.

Hattori Hiro sat up in the darkness and pushed his quilt aside. His cat, Gato, tumbled to the floor. She mewed in protest.

Careful footsteps passed the door to Hiro's room. He recognized the pace of Ana, the housekeeper who cooked and cleaned for the Portuguese priest whose home they shared. Her rapid response told Hiro sunrise must be close at hand. Only a person already awake and dressed would reach the door so quickly.

"Hm. Unreasonable hour for visitors." Ana's irritated mutter carried through the walls.

Her footsteps faded into the entry. Moments later, Hiro heard the creak of a door and Ana asking, "What do you want?"

"My name is Jiro," a male voice said. "Please . . . I need to see the foreign priest."

Hiro crossed his room and opened the paneled door to hear more clearly. Unexpected visitors brought news, but also threats, and though most people thought him merely a translator, Hiro was also a *shinobi*— a ninja spy and assassin—hired to protect the priest.

"Return at sunrise," Ana said. "Father Mateo is asleep."

"I beg you," Jiro said, "please let me in. I cannot wait for dawn."

The paneled door beside Hiro's room slid open with a muted rattle.

"It's all right, Ana," Father Mateo called, "please show him in."

Hiro shut his door, slipped on his favorite gray kimono, and wrapped an *obi* around his waist. He checked the samurai knot atop his head. As he expected, not a hair lay out of place.

Dressed and ready, he entered the common room.

Father Mateo knelt by the hearth, across from the man who called himself Jiro.

The visitor had gangly arms and narrow shoulders that tapered to bony wrists. His skinny hands protruded from his sleeves like twigs from a bank of snow. He wore a fine but faded kimono that seemed to be recently slept in, and his close-cropped hair stuck out at odd angles above a slender face that Hiro recognized at once.

Jiro was the apprentice of a prosperous merchant and moneylender who owned a shop in Kyoto's Sanjō Market. Hiro and Father Mateo had met the youth, and his master, while investigating the murder of a brewer several weeks before.

As he walked to the hearth, Hiro wondered why his investigations returned to haunt him like hungry ghosts. He hadn't come to Kyoto to help the families of murdered strangers, and although he enjoyed the hunt for a killer, it attracted more attention than he liked.

Father Mateo smiled at Jiro. "Good morning. Aren't you Basho's apprentice?"

"Yes, sir." Jiro bowed his head. "I feared you wouldn't remember me. Please, I need your help."

Ana stood near the entrance, watching the youth with a wrinkled frown that made her opinion perfectly clear: no one should bother the Jesuit before dawn and without an appointment.

For once, Hiro agreed with her. Predawn visitors never brought good news. He gave the woman a barely perceptible nod, and her frown deepened into a disapproving scowl. She circled the room along the wall and exited through the door that led to the kitchen.

Gato trotted after her, tail high.

"Has something happened?" Father Mateo asked Jiro.

The young man drew a breath and blurted out, "Last night I killed a girl and left her body by the river."

"The priest does not help murderers," Hiro said. "You need to leave."

"Hiro." Father Mateo raised his scarred right hand.

Hiro bristled at the gesture, even though the Jesuit meant no insult. When distracted or surprised, Father Mateo often forgot the rules of Japanese etiquette.

The priest turned to Jiro. "What help do you think I can offer?"

Jiro ducked his head. "I don't want to die for a crime I didn't commit."

"You just confessed to killing a girl," Hiro said. "Did you do it or not?"

"That's the problem." Jiro looked up. "I don't remember."

Hiro raised an eyebrow. "Either you killed a girl or you didn't. It's not the sort of thing you forget overnight."

The delicate odor of steaming rice wafted into the room. Ana must have started cooking before the visitor arrived. Hiro's stomach growled. Hunger always shortened his temper, but Hiro didn't care. A samurai had no obligation to heed a commoner's plea at all, let alone before the morning meal.

"Tell us everything you remember," Father Mateo said. "Would you like some tea?"

"No, thank you," Jiro said. "I couldn't impose upon your kindness."

Just our sleep and safety, Hiro thought.

"Tell us what happened," Father Mateo said, "and we will help you, if we can."

Hiro didn't argue. There was time enough to send Jiro away when he finished with his tale.

"Last night," Jiro said, "I went for a drink at a sake shop in Pontochō. I'd never been to one before, but yesterday morning a customer gave me some silver coins for delivering a package." After a pause, he added, "I didn't spend them all on sake."

Hiro loathed the pleasure districts, especially crowded Pontochō, but couldn't fault the boy's attraction to lovely women and cheap sake. Most men found the entertainment quarters irresistible.

"You met a girl in Pontochō?" Father Mateo asked.

Jiro blushed. "I could never afford the girls in Pontochō. I drank three flasks and left the sake shop."

"Three?" Hiro asked. "That seems a lot for a youth your age and size."

"I didn't drink them alone," Jiro said. "I split them with the man who shared my table. Even so, I left the shop almost too drunk to walk. I didn't realize how much sake a silver coin could buy."

"Is there a girl in this story somewhere?" Hiro asked.

Father Mateo frowned.

Jiro bowed his head. "I'm sorry. I will speak more clearly. I left the teahouse feeling sick, and went to the river to get some air. The guards on the bridge didn't stop me—I think they knew that I was drunk."

"That, or they knew your story would take all night," Hiro muttered.

Father Mateo gave Hiro a look, but Jiro apparently missed the comment.

"South of Shijō Road, I saw a beautiful girl by the river." The young man's voice grew soft with memory. "Moonlight glimmered on her hair and set her skin aglow. She seemed like a dream, but when she turned I recognized her face."

Hiro fought the urge to stifle the youth's romantic fancy. It seemed young Jiro had spent many hours with poems, and far too few with real girls.

"You knew the woman?" Father Mateo asked.

"Her name is Emi," Jiro said. "She lived in a teahouse in Pontochō and worshipped at Chugenji, the little shrine just east of the river at Shijō Road. We met there a couple of weeks ago, and after that I saw her several times."

"The girl is an entertainer?" Father Mateo asked.

"Yes," Jiro said. "That is, she was, but I don't know which house she worked for. She said she didn't want the owner learning we were friends."

"A teahouse owner can bill a man for spending time with an entertainer," Hiro explained to Father Mateo. "Even if they meet outside the teahouse."

Father Mateo nodded and turned to Jiro. "Please continue."

"Emi hated the teahouse," Jiro said. "The owner didn't like her, and the other girls were mean. She planned to escape, but couldn't afford to buy her contract back."

Hiro wondered if the girl had asked the youth for money. Entertainers often spent a lifetime working off the costs of education and room and board. The lucky ones found a wealthy patron or acquired sufficient fame to earn their independence. But for girls with lesser skills and plainer faces, life in a teahouse could, indeed, be cruel.

"Then, last night, Emi said she'd found a way to buy her freedom." Jiro sounded on the verge of tears. "She wouldn't tell me how, or why, but said the teahouse owner had agreed to let her go."

Father Mateo smiled at the boy. "You wanted to marry her, didn't you?"

Jiro's cheeks flushed red. The color went all the way to his ears. "She was a beautiful teahouse girl. I'm . . . I didn't know if she would have me."

"So you asked, and she refused, and then you killed her." Hiro hoped the accusation would speed up the narrative.

The color drained from Jiro's face. "No . . . at least, that's not the way I remember it. We sat together by the river. She told me about her plans to move to Edo. I felt dizzy from the sake and lay down, in hopes of feeling better.

"Next thing I remember, I woke up and found her dead."

CHAPTER 2

A door on the opposite side of the room rattled open, revealing a portly Portuguese man in a knee-length linen shift. His rounded belly protruded before him, causing the nightshirt to stretch across his stomach and then droop like a wrinkled curtain.

"So, what happened?" the man demanded. "Did you kill the girl or not?"

"Luis!" Father Mateo exclaimed.

Luis Álvares folded his arms across his ample belly. "He woke me at this indecent hour—the least I deserve is to hear the rest of the story."

Hiro stared at Luis's feet to avoid the unfortunate sight of the man as a whole. In the years since Hiro arrived in Kyoto, he had never seen the merchant barefoot. Luis's hairy toes repulsed and intrigued the shinobi in equal measure.

"I don't know if I killed her," Jiro said. "I don't remember anything after lying down on the riverbank."

"You're certain the girl was dead? She wasn't sleeping?" Father Mateo asked.

"She wasn't breathing," Jiro said. "Her eyes were full of blood."

"Why do you think we can help you?" Hiro asked.

Jiro gave him a pleading look. "You helped the brewer, Ginjiro— please, I don't know what to do."

"Turn yourself in and confess to a drunken accident," Hiro said. "Perhaps the magistrate will show mercy and grant you an easy death."

"What if he didn't kill her?" Father Mateo looked dismayed.

Luis snorted. "Who else could have done it? A river spirit?" He waved a dismissive hand. "Don't be ridiculous, Mateo. Your translator's right. The boy is guilty. I'm going back to sleep."

Luis returned to his room and shut the door.

Hiro recognized the determined look on the Jesuit's face. Father Mateo intended to help the youth, despite the evidence—and the potential danger.

"Kyoto is barely safe for the innocent, let alone the guilty." Hiro spoke quickly, in Portuguese, to stop the priest from making a foolish promise. "We must not intervene where we don't belong."

"The boy needs help," the priest replied. "If we refuse, he faces execution."

"He forfeited his life when he took another. As I said, this is not our concern."

Jiro bowed his head and waited, unable to understand the conversation.

"I choose to make this matter my concern." Father Mateo turned to Jiro and switched to Japanese. "I will help you, but I cannot shield a guilty man from justice. If you killed her, you must answer for the crime."

Tears welled up in Jiro's eyes as he looked at the priest. "I wish I never drank sake. I wish I went home by another path. . . ." He paused to recover control and bowed his face to the floor again. "Thank you for helping me. Thank you both."

Hiro felt an unexpected spark of compassion. The parallel scars on his shoulder, and the matching ones on his inner thigh, were constant reminders that all men's indiscretions had a price.

"We will help you discover the truth." Father Mateo rose and smoothed his kimono. "Take us to the place where you woke up and saw the girl."

Jiro shook his head. "I can't go back. The police—"

"—will find you one way or the other," Hiro finished. "You asked for help. Now do as you are told."

Hiro hoped their investigation wouldn't involve the Kyoto police and wouldn't draw the attention of Matsunaga Hisahide, the warlord who seized the Japanese capital after the shogun's death three months before. Officially, the emperor hadn't named a successor shogun, but Hisahide claimed the title—over the objections of the former shogun's clan. With Kyoto's future uncertain, and rival samurai threatening war, wise men took great care to avoid attention.

"Shall we go?" Father Mateo's question interrupted Hiro's thoughts.

"One moment." Hiro returned to his room and fastened a pair of swords to his obi. He also slipped a star-shaped metal *shuriken* and a dagger into hidden pockets in his sleeves.

He rejoined the others and left for the scene of the crime, thoughts of breakfast temporarily forgotten.

CHAPTER 3

Hiro, Father Mateo, and Jiro reached the Kamo River as the sun appeared on the eastern horizon. Dawn sent reddish sparkles over the flowing river and burnished the wooden bridge that spanned the flow at Marutamachi Road.

The armored samurai guarding the bridge walked up to meet them. He didn't bow or offer a greeting, but Hiro didn't expect any trouble. The tensions that followed the shogun's death had eased as Hisahide's samurai learned to recognize the people who lived in the wards they guarded.

The samurai indicated Jiro. "Who is this man? He said he knew you, and had an appointment, or I would not have let him pass. The shogun disapproves of people traveling before dawn."

Hiro waited for Father Mateo to respond. A translator had no right to speak before his master, and Hiro couldn't risk revealing his true identity. He wondered whether Father Mateo realized that Jiro's life depended on the answer. No commoner lied to a samurai and lived.

"I apologize for his unfortunate timing." Father Mateo bowed. "I am a priest. This young man summoned me to attend the dead."

Hiro admired Father Mateo's growing talent for walking the line between pragmatism and honesty. A parallel but nonresponsive truth was not a lie.

"I will not delay you further." The samurai looked at Jiro. "In future, wait for dawn to get the priest."

"Yes, sir." Jiro bowed so deeply that he almost tumbled over.

The samurai nodded to Father Mateo and looked away. Hiro received no recognition, but didn't mind. As a rule, the shinobi preferred to pass unnoticed.

Jiro turned south on the path that paralleled the western bank of the Kamo River. Hiro and Father Mateo followed. At every bridge, they stopped to explain their business to the samurai on guard. Fortunately, no one questioned Father Mateo's story.

A trio of samurai stood on the riverbank south of the bridge at Shijō Road. The larger two wore wide-shouldered tunics with pleated *hakama*. Plenty of samurai wore pleated trousers, but these men also carried hooked metal nightsticks, which identified them as *dōshin*—low-ranked members of the Kyoto police.

The third samurai wore a tunic sewn from alternating stripes of brilliant green and orange silk. A pair of swords hung from his patterned obi. The gaudy clothing and lack of a nightstick marked him as a *yoriki*, or assistant magistrate.

All three samurai had their backs to the path. They stared at a rumpled lump on the ground, about the size and shape of a human body.

The yoriki turned as Hiro and the others approached. His expression changed from surprise to recognition, and then annoyance. "Not you again."

Hiro had much the same reaction, though he kept his face a neutral mask. In an unfortunate stroke of luck, the girl had died within the jurisdiction of the yoriki who handled the brewery killing the month before. He hadn't approved of Hiro and Father Mateo's involvement then, and he clearly wasn't pleased to see them now.

Father Mateo bowed to the yoriki. Hiro followed suit.

Jiro bent forward and held his bow, awaiting permission to rise.

"Good morning," Father Mateo said. "We understand a girl was murdered here."

"You understand incorrectly," the yoriki said. "There was no murder."

"What?" Jiro spoke—and straightened—in surprise. A moment

later he fell to his knees and pressed his forehead to the ground. "A thousand apologies for my rudeness."

The yoriki ignored him.

Father Mateo leaned sideways in an attempt to see around the samurai. "That certainly looks like a corpse to me."

The yoriki stepped aside and motioned for the dōshin to clear the way.

A girl of no more than sixteen years lay on her back with her arms at her sides. Faint green grass stains streaked her gold kimono. A pale blue obi trailed at her side, and bits of hair strayed loose from her long black braid.

Angry rope burns crossed her neck, with darker bruising spreading out around them. Moon-shaped cuts and vertical scratches around the bruises revealed the girl had struggled with her killer.

Hiro noticed a leather thong around the victim's neck. It disappeared into her robe, suggesting a pendant tucked within her clothes. Based on the size and shape of the burns and bruises, the thong appeared to be the murder weapon.

Above the victim's mangled neck, a set of delicate features balanced in her oval face. The girl had a loveliness, and an innocence, even death could not erase.

Then Hiro saw her eyes.

Hemorrhages bloomed within the whites, the color startlingly vibrant even hours after death.

Father Mateo gasped and backed away. He made the sign of the cross and clasped his hands together as if in prayer.

Hiro watched the Jesuit with surprise. Father Mateo had never reacted dramatically to a murder victim, even though most of the bodies they had seen looked worse than this one.

He wondered if the Jesuit had seen this girl before.

"Do you know her?" the yoriki demanded.

Father Mateo shook his head. "No, I . . . simply wasn't prepared to see a girl so young. How can you say this wasn't murder? Clearly, she did not die of natural causes."

"The girl is an actor's child," the yoriki said, as though this answered the Jesuit's question.

Jiro's head rose up in surprise, but he pressed it to the ground again at once.

"An actor's daughter?" Father Mateo looked confused.

"Actors stand outside the social order," Hiro said in Portuguese.

"What does her status have to do with the nature of her death?" Father Mateo spoke in Japanese and to the yoriki.

"Actors' daughters do not matter to the law." The yoriki spoke slowly, as if addressing an unusually stupid child.

Father Mateo's look of confusion changed to one of anger.

Before the priest could argue, Hiro said, "Then you consider the matter closed."

The yoriki nodded. "My office has more important business than finding out who dumped this pile of filth on the riverbank."

"And yet, you spared three men to come and stare," Father Mateo said. "How do you know the girl is an actor's daughter? She didn't tell you."

The yoriki gestured toward the bridge that crossed the river at Shijō Road. "After she didn't come home last night, her parents sent her siblings out to find her. The sister arrived just after we did. We are only here to ensure the family removes the corpse before it stinks."

"How thoughtful." Father Mateo's frozen tone revealed unusual self-restraint.

Hiro glanced at Jiro, wondering whether the boy had lied to them about the girl's profession. Entertainers lived at a teahouse, never in their parents' homes. The youth's reaction indicated surprise, but ignorance was easily faked.

He also wondered what Father Mateo intended to do when the family arrived—assuming the yoriki let them stay, which, under the circumstances, seemed unlikely.

Father Mateo hadn't finished. "Your words imply you don't intend to investigate this murder."

"Her life meant nothing," the yoriki said. "No investigation is required."

CHAPTER 4

The yoriki looked down at Jiro. "Who are you? Identify yourself."

The young man kept his face to the ground. "A merchant's apprentice, sir, called Jiro. I work for Basho, in the rice-sellers' street."

"You have no business here," the yoriki snapped. "Be on your way."

Jiro stood and scurried off without a backward glance.

Hiro noted the look of relief on the young man's face as he departed—unusual for someone who just discovered the girl he loved was a liar. And yet, had Jiro known the truth, he wouldn't have bothered to ask the priest for help.

Either way, the youth's reaction didn't fit the facts.

Fortunately, Jiro's suspicious behavior no longer mattered. Hiro had no intention of investigating a crime without a reason.

"Someone killed her." Father Mateo gestured to Emi's body. "How can you claim there was no crime?"

The yoriki stared at the Jesuit. "Her death is of no consequence. *To anyone.*"

Hiro caught the warning in the words. The yoriki had allowed them to investigate the brewery murder, mainly because his supervisor—the magistrate—respected the foreign priest. However, that crime involved the death of an artisan, not an actor. Father Mateo might object, but to the Japanese the social status of the victim made a difference.

One of the dōshin caught the yoriki's eye and nodded toward Shijō Road. A man and two women had just stepped off the bridge.

The man had a narrow face and a slender build. He walked with his shoulders rounded forward, face turned down, and heavy feet, as if his grief weighed more than he could bear. The woman to his left had graying hair and a work-worn face that retained the shadow of its former beauty. She leaned on a teenage girl whose features echoed hers in a plainer way.

When they had almost reached the body, the older woman fell to her knees. She covered her mouth with her hands and sobbed as tears spilled down her cheeks. The daughter knelt beside her mother, leaving the man to approach the scene alone. As he reached a respectful distance, he knelt and pressed his face to the ground.

After a moment long enough to reinforce his status, the yoriki said, "I assume you have come to claim this body?"

The man pushed himself to a kneeling position, but kept his face turned down.

"Speak up," the yoriki snapped. "I don't have time to listen to your silence."

"Noble yoriki," the man replied, "this girl is my daughter Emi."

A muffled sob escaped the lips of the woman behind him.

The man tensed. "Please forgive my wife," he said, "she means no disrespect. Sometimes a woman can't control her tears."

"What is your name and occupation?" the yoriki demanded.

"I am Satsu, an actor, from the Yutoku-*za*."

Hiro's stomach dropped at the name of the actor and his guild. He wished he had made the Jesuit stay at home.

Father Mateo leaned toward Hiro and whispered, "What are they waiting for?"

"Permission," Hiro whispered back. "The family cannot move the body until the yoriki consents."

The yoriki turned to Hiro. "Tell your master he may leave. No one here requires his aid."

"I have no intention of leaving," Father Mateo said. "This family needs my help."

The yoriki laid a hand on his sword. "This matter does not concern you. I have decided. My word is law." He looked at Hiro. "Translate to ensure he understands!"

Hiro complied, to avoid a fight and to give the Jesuit time to reconsider. In truth, the yoriki couldn't forbid an investigation—only the magistrate had that power—but magistrates tended to approve the decisions a yoriki made in the field.

Also, people shouldn't pick fights with men who could arrest them.

When Hiro finished translating the order into Portuguese, Father Mateo bowed and said, "Perhaps you misunderstood my intentions. I merely wish to pray with this family and comfort them in this difficult time."

"These people do not warrant a priest's attention," the yoriki said.

"What about the ground beneath the body?" Father Mateo gestured toward, but did not look at, the murdered girl. "Only a priest can cleanse the defilement after the family moves her."

"A *Japanese* priest," the yoriki said. "Our *kami* do not speak your foreign tongue."

"The Christian God inhabits Japan as well as other places," the Jesuit said. "Would you knowingly risk his wrath by refusing me?"

Hiro admired the Jesuit's gamble but doubted it would work. The yoriki didn't strike him as the type of man who feared a foreign god.

"I do not want to waste the morning arguing with you." The yoriki turned to the pair of burly dōshin. "Go to Kenninji and fetch a priest to cleanse the ground. Tell him the Yutoku-za will cover the donations."

The dōshin bowed. As they swaggered off, the yoriki turned to Hiro. "Ensure your master does no more than pray. I will hold you both responsible if he tries to investigate."

Hiro bowed to avoid a reply. Until he heard the actor's name, he might have agreed to prevent an investigation. Now, he made no promises.

The yoriki turned and walked away without another word.

A keening wail rose from Satsu's wife as she crawled to her murdered daughter's side. Her grief brought unexpected tears to Hiro's eyes. He had seen, and heard, such pain before, on the day that he—the second son—became his mother's eldest living child.

He forced the memory away, and his emotions with it.

Satsu said, "Chou, help your mother. I will carry Emi. We must go before the samurai return." The actor kept his face turned down, shielding it from view.

Father Mateo took a step toward the family. "If you please, may I speak with you before you go?"

Satsu bowed his head to the ground. His wife and daughter bowed as well.

"Forgive me," Satsu said, "but a man like you would only defile himself with the likes of us. Please allow us to take our dead and leave."

CHAPTER 5

"**N**othing outside a man can defile him," Father Mateo said. Chou looked at the Jesuit. "Truly?"

Satsu's wife reached out and slapped the girl across the face, her movement as fast as a striking snake and just as startling. Satsu's daughter clutched her cheek in pain.

"Please don't kill her!" The woman wailed as she resumed her prone position.

Father Mateo seemed confused, but Hiro understood. By law, a commoner had no right to question the word of a samurai, and the priest, though not actually samurai, had equivalent status—at least, in a commoner's eyes.

"I will not harm her," Father Mateo said. "I simply wish to talk with you, and pray. If not here, perhaps we could follow you home."

Hiro frowned. The Jesuit did not understand the problem his words created. These people could not refuse his request, but their house would not be prepared to receive a man of samurai rank. Accepting would also place the family at risk, if the yoriki discovered what they'd done.

"Let them go," Hiro said. "We should leave them to their grief."

Father Mateo lowered his voice and switched to Portuguese. "Have you no conscience? But for us, this girl will have no justice."

"The law does not entitle her to justice." Hiro wanted to agree with the priest, but he would not place this family at risk.

"The girl is not a pile of trash, or a beast," the Jesuit said. "Her life had meaning. No one had the right to take it from her."

"You heard the yoriki. He forbade—" Hiro fell silent at the sight of Satsu's face.

The actor had risen to his knees. He looked at Hiro with surprise—and recognition. Hiro searched his memory, but couldn't place the actor's face beyond a fuzzy memory he did not trust as truth. Still, in combination with the name . . .

Father Mateo followed Hiro's gaze.

This time, Satsu didn't hide his face. "I apologize, noble sir, if you find me rude, but . . . *do I hear Iga's shadow in your speech?*"

The coded question identified Satsu as an Iga shinobi in need of aid. It would have obligated Hiro even if he hadn't recognized the actor's name.

Once again, he wondered how Satsu knew him.

"What do you care if my speech bears Iga's shadow?" Hiro asked.

"After so many years away, even the shadow of home seems bright as sunlight," Satsu said. "It drew me, as twilight draws the shadows close."

Father Mateo looked from Hiro to Satsu, puzzled.

"I am only a humble man," the actor continued, "but I would be honored, and grateful, if you and the priest would accompany me home."

Hiro nodded. He didn't know what Satsu wanted, but as long as it didn't endanger Hiro's mission to protect the priest, he had an obligation to assist. Since Father Mateo seemed inclined to help the family anyway, it wouldn't hurt to hear the actor out.

"What changed his mind?" Father Mateo asked in Portuguese as he and Hiro followed Satsu's family across the bridge at Shijō Road.

The samurai on guard had let them pass without a word. The mourning family, and the corpse, required no explanation.

"Do you intend to investigate this murder?" Hiro asked.

"Of course I do," the Jesuit said, "regardless of the yoriki's threats."

"What will you do with the killer?" Hiro asked. "You can't turn him in to the magistrate. The yoriki would arrest us both for disobeying orders."

"When did you start to worry about the yoriki?" Father Mateo asked.

Instead of answering, Hiro looked at the family ahead on the bridge.

Satsu's living daughter, Chou, walked behind her father with an outstretched arm around her mother's shoulders. Just in front of them, Satsu carried Emi in his arms. The stiffness that followed after death had already frozen Emi's muscles, but Satsu had no trouble balancing her tiny frame. Etiquette didn't allow the other men to offer help, but Hiro suspected Satsu would have refused it anyway.

"What happened back there?" Father Mateo glanced over his shoulder toward the river. "One moment you tell me to leave him alone, the next you're talking nonsense, and now—" His eyes widened with realization. "Shadows of Iga . . . Satsu . . . He's like you?"

Hiro appreciated the priest's decision not to say "shinobi." Wise men didn't use the word aloud. He was also impressed. The Jesuit had made the connection faster than Hiro anticipated.

"Do you know him?" Father Mateo asked. "You treated him like a stranger."

Hiro increased his pace as Satsu's family reached the eastern end of the bridge. He didn't want to lose them in the narrow streets beyond the river.

"He is a stranger," Hiro said, "and also my uncle, on my mother's side."

CHAPTER 6

"That man is your uncle?" Father Mateo stared at Satsu. "How do you know, if he's a stranger?"

Hiro answered in Portuguese. "When I left home, my mother mentioned her brother had come to Kyoto years ago. She told me the name that he assumed and that he had joined a school of actors called the Yutoku-za."

"Why haven't you mentioned him?" Father Mateo asked.

"And risk his safety? Two men keep secrets only if one is dead." Hiro hoped the priest would understand the awkward phrasing. Despite three years of study, and his aptitude for languages, he sometimes failed to express himself precisely in Portuguese.

"Can we trust him?" Father Mateo asked.

Hiro shrugged. "I don't."

"Then why go with him?" Father Mateo asked.

"You're the one who wanted to follow him home."

"He wasn't dangerous then," the Jesuit said.

Hiro raised an eyebrow. "I assure you, he was no less a threat before you knew the truth. I do not trust him, but he asked for help, so I must hear him out. If he refuses to answer my questions, or threatens us in any way, I will kill him—and his family—at once."

"You'd kill your own uncle?" Father Mateo sounded horrified.

"I am paid to keep you alive," Hiro said.

"Though we don't know why, or by whom," the priest interjected. "Surely family supersedes the orders of a stranger."

"Duty knows no family, and duty must prevail." Hiro paused to let the words sink in. "My orders are to protect you, and I will not hesitate to kill anyone who threatens that objective."

"If you don't know Satsu, how did he know you?" Father Mateo asked.

Hiro noted the change of subject, a tactic the Jesuit often used to avoid unpleasant topics—like whether or not his friend would run a sword through a relative's heart.

"That's a question I intend to ask him."

Satsu's recognition didn't surprise Hiro nearly as much as the fact that the actor requested help. No shinobi would risk exposure over a simple murder. But Hiro wouldn't speculate about the cause until he talked with Satsu. Speculation led to assumptions. Assumptions caused mistakes.

"This doesn't seem suspicious to you?" Father Mateo asked.

"No more than any other family asking us for help."

Satsu stopped in front of a wooden building on the north side of the street. It was larger than Hiro expected, though theater troupes did need significant room for practice and storage spaces. An indigo *noren* hung in the entry. Characters running down the fabric panels read "YUTOKU-ZA, PERFORMERS OF *NŌ*."

Satsu spoke to his wife and Chou, who bowed and entered the building while the actor stood outside with Emi's body.

Hiro stopped a short distance away. "We should give them time to make arrangements."

"Do they live there?" Father Mateo asked. "That looks like a business."

"Actors live with their troupes," Hiro said. "The building most likely belongs to the man who leads the Yutoku-za."

Chou reappeared in the doorway. Satsu followed her inside.

Father Mateo started forward, but Hiro stopped him. "Wait. He will come to us."

More than courtesy prompted the words. The street gave Hiro room to maneuver. Defending against attack would prove more difficult indoors.

As he waited for Satsu, Hiro watched a handful of people enter and leave the tiny shrine across the road. Unlike the larger temples, which had landscaped grounds and many buildings, this one encompassed only a single yard and a couple of tiny structures. Lettering over the entrance gate identified the temple as Chugenji.

"Is that a shrine?" Father Mateo asked.

Hiro nodded. "Most likely, it honors a local kami or lesser deity not important enough for a larger place."

Before the priest could answer, Satsu arrived at Hiro's side. He bowed low and held the gesture before he rose. "Forgive me, but Botan is teaching a lesson, and we have disturbed the house already, with Emi's body. Perhaps we could talk on the grounds of Kenninji instead of here?"

"Of course," Hiro said. "The temple grounds are pleasant in the autumn."

"This hardly seems an appropriate time for a foliage viewing," Father Mateo said.

"He wants to speak with us privately," Hiro said in Portuguese. "His home has too many curious ears for the words he wants to say."

Satsu bowed. "Please, I would be honored to show you the temple grounds. That is, if you don't object to an actor's company."

Hiro made a permissive gesture, and Satsu led the way.

They had barely traveled a block to the east before Father Mateo said, "Tell me, Satsu, how long have you acted with the Yutoku-za?"

Satsu glanced at Hiro, who walked on the other side of the priest.

Hiro pretended not to see him. For once, Father Mateo's curiosity came in handy. The answer would give Hiro a chance to evaluate Satsu's honesty, though he suspected most of the story would be untrue.

"Twenty years," Satsu said. "Nori, my wife, is the only child of Botan, who leads the Yutoku-za and acts the role of *shite* in the plays." Satsu looked at Father Mateo. "Do you understand the various roles in a nō performance?"

"I know of nō," Father Mateo said. "It's a kind of Japanese play, performed on a special stage. I saw it once, some years ago, though I confess, I did not understand it well." After a pause, he added, "However, I found it quite intriguing."

Satsu nodded. "Nō is a purely Japanese art. I can understand how it might confuse a foreigner." At the corner, he turned right and led them south, toward Kenninji. "The shite performs the leading role, the most demanding part of the play, and also the most important. Only the greatest actors have the chance to become shite."

"The role is also hereditary," Hiro said. "At least, that is my understanding."

"Yes," Satsu replied. "I normally act in the chorus."

"And yet you married a shite's daughter," Father Mateo said.

Satsu shrugged. "In my youth, I had talent. Botan accepted me as an apprentice, and his son-in-law, before we realized my limited skills would not allow me to succeed him."

Hiro recognized the lie. The leader of a theater troupe would never marry his only child to a man who lacked the skills to succeed him. Not unless that man had something exceedingly valuable to offer.

"Fortunately," Satsu continued, "my son shows promise, which lessens the shame of my personal failure."

Father Mateo asked no further questions. A father would not brag about his son's accomplishments in public, and Satsu's mention of personal failure made inquiries on that topic equally awkward.

Hiro admired Satsu's skill at ending the unwanted conversation.

A few blocks to the south, they reached the massive wooden entrance to Kenninji. Its sloping, black-tiled roof rose more than three stories above the ground. Father Mateo craned his neck to examine the decorative latticework as they approached the sliding door that led into the gate and to the temple grounds beyond.

A pair of samurai stood guard outside the entrance, wearing kimono emblazoned with the Matsunaga crest. They barely seemed to notice the three men passing.

"Curious that they do not care about our names and business," Father Mateo murmured.

Satsu smiled. "Those who pass inside the gates to pray are not the true concern. Wise men fear the ones who live within."

"You mean the monks?" Father Mateo asked.

"Most of the warrior monks have fled to the countryside," Satsu explained, "but who can tell how many remain in the city, hiding and awaiting a chance to strike?"

Father Mateo gave Hiro a curious glance.

"Later," Hiro murmured in Portuguese.

The foreign word drew a glance from Satsu, though Hiro saw no comprehension in the actor's eyes.

"The monks have no known argument with Matsunaga Hisahide," Satsu added as he led them through the temple grounds. "However, less-important events than Shogun Ashikaga's recent death have sparked rebellions in the past."

Hiro and Father Mateo followed the actor through another building and into a landscaped garden. Covered wooden walkways surrounded the space. A group of stones rose up from a grassy hillock at the garden's center. Closer to the walkways, maples blazed with autumn's fire, their changing leaves a brilliant splash of red and gold.

Father Mateo paused at a railing. He shook his head, at a loss for words.

Hiro understood. Like most Zen gardens, the landscape inspired thought and, in this season, awe. He paused to appreciate the scene, but did not lose himself in its beauty.

Satsu might be family, but even so, he did not trust the actor . . . yet.

CHAPTER 7

After a moment long enough to show respect for the garden, Hiro said, "Enough pretense. What is your connection to Iga Province?"

Satsu continued to watch the garden, as if reflecting on the autumn landscape.

Hiro laid a warning hand on the hilt of his katana. "Answer my question or I will kill you, and then I will kill the rest of your family also."

"Hiro!" Father Mateo sounded shocked.

"If you are who I believe, you are not bluffing," Satsu said. "May I speak freely, without regard for rank?"

"There's no one here but us and the priest," Hiro said. "You may say what you like. But I warn you, I have no patience for strangers' lies."

"I probably do seem strange to you, though you're not strange to me." Satsu smiled. "You look exactly like your father."

"My father will be pleased to hear you think so," Hiro said.

"Your father is dead, Hattori Hiro," Satsu replied, "though I hope my youngest sister lives."

The answer passed the initial test, but Hiro wasn't finished. "Tell me why I shouldn't turn you over to the shogun's samurai."

"Matsunaga Hisahide is not the shogun," Satsu said, "no matter how loudly he claims the title. And you won't turn me in. My sister's son could never be a traitor."

Hiro noticed Father Mateo watching the exchange with interest.

"I accept that you know me," Hiro said. "Now explain why I should trust you."

Satsu snorted. "No one trusts an actor."

"You're no actor," Hiro said. "Not if you were born in Iga."

"Iga has more than its share of actors," Satsu countered, "most of whom will never set a foot upon a stage. However, I am an actor, as well as shinobi."

"Does your father-in-law know what you are?" Hiro asked.

"Of course not," Satsu said. "I arrived in Kyoto with documents establishing my lineage as the cousin of a shite from an acting troupe in Edo."

"Forged," Hiro said.

"He is, in fact, my cousin," Satsu said, "and also one of us—like me, inserted long ago and living in disguise, in case of need. But to answer your question directly, no, neither my wife nor her relatives know about my other profession. I would prefer it remained that way."

"If you want to stay hidden, why did you reveal yourself to us?" Father Mateo asked.

Hiro found the reversal of roles amusing. Normally, Hiro questioned people, trying to keep the Jesuit out of trouble. Now, it seemed, the priest was returning the favor.

"Someone killed my daughter." Satsu glanced across the garden, as if ensuring they remained alone. "I want to know who, and why, and if Emi's murder puts others at risk."

"Why would her death threaten others?" Father Mateo asked.

"A week ago, a stranger approached the Yutoku-za." Satsu turned to Hiro. "He demanded money and said if Botan didn't pay him, he would tell Matsunaga-san that we were hiding spies within the troupe."

"Sounds like standard bribery," Hiro said, "unless you're sloppy and were seen."

Satsu folded his arms across his chest. "Twenty years, and not a hint of an accusation before now." He shook his head. "I didn't think anything of it until this morning, but then, with Emi's death—I had to wonder. Did the killer figure out the truth? And then I saw the coin."

"What coin?" Father Mateo asked.

"Botan believed himself innocent, but he paid the extortionist anyway," Satsu said. "He couldn't risk the shogunate samurai closing down the troupe. He didn't have the money to pay the entire sum the man demanded, but what he paid, he paid in golden coins . . . exactly like the one on the leather thong that killed my daughter."

Father Mateo looked at Hiro. "Do you understand what he's talking about?"

Hiro suspected he did, but had no intention of offering an explanation.

"My daughter had a leather thong around her neck," Satsu continued. "A coin was strung on the leather, like a pendant. I saw it when I took her body home."

"Couldn't the coin have belonged to your daughter?" Father Mateo asked.

Satsu shook his head. "Emi did not own a golden coin. The killer must have left it on her body for some reason. Maybe he wants more money and murdered Emi to scare us into paying. Either that, or he knows who I am and killed my daughter to warn me I am next. The former places my troupe at risk. The latter might endanger every Iga shinobi in Kyoto, depending on how much the killer knows.

"That's why I need your help. I need to find the link between the killer and the coin, and I can't investigate it on my own."

Hiro didn't trust Satsu, but couldn't ignore the possibility that the actor spoke the truth. Matsunaga Hisahide had ordered his men to hunt for spies, and it did seem a strange coincidence that someone accused Botan of hiding shinobi.

"What makes you think we can help you?" Father Mateo asked.

"All the entertainers know about the *ronin* and the priest who help the wrongfully accused." Satsu gave a mirthless laugh. "It didn't occur to me that the 'masterless samurai' might have been a shinobi in disguise until this morning, though it should have. Most true ronin wouldn't serve a foreign master."

After a pause, he added, "How did you learn about Emi's murder?"

"A friend of your daughter," Father Mateo said.

Hiro frowned at the priest with irritation.

"Impossible," Satsu said. "Emi had no friends outside the troupe, and no one from the Yutoku-za would talk to an outsider."

"Then you tell us how we learned about her murder," Father Mateo said.

Satsu frowned. "I want his name—and don't deny it was a man. My daughter would not have concealed a woman's friendship."

"Tell us the name of the man who bribed the theater troupe," the Jesuit countered.

"I don't know it," Satsu said. "Botan spoke with him alone and claimed he was a bandit. I didn't believe him—bandits don't threaten to turn you in to the shogun. I pushed the issue as far as I could, but Botan wouldn't change his story. He also claimed he didn't know the man, and that part I believe."

"Then we need to speak with Botan," Hiro said.

"I want the name of the man who told you about my daughter's murder," Satsu said.

"Not until we determine whether or not he deserves to die." Hiro had no intention of giving a grieving father enough information to kill the only potential witness—and suspect—he currently had to investigate.

"Then you will help me?" Satsu asked.

Hiro nodded. To his surprise, he wanted to know the truth about Emi's murder, and not just because of the danger it might present to his clan, the Iga *ryu*. Although he had never met the girl, the blood of his family flowed in her veins.

Her death required an answer, and he would find it.

"We will help you," Hiro said, "on one condition. Our assistance must remain a secret. We will not incur the yoriki's wrath, or the magistrate's, for conducting a forbidden investigation."

"I will honor that condition," Satsu said.

"Very well," Hiro said. "We need to examine the body."

Satsu bowed. "I will take you to her."

CHAPTER 8

As they approached the building that housed the Yutoku-za, Hiro turned to Father Mateo and whispered, in Portuguese, "Do not contradict me, regardless of what I say."

"If I wanted to argue with you in public, I would have done it back at the temple." Father Mateo glanced at Satsu. "I don't trust him."

"I don't either," Hiro replied, "but I have an obligation, at least for now."

Before the priest could answer, Hiro stepped behind Satsu and shoved him hard. The actor staggered forward, striking the wooden door of his home and falling to the ground.

"What do you mean you can't do it today?" Hiro demanded, loudly enough for people on the street to hear. "You told me you could arrange a performance!"

Satsu rose to his knees. "I'm sorry. Please come inside. We will make the arrangements immediately." He bowed his forehead to the ground. "Forgive my insolence."

The change in his voice, and his instant cooperation, reinforced Hiro's suspicion that Satsu was a persuasive liar.

"What are you doing?" Father Mateo whispered in Portuguese.

"I said, don't argue," Hiro whispered back. "We need an excuse to enter the house so the neighbors don't suspect our real purpose."

Slowly, the door swung open, as if the person on the other side had heard the commotion. Satsu's daughter, Chou, appeared in the doorway. She bowed to the visitors, looked at her father on the ground, and withdrew into the house without a word.

Satsu scrambled to his feet, bowed low, and led the men inside.

As he followed, Hiro wondered why Chou had answered the door. Satsu's daughter should have been helping her mother with the body.

Just beyond the narrow entry lay an enormous common room with a central hearth. The room would have seemed out of place in a standard home, or even a teahouse, but the size made sense for a theater troupe, where several generations of multiple families shared the space. Clean *tatami* covered the floor, and sliding doors in every wall led off to rooms beyond. A colored scroll hung in a decorative alcove across from the entry. The scroll depicted a scene from a play, though Hiro couldn't identify either the characters or the source.

A kettle hung above the fire, suspended from a chain attached to the ceiling beams. Chou removed the kettle and knelt beside a teapot and a tray of porcelain cups.

"Three cups, but the girl is alone in the room," Father Mateo whispered in Hiro's ear. "Satsu knew we would return."

Hiro had noticed that too, and didn't like it.

"May I offer you gentlemen tea?" Satsu asked.

"No," Hiro said. "Just take us to the body."

Satsu bowed. "As you wish, sir. Please follow me."

He led them to a sliding door on the eastern side of the room, pulled it open, and stepped away so Hiro and Father Mateo could enter first.

A brazier cast a golden light across the room where Emi lay. Inexpensive tatami filled the air with the scent of grasses. A hint of sandalwood incense also lingered in the room, but faintly, like the ghost of a prayer almost forgotten.

Emi's body lay on a woven mat at the center of the tiny room. Nori knelt beside her daughter, head bowed down in grief.

"Nori," Satsu said, "please leave us. Chou will pour you tea."

The woman rose, bowed deeply to Hiro and Father Mateo, and left the room without a word.

Hiro walked to the body and bent to examine Emi's corpse.

The grass stains streaking the sides of Emi's kimono barely showed in the brazier's flickering light. Hiro would have missed them if he hadn't known to look. He pulled at the girl's kimono enough to reveal that the grass stains continued onto the back of the garment.

"What do you see?" Father Mateo asked.

Hiro withdrew his hand and gestured. "Grass stains, here—and on her back. The killer must have held her arms and dragged the body along the ground."

"How can you tell?" the Jesuit asked.

"No stains on the sleeves," Hiro said, "and none on her shoulders, suggesting those parts of her body didn't touch the ground while she was moved."

He didn't mention, but did observe, that the stains conflicted with Jiro's story, unless the killer lured the girl away and then returned her corpse to Jiro's side without him waking up.

Hiro saw no open wounds on Emi's hands, but noted a pair of broken fingernails.

Father Mateo shuddered. "Do you know what happened to her eyes?"

The crimson blooms in the whites of her eyes retained their shocking impact even in the darkened room.

"Strangulation," Hiro said. "It is common, in such cases, for the victim's eyes to bleed."

Satsu nodded, confirming the words.

"You've seen it before?" the Jesuit asked.

"It's worse when the victim struggles," Hiro said. "She struggled hard."

Father Mateo turned away.

"Her neck confirms she died by strangulation," Hiro said. "The marks from the leather strap, and the bruising. Also, see the scratch marks here, and there"—he gestured to vertical scratches on Emi's neck—"she tried to get away, but failed. Her fingernails made those moon-shaped cuts as she struggled to free herself from the killer's grip."

Father Mateo didn't answer. Hiro wondered why the Jesuit wouldn't look at the murdered girl, though he doubted the priest's objections matched his own. Hiro considered strangulation messy, slow, and painful. He preferred a faster, simpler method when he had to kill.

Gentle footsteps approached the room. Chou appeared in the doorway, bowed, and stood at her father's side.

"Show me the coin," Hiro said.

"I tucked it back where I found it," Satsu said, "beneath her clothes." He turned to his daughter. "Show him, Chou."

The girl approached and knelt on the opposite side of her sister's body. She bowed her forehead to the floor. "Will you permit me to assist you, sir?"

Hiro made a noise to show assent.

Chou rose to a sitting position, but kept her face turned down to show respect. She tenderly slipped the end of the thong from under Emi's garment. As Satsu described, the leather strip passed through a hole at the center of a golden coin, allowing the coin to serve as a make-shift pendant.

Hiro spoke to Father Mateo. "The width of the leather strip is a match to the injuries on the victim's neck." He looked at Satsu. "I will take the leather with me—along with the coin."

Satsu nodded. "As you wish, sir."

Chou attempted to untie the leather strip from her sister's neck. The knot that bound the thong had tightened, possibly during the murder; it proved difficult to loosen. When she finally freed the leather, Chou offered it to Hiro with both hands.

"Do you know where your sister got this?" Hiro asked as he accepted the coin.

Chou shook her head but did not look up. Something—likely her mother's slap—had made her remember that actors' daughters did not speak boldly to samurai.

"She didn't tell you about it?" Satsu asked. "You are certain of this?"

"I never saw it . . . before . . ." Chou's voice trailed off, and her eyes filled with tears as she looked at her sister's body.

Satsu gave Hiro a meaningful look. Chou's answer reinforced his assertion that Emi had not owned a golden coin.

Hiro retied the knot to keep the coin from sliding off and tucked the coin and thong into his sleeve. "Why did your sister go to the river yesterday, in the evening?"

"With respect, we did not know she went there," Satsu said.

"I did not ask you." Hiro let an edge of frustration creep into his voice. "I asked your daughter."

CHAPTER 9

"She wouldn't—" Satsu began, but stopped as Chou began to speak.

"Sometimes Emi had trouble sleeping. She walked by the river to clear her head." Chou turned to her father and bowed her face to the tatami. "I am so sorry. I should have told you."

Rapid footsteps thumped in the outer room.

Hiro drew his sword and leaped to the doorway. He pressed the katana's blade to the neck of the man who appeared in the entrance.

The newcomer froze, terrified by the unexpected steel against his skin. His eyes went wide, but he did not move or speak.

"Who are you?" Hiro demanded.

The man had a delicate build, effeminate features, and a mane of shimmering hair that nearly reached his waist. His narrow chin could not yet grow a beard.

He straightened. "I am Yuji, shite of the Yutoku-za." His red-rimmed eyes had the look of recent tears.

Hiro did not like the arrogant tone in the young man's voice. "You lie. The shite of this troupe is named Botan."

"I am his eldest apprentice, betrothed to his granddaughter," Yuji said.

Satsu bowed. "It is the truth."

Father Mateo extended his hands to Yuji. "I am so sorry for your loss."

Hiro narrowed his eyes but sheathed his sword.

"My loss?" Yuji looked confused and frightened in equal measure.

"You haven't heard? Oh . . ." Father Mateo ran a hand through his hair. "I am so sorry."

Understanding transformed Yuji's face. "I am betrothed to Botan's *eldest* granddaughter—Chou." After a pause, he added, "Not that Emi's death does not upset me."

"Why were you running?" Hiro asked.

Yuji's eyes filled with tears as he saw the corpse. "I learned of the tragedy only now, after I finished my lesson with Master Botan. I had to see . . ." He raised a hand to his mouth and shook his head.

"I told Haru—my son—to wait outside the practice room and deliver the message after the lesson finished," Satsu said.

Father Mateo looked horrified at the thought of delaying such important news.

Hiro accepted that actors didn't behave like normal people. "How old is your son?"

"Haru?" Satsu asked. "He is eight, sir."

The answer eliminated the boy as a suspect. A child that age could not subdue and strangle a woman of Emi's size.

"Very well. We have what we came for." Hiro glared at Yuji. "Clear the way!"

The young man scuttled sideways, like a crab, and Hiro left the house with Father Mateo following in his wake.

When they reached the bridge at Shijō Road, Hiro started across the river.

"Where are we going?" Father Mateo asked.

Hiro didn't answer. The samurai guarding the bridge had already started in their direction.

"Good morning," the samurai said.

Hiro bowed. "Good morning. I believe I dropped my dagger on the other side of the river."

"You were the ones who spoke with the yoriki earlier," the samurai said.

Hiro nodded. "I just noticed the dagger missing, so we returned. It's a family heirloom."

The samurai looked over his shoulder. "The priests haven't come to cleanse the ground. You might still find your dagger there, assuming a beggar hasn't found it first." He stepped away. "I hope you find it."

"Thank you." Hiro continued across the bridge with Father Mateo.

When they reached the western bank of the river, Hiro walked off the path and past the place where they had first seen Emi's body.

"What are you doing?" Father Mateo asked.

Hiro frowned at the grass. "Trying to see where the murder happened, and failing." He shook his head. "It's useless. There's broken grass near where she lay, but the trail fades away too quickly. I cannot tell how far the killer dragged her."

Father Mateo looked at the river. "Why would the killer risk moving her back to Jiro?"

"Your question assumes Jiro isn't the killer," Hiro replied without looking up.

"Why do you doubt his story?" Father Mateo asked. "I think Satsu lied to us. He may be your uncle, but I don't trust him."

"I already told you, I don't trust him either," Hiro said.

"Why help him, then?" the Jesuit asked.

"Three reasons." Hiro held up a matching number of fingers. "First, because the code of the ryu requires it. Second, because he *is* my uncle, which also makes his daughter my cousin. And, finally, because someone may have identified Satsu as a shinobi from the Iga ryu. If one of us is compromised, the rest could be in danger."

"That's an assumption," Father Mateo said.

"Perhaps you cannot understand, but I have an obligation," Hiro said. "Why do you object to helping Satsu?"

"Because I think he killed the girl himself." Father Mateo crossed his arms. "I think he learned about Jiro, and he couldn't allow his daughter to love a merchant."

"If that's the case, he wouldn't ask for help." Hiro palmed his dagger and pretended to pick it up from the ground, in case the guard was watching. "What's truly the problem? You've never reacted this way to a murder before."

Father Mateo shook his head and ran a hand through his hair again.

Normally, Hiro disapproved of the Jesuit's nervous gesture, which samurai would consider a sign of weakness. Now, however, it revealed that something about the crime was unusually troubling to the priest. Hiro didn't press the issue. He could bring it up again when time had given the Jesuit some distance.

"I can hunt for Emi's killer alone," Hiro said, "if you would rather not participate."

Father Mateo turned away from the river, but didn't answer.

CHAPTER 10

Hiro matched Father Mateo's pace as they followed the Kamo River north, toward home. As they walked, he listened to the muffled crunch of dirt and fallen leaves beneath their sandals. The autumn air had a tang of smoke, along with the musky scent of dead and decomposing leaves.

Father Mateo didn't speak until they had almost reached the bridge at Marutamachi Road.

"I will help," the Jesuit said.

"With the investigation?" Hiro asked.

Father Mateo nodded. "Emi deserves it, whether or not her father does."

As Hiro hoped, the Jesuit's normally helpful nature had reasserted itself.

"Where should we start?" Father Mateo asked.

Hiro deferred his answer until they had crossed the bridge and entered the empty street beyond. Once they were alone he said, "We start with the coin. The killer left it behind for a reason, and Satsu suggested we follow that link. Whether or not he lied to us, it's the logical place to begin."

"Do you think the killer panicked and left it?" Father Mateo asked.

Hiro shrugged. "Inexperienced killers panic. Trained ones misdirect."

Luis looked up from his seat near the hearth as Hiro and Father Mateo entered the house. The merchant wore a purple tunic cut in the foreign style he favored. Its bulbous, puffy sleeves reminded Hiro of overripe plums. Beneath the tunic, form-fitting hose directed unfortunate attention to the merchant's bulging thighs.

"Didn't expect you back so soon," Luis said through a mouthful of rice. "Did the magistrate hang the boy without a trial?"

"The yoriki released him," Father Mateo said. "Unharmed."

"What? He confessed to murder," Luis protested. "Never seen a samurai pass up the chance to cut off someone's head."

"A beheading could be arranged," Hiro said. He often wished the Jesuit didn't like the obnoxious merchant quite so much.

"See?" Luis raised a hand toward Hiro. "He makes my point exactly."

"The yoriki elected not to investigate," Father Mateo said. "It appears the girl was an actor's daughter, not a teahouse entertainer."

"An outcaste?" Luis said. "You know, they have a word for that. It translates, 'pile of—'"

"Thank you, I've heard it." Father Mateo cut Luis off before he could speak the offensive word.

"That's not the proper term anyway," Hiro said. "For actors, we use—"

"Don't encourage him," Father Mateo said.

Hiro shrugged. He intended correction, not encouragement.

"Well, at least you won't end up involved in another investigation," Luis said. "Far too much of that nonsense going on lately."

Father Mateo glanced at Hiro, who reminded himself to teach the priest that ill-timed glances often suggested guilt.

"Excuse me," Father Mateo said. "I need to eat, and then attend to my morning prayers."

"Offer one up for me," Luis said. "I'm spending the day at the city gates, waiting on a shipment from Yokoseura. Have to meet it personally—new orders from the shogun."

Hiro had heard enough, so he went into the kitchen, where Ana prepared him a bowl of rice. As he ate, she prepared a tray for Father

Mateo and carried it into the common room, walking with a stiffness that betrayed her loathing for the merchant's constant griping.

She returned and scrubbed a teapot with frustrated vigor.

Luis's voice carried over the rafters. He grumbled to Father Mateo about the "obnoxious regulations" Matsunaga Hisahide placed on weapons shipments to Kyoto.

If someone gave that man a kingdom, he would complain about the distance he rode to claim it, Hiro thought.

After finishing his rice, Hiro went to his room and put on a tunic and practice trousers. He stepped out through the veranda door, trading the merchant's whine for the burble of Father Mateo's koi pond and the whisper of breezes through the cherry trees that lined the garden.

He wondered, yet again, at Father Mateo's exceptional patience. Luis's sales financed the Jesuit's work in Japan, and from that perspective Father Mateo needed the merchant, but their relationship went beyond financial dependence. Hiro didn't understand how, or why, but he did recognize that only a rare and unusual man could consider Luis Álvares a friend.

After Hiro finished his meditation and weapons practice, he changed back into his gray kimono and stood outside the door that led to Father Mateo's room.

"I'm going to visit Jiro now." He spoke with just enough volume for his voice to carry through the door, but not enough to disturb a meditation.

The door slid open, and Father Mateo appeared. "Jiro? Why now?"

"At this hour, the rice shop will be crowded," Hiro said, "which means our talk will not attract attention. The boy has less incentive to lie if his master isn't part of the conversation."

Father Mateo rubbed his hands. The smallest finger on the priest's right hand did not bend properly into the gesture.

"You haven't recovered use of that finger?" Hiro wondered why he hadn't noticed.

Father Mateo raised his hand. "This one?" He tried to bend it, and winced. "I can force it farther, but it hurts. It hasn't healed as well as the others. The bone seems out of place."

Earlier, in the summer, the neighbor's Akita had broken free and attacked the priest. Fortunately, Father Mateo suffered only broken hands and a bite that left a scar across his neck.

"The finger may need breaking again, in order to set it straight." Hiro reached for the Jesuit's hand. "I can do it."

"You most certainly will not!" Father Mateo pulled his hand away.

"I didn't mean right now," Hiro said. "I was simply going to examine it."

Father Mateo clasped his hands together. "Thank you, but that won't be necessary."

"The examination?" Hiro asked. "Or the breaking?"

"Either." Father Mateo changed the subject. "Do you think Jiro will speak with us? He heard the yoriki say we can't investigate."

"Don't worry." Hiro drew the coin and strip of leather from his sleeve. "He'll talk when I ask if he wants his *koban* back."

CHAPTER 11

"I'm sorry, but that isn't mine." Jiro shook his head, eyes fixed on the golden coin that dangled before him on its leather thong.

Hiro swung the pendant gently. "Didn't you mention receiving a tip from a wealthy customer yesterday?"

Jiro glanced nervously into the crowded rice shop.

As expected, Basho's apprentice had scurried forward the moment he caught sight of Hiro and Father Mateo in the entrance. He spoke in the muted tones of a man who didn't want anyone hearing his conversation.

"I did," Jiro said, "but the customer paid me in silver, not in gold."

"So you didn't give this to Emi?" Hiro lowered the coin to his other palm and closed his hand around it so the gold would not attract undue attention.

"I have never owned a golden coin, and—if I may speak honestly— I wouldn't waste one on a girl," Jiro said. "I would buy myself a new kimono first."

"You're lying," Hiro said. "Perhaps Basho can help us learn the truth?"

"No, please!" Jiro glanced into the shop again. "The coin's not mine, but I know where it came from. I'll meet you later, and tell you, but please—I beg you—don't tell my uncle about Emi."

"He's your uncle?" Father Mateo asked. "You never told us that before."

Jiro shrugged. "It didn't seem important."

"How do I know you'll keep your word?" Hiro let suspicion creep into his voice even though he believed that Jiro would follow through.

The fear on the young man's face was real. He wouldn't risk them coming back and talking to Basho.

"I promise, I'll meet you," Jiro said. "I couldn't run if I wanted to. I haven't got a travel pass, and Basho won't loan me his without a reason. Especially not at harvest time, with rice coming in from all the farms. I'll tell you everything, but please, don't make me say it here."

Not many men would dare to ask a samurai to wait. Hiro paused as if considering Jiro's request and inhaled deeply, enjoying the grassy-sweet scent of the rice shop. His stomach might prefer noodles, but few aromas pleased Hiro's nose as much as the smell of freshly polished rice.

"Very well," he said. "Meet me at Ginjiro's brewery, tonight, just after sunset. If you fail to appear, or lie to me, I will tell your master everything—including my suspicion that you killed the girl because you discovered she wasn't truly an entertainer."

Jiro bowed from the waist. "I'll be there. I swear it . . . and thank you. I'm in your debt."

Under the circumstances, Hiro drew no inference from the young man's failure to deny the murder allegation. Commoners had no legal right to contradict a samurai, and Jiro had already claimed he didn't know what actually happened by the river.

Father Mateo gestured to a nearby barrel. "Please deliver a bag of that rice to my home on Marutamachi Road." He pulled a silver coin from his purse and handed it to Jiro.

"Thank you." Jiro bowed again and accepted the coin with both hands. "I will arrange delivery today."

As they left the shop, Hiro said, "I wonder what Ana will think when that rice arrives, considering that your barrel is currently full."

"I know the barrel is full as well as you do," Father Mateo said, "but the purchase gives Jiro an explanation for our appearance at the shop."

"I was planning to buy some rice for that very reason," Hiro said, "but I'm surprised you thought of it, and that you willingly helped the boy to lie."

"On the contrary." Father Mateo smiled. "I saved him from a lie. We did, in fact, buy rice." The smile faded. "Do you think he told the truth about the coin?"

"I'm not certain," Hiro said. "His hands kept fidgeting as we spoke, but any number of things could have made him nervous."

"Talking with a samurai, for one," the Jesuit offered.

"Or killing a girl by the river," Hiro countered.

"Why did you agree to talk with him later?" Father Mateo asked. "You normally want answers on the spot."

"I saw no point in causing trouble prematurely," Hiro said. "Whatever relationship Jiro had with the girl, it's over now. We've plenty of time to talk with Basho if the evidence proves that Jiro is a killer."

Just before sunset, Hiro left the Jesuit's house and walked toward the river. Father Mateo disapproved of sake shops, and had a prayer meeting anyway, so Hiro went to meet Jiro alone.

He reached the bridge as sunset lit the evening sky ablaze.

The samurai guard on duty stepped forward. "Where are you going?"

Hiro bowed. "To a sake shop, west of Pontochō."

He expected the guard to let him pass, but the samurai didn't move.

"Don't you get tired of being a ronin, or serving a foreign priest?" he asked.

"Pardon me?" Hiro felt an instinctive, warning twitch in his stomach. Other samurai didn't normally mention a ronin's status, except to insult him or start a fight.

"What if I could offer you a chance to serve a noble lord?" the samurai asked.

The question made Hiro suspicious. A masterless samurai didn't usually have a chance to redeem his honor, or to serve another lord. A ronin remained a ronin until he died.

"Which of the *daimyo* has opened his ranks to ronin?" Hiro asked.

"Shogun Matsunaga needs an army to hold Kyoto against his enemies," the guard explained. "He has issued an invitation to every samurai in the city. The shogun is generous. He rewards his warriors' faithful service. Distinguish yourself, and he might restore your honor.

"You must provide your own weapons and armor, of course, but that—and your pledge of fealty—is all that Matsunaga-*san* requires. A rare opportunity for a man like you."

Given his past experiences with Matsunaga Hisahide, Hiro suspected the "invitation" would not apply to him as to other men. However, he had no intention of mentioning this to the samurai guard.

Instead, he bowed. "Thank you. I will consider the shogun's offer."

"Do more than consider," the samurai said. "Soon the Miyoshi army will march on Kyoto. Wait too long, and you will miss your chance to survive the coming war."

"A man's allegiance does not assure his survival in times of war," Hiro said.

"And yet, it can ensure his death," the samurai countered.

Hiro nodded. "I appreciate the warning."

"Appreciation won't save your life. Accept the shogun's offer while you can." The guard stepped back, and Hiro continued across the bridge.

When he reached the western bank, he started south on the path that paralleled the river. As he walked, he considered the samurai's words.

Matsunaga Hisahide had seized control of Kyoto after the former shogun's alleged suicide three months before. The emperor had not officially given Hisahide the shogunate, but it would happen unless another claimant seized the capital city soon. Hiro didn't care who became the shogun, as long as Father Mateo remained alive and out of danger. Warlords had ruled Kyoto for over a century, and, though some men might argue otherwise, Hiro saw little difference between Hisahide and any other.

Hiro turned west at Shijō Road. A block from the river, he passed the entrance to Pontochō. Few customers walked the narrow alley at this early hour. The pleasure district's bars and teahouses didn't fill up until after dark.

A ragged beggar emerged from the shadows near the alley entrance. He wore a dingy, hooded robe with a cowl that hid his face. He started toward Hiro, head bowed and hands extended. "Sir?"

A dōshin raced across the street, brandishing his *jitte*. "Leave the samurai alone! Get out of here, you filthy trash!"

CHAPTER 12

The beggar paused a bit too long. The dōshin's nightstick struck his shoulder with a thump that promised an ugly bruise. The beggar doubled over and raised his hands to shield his head. "I'm sorry, sir! I'm sorry!"

The quavering voice sounded slightly familiar, though Hiro couldn't place it.

"Get out of here!" the dōshin ordered. "I've told you filth a thousand times—no begging in Pontochō during business hours!"

The beggar whimpered and turned to flee.

As the dōshin raised his jitte again, a winged shadow streaked from the sky and struck the policeman's face. He staggered backward with a startled cry.

The bird beat its wings on the dōshin's head. Its talons scratched his cheek, and then the bird flew off toward the river, as suddenly as it appeared.

Hiro noted the beggar had used the distraction to escape.

The dōshin raised a hand to his cheek. "A demon! It attacked me!"

"A crow, not a demon." Hiro gestured toward the roof from which the bird had come. "Most likely, it nests in the rafters."

The dōshin glanced upward nervously, as if expecting another attack. "A crow? I've never seen one do that before."

Hiro had, though not to a person. In Iga, he'd often seen the adult birds defending their nests against predators. Father Mateo had said that Western people considered crows an evil omen, but in Japan they were harbingers of the gods. Hiro admired the large black birds. Like shinobi, they protected their own. He did find it odd that the crow appeared at the moment the beggar needed help. Especially since, despite his words, he saw no nest nearby.

Hiro continued toward Ginjiro's as the sunset torched the sky. A couple of blocks past Pontochō, he turned and continued south. Just before he reached the brewery, Hiro stopped to buy a bowl of noodles from his favorite roadside vendor. Nothing tasted better than steaming *udon* in a savory, fishy sauce. He finished his treat as the sky grew dark and the golden glow of lanterns lit the street. With a nod, he returned the bowl to the vendor and resumed his walk.

Most of the shops had opened, but few customers walked the street. Laborers ended work at sunset, as did many samurai, and getting to the restaurants took time. Flickering, inviting light emerged from doorways along the street, blocked in places by the shadowed forms of business owners watching passersby with hopeful eyes.

"You! Ronin!"

The voice made Hiro pause. He turned to see one of the yoriki's henchmen walking toward him. He waited as the dōshin approached, but didn't speak or bow.

"What are you doing out without your master?" the dōshin demanded.

I could ask the same of you, Hiro thought, but opted for something less likely to cause a fight. "I do not work in the evenings. I came out for a flask of sake."

"We don't want your kind in this ward. If you want sake, go to Pontochō."

"This street serves every class of man, from samurai to farmer." Hiro struggled to retain his calm demeanor. "You have no right to order me to leave."

"I could arrest you for causing trouble." The dōshin's upper lip curled with disdain. "Yoriki Hosokawa says you're troublemakers—you and the priest."

"Did he order you to follow me?" Hiro asked. "Or did you simply see me walking and decide to create a problem where none existed? I will remind you, in case you'd forgotten, that Magistrate Ishimaki respects me . . . and the foreign priest."

"That won't save you from interrogation," the dōshin threatened. "We have orders to make sure you're not conducting an investigation."

"Does this look like an investigation?" Hiro made an expansive gesture. "It looks to me like a man in search of a drink."

"I'm watching you," the dōshin snarled. "Do not forget your place."

"Words every man should remember," Hiro said.

After an uncomfortable moment, the dōshin scowled and stomped away. When he disappeared up the street, Hiro continued toward his destination.

Ginjiro's brewery featured an open storefront with a raised, tatami-covered floor where patrons could sit and enjoy their drinks with a view of the usually bustling street. As Hiro approached, he noticed Ginjiro standing behind the wooden counter that ran along the left side of the shop. Charcoal braziers cast a golden glow on the honeyed wood and chased the shadows from the knee-high floor where patrons gathered during business hours.

The shop was empty of customers, but the brewer wasn't alone inside. A bald-headed monk knelt in the corner nearest the street, as far from the counter—and Ginjiro—as possible. He wore a filthy, grease-stained robe, and his age-lined face had a patient, if vacant, expression. When he noticed Hiro, his countenance lit up with a smile that revealed his lone remaining tooth.

"Hiro-*san*!" the monk exclaimed. "A thousand blessings on you this fine evening!"

"And on you, Suke," Hiro said. "Are you well tonight?"

Suke's smile vanished. "In truth, I have a terrific thirst. I'd bless a man a hundred times for buying me a drink."

"And two hundred for a flask?" Hiro slipped off his sandals and knelt up onto the knee-high floor but did not remove his katana because he didn't intend to stay.

"A man of my humble means could never expect such generosity," Suke said, "but if your words are an offer, I won't refuse."

Ginjiro bowed as Hiro reached the counter. "Good evening, Matsui-*san*."

Like most people in Kyoto, the brewer knew him only as Matsui Hiro, the masterless samurai who served the foreign priest—an identity Hiro had adopted upon his arrival in Kyoto, to ensure his shinobi status remained a secret.

Ginjiro bowed again, more deeply. "Thank you again for helping me—"

Hiro cut him off. "No further thanks is necessary. What is past is finished."

The brewer's gaze flickered to the swords in Hiro's sash. "How may I help you?"

"Draw a flask for Suke," Hiro said, "and bring him a bowl of rice, along with whatever else you have tonight."

Ginjiro frowned at the monk in the corner. "It's early. Nothing is ready but soup and pickled vegetables."

Hiro ignored the brewer's scowl. Ginjiro pretended to disapprove of Suke's constant presence, but he never sent the monk away and always ensured that Suke had food to eat if no one bought it for him.

"Soup and vegetables will do, along with a bowl of rice." Hiro set a pair of silver coins on the wooden counter. "I cannot stay, but this should cover the expense."

"And then some." Ginjiro took the coins. "I will see that he gets food."

"And sake!" Suke called from his corner. "Hiro mentioned sake."

He might have lost his hair and teeth, but there was nothing wrong with Suke's ears.

Footsteps approached the brewery, and Hiro turned to see Jiro outside the shop. The young man bowed, but seemed unwilling to step inside.

Hiro left the shop and slipped on his sandals. "Would you like some noodles?"

"Noodles?" Jiro seemed confused.

"You do eat udon, don't you?" Hiro started toward the nearest vendor. It wasn't his favorite, but then, he had eaten already.

At the cart, he paid for a bowl of noodles and told the merchant to give the food to Jiro.

"Eat," Hiro said. "We'll talk when you finish."

Jiro looked nervous, but hesitated for only a moment before he wolfed the noodles down.

Hiro stifled a smile. Given Jiro's age and build, as well as his occupation, Hiro suspected the youth was often hungry. He also hoped the unexpected treat would loosen Jiro's tongue. In Hiro's experience, hungry men let down their guard in the presence of tasty food.

As he waited, Hiro inhaled the mingling scents of steaming noodles and grilling fish from carts along the street. The salty-sweet odor of roasting meat and a plume of smoke from a charcoal fire combined with other aromas, and Hiro's mouth began to water. He resisted the urge to indulge in yet another bowl of noodles.

When Jiro had almost finished, Hiro said, "Tell me what you know about the coin."

Jiro shrugged. "I never saw it before this morning."

"That's not what you told me earlier," Hiro said.

Jiro flushed. "I wanted you to leave before Basho noticed you at the shop."

"I know the coin belonged to Emi," Hiro said. "She was wearing it when she died."

"That isn't possible." Jiro seemed alarmed. "Emi needed money to buy her freedom from the teahouse. She would not have kept a golden coin as an ornament."

"She did not need to buy her freedom," Hiro said. "She was an actor's daughter, not a teahouse girl. She lied to you—unless you lied to me."

CHAPTER 13

Jiro slurped down the last of his noodles and returned the bowl to the vendor.

"I'm only going to ask this once," Hiro said as they started down the street. "Did you give the coin to Emi?"

"No, sir," Jiro said. "Not that it matters."

Hiro stopped walking and turned on the youth with a glare.

"I apologize." Jiro ducked his head and raised his hands in self-defense. "I did not intend—"

"Your intentions are irrelevant," Hiro snapped. "Do not forget your place again. Does Basho know you had an affair with a riverbank girl?"

Jiro straightened, but kept his face turned downward. "There was no affair—nothing for him to know—I swear. We spoke at the shrine a couple of times, and once by the river, but nothing more. I never even told her how I felt—"

"I don't believe you," Hiro interrupted.

"I promise, sir, I'm telling the truth. Emi told me she worked in a teahouse. We only talked a few times, by the shrine and the river. We walked together . . . and talked . . . but nothing more. . . ." Jiro started breathing hard. His hands were shaking. "Please, you must believe me. This apprenticeship is all I have. I had to come to Kyoto because my parents can't afford to feed me. If you talk to Basho . . . if he fires me . . . I have nowhere else to go."

"A persuasive story," Hiro said, "except that I don't believe it. You will have to do better than merely repeating the lies you've told before."

Jiro struggled to control his breathing. "I admit, I did love Emi. I wouldn't have cared that she was an actor's daughter. But she really

58

did say she lived in a teahouse. I learned the truth from the yoriki this morning—just like you did." He wiped a tear from his eye.

Hiro examined the coin for a moment and then returned it to his sleeve. "If I discover you've lied to me, I will tell Basho that you had an affair with an actor's daughter and killed her so he wouldn't learn the truth."

Jiro shook his head, too stunned to speak.

"I do not care if the story is false," Hiro added. "Basho will believe it, and you will have to deal with the consequences."

"Please, sir, no." Jiro fell to his knees and pressed his forehead to the ground. "I beg you. You must believe me. I told the truth."

"Then you have nothing to worry about." Hiro made a dismissive gesture. "Go."

Jiro climbed to his feet and scurried away.

Hiro knew the youth had not revealed everything he knew, but he did believe that Jiro loved the girl. Unfortunately, that didn't eliminate the possibility that he killed her.

Jiro had barely disappeared when a voice across the street said, "Matsui-*san*!"

Hiro spun, expecting another dōshin. Instead, he saw a familiar, middle-aged man in a carpenter's tunic and baggy trousers.

The carpenter's gnarled hands revealed years of manual labor, but his eyes had an intelligent gleam that spoke of knowledge beyond his planes and chisels.

Etiquette didn't permit a bow, but Hiro nodded as the man approached. "Good evening, Ozuru. I didn't expect to see you here."

Ozuru bowed from the waist. "I'm glad I found you, Matsui-*san*."

"Truly?" Hiro asked. "I seem to remember, the last time we met, you said we would not meet again."

"I have not come of my own accord." Ozuru was no more a carpenter than Hiro was a translator, although the two men came from different clans.

Hiro felt his pleasant evening slip away, and cast a longing look at the glow of Ginjiro's brewery down the street. "What message does Matsunaga-*san* have for me this time?"

"Hisahide did not send me." Ozuru began to walk away. "And what I have to say, I can't say here."

After a moment's hesitation, Hiro fell in step with the older man.

At Sanjō Road, Ozuru turned right, toward the river. Hiro followed, hoping the "message" didn't involve an ambush. The fight itself didn't worry him. He could probably kill Ozuru. However, he would rather not be responsible for starting a war between the shinobi clans.

When they reached the Kamo River, they stopped in front of the bored-looking samurai guarding Sanjō Bridge.

"What is your business this evening?" the samurai asked.

Hiro bowed. "I am Matsui Hiro, translator for the foreign priest who lives on Marutamachi Road. The priest has need of a carpenter, and summoned this man for an estimate."

"At night?" the samurai asked.

Ozuru bowed and kept his face bent down in deference. "Please forgive me, sir. I work all day and can only discuss new jobs at night."

The samurai looked at Hiro. "Wise to escort him. I wouldn't have let him pass the bridge alone."

"Has the shogun instituted a curfew?" Hiro loathed referring to Hisahide as the shogun, but anything less would raise unwanted questions about his loyalty.

"Not officially," the samurai said, "but there have been . . . incidents . . . on the bridges after dark."

Hiro nodded. "Shall I escort the carpenter home as well?"

"As long as he returns by this road, I'll remember him, but I go off duty when the bells ring midnight."

Hiro nodded again. "Our meeting will not take that long."

Ozuru turned north, to follow the path on the western side of the river. Hiro started across the bridge. He doubted Ozuru intended an ambush, but had no intention of letting a possible adversary choose the path. Ozuru had no choice but to follow.

The path beside the river was dark and empty. Cherry trees stretched their limbs overhead like grasping witches from a children's tale. A gentle breeze blew off the river, making the branches waver as if preparing to seize their prey.

"You know I won't allow you to follow me all the way to the Jesuit's home," Hiro said as they walked beneath the trees.

Ozuru nodded. "No more than I would permit you into the shogun's compound after dark."

"Then Koga is loyal to Hisahide," Hiro said.

"My clan is loyal to itself alone," Ozuru answered. "Were it otherwise, I would not be here now. I bear a message from the Koga ryu."

"You expect me to believe that Koga's leader has something to say to me?" Hiro barely managed to stop himself from calling Ozuru a liar.

The older man paused beneath a tree whose spreading branches cast the road in darkness. "No, but Koga's leader recently sent a message to Hattori Hanzo. Since that message affects your interests, I thought you would want to hear it as soon as possible."

Hiro reached up his kimono sleeve and touched the shuriken hidden there. At this range, and in the dark, he wasn't taking any chances. Hattori Hanzo was the head of the Iga ryu, as well as Hiro's cousin, but even if the Koga leader had sent Hanzo a message, that fact didn't make this meeting any safer.

"I heard you reach for a weapon," Ozuru said. "I assure you, I do not want a fight. However, if it comes to that, you will not take my life."

"You are not the first man to wrongfully think he can beat me," Hiro said, "and, I promise, you won't be the last."

CHAPTER 14

"Perhaps you should hear my message before we duel to the death?" Ozuru's tone revealed he was smiling.

"I am listening," Hiro said.

"Hisahide holds Kyoto, but his claim on the shogunate is not secure. A number of other daimyo have laid claim to the title also. Koga has not decided, yet, which samurai lord to support. I understand that Iga has not either."

Hiro saw no harm in admitting the truth. "I've heard nothing of Iga's decision, one way or another."

"After the shogun's death, Hattori Hanzo sent a message to Koga, requesting a meeting and suggesting an alliance. He wishes to prevent our clans from fighting one another when the daimyo go to war."

"Hattori Hanzo has no fear of Koga," Hiro said.

"Fear is not the only reason leaders seek a truce. With the shogunate contested for the first time in a century, who knows how many pointless deaths an alliance between the shinobi could avoid?"

Hiro didn't answer. Ozuru's story seemed entirely too convenient.

"I find your silence reassuring," Ozuru said. "Only an intelligent man takes time to consider unexpected news."

Hiro raised an eyebrow, though Ozuru couldn't see him in the darkness. "An intelligent man might also ask why one low-ranked shinobi would discuss this kind of news with another. Until our leaders make decisions, clan affairs are none of our concern."

Ozuru released an exasperated sigh. "Enough pretense. Only a senior shinobi gets assigned to protect a critical foreign target."

"You overestimate my importance," Hiro said, "and that of the priest."

"You underestimate my intelligence—and my sources," Ozuru countered. "Koga's ambassador is preparing to leave for Iga, even as we speak. During negotiations, every Koga shinobi has orders to act as if an alliance is in effect. You, my Iga brother, are now my ally—at least until my commander tells me otherwise."

Hiro didn't trust assumptions, beautiful women, or men from rival clans. All of them had proven far too deadly in the past.

"You risked a meeting just to tell me our clans *might* form an alliance?"

"That isn't a sufficient reason?" Ozuru asked.

Hiro had tired of verbal sparring. "No."

"Proving yet again that you're no novice," Ozuru said. "I also came to warn you that Hisahide plans to kill the Portuguese merchant and priest you guard."

Hiro felt a surge of nervous energy. If Ozuru spoke the truth, Father Mateo needed to escape from Kyoto immediately. But if the other shinobi lied, a sudden departure would send them directly into a Koga ambush.

"When does he plan to do it?" Hiro asked.

"I do not know, but soon. He sent a messenger to the foreign settlement at Yokoseura, carrying a license for another Portuguese merchant to sell firearms in Kyoto."

"Eliminating his need for Luis Álvares," Hiro said.

"An intelligent inference, and an accurate one."

"Harming the merchant, or the priest, would anger the Portuguese king," Hiro said. "Surely Hisahide wouldn't risk a second war."

"The foreigners' country lies on the opposite side of a hostile and unpredictable ocean. Hisahide has more pressing concerns than the anger of a distant foreign king." After a pause, Ozuru continued, "The Miyoshi daimyo has summoned his army and sent out word that he's hiring mercenaries. Also, Shogun Ashikaga's brother has renounced his vows and left his monastery."

"Oda Nobunaga will not let this war resolve without him," Hiro added. "That means at least a three-sided fight for Kyoto."

"If not more," Ozuru said. "Those three are not the only claimants to the shogunate."

"When does Hisahide expect the new merchant from Yokoseura?" Hiro asked.

"By the end of the week," Ozuru said. "Your merchant will suffer a most unfortunate accident soon thereafter."

"At your hands?" Hiro would rather not kill Ozuru, especially not to benefit Luis Álvares. However, he could not tolerate threats against Father Mateo's household.

"Only a fool would send an assassin to kill a merchant," Ozuru said, "and, whatever you think of Hisahide, he is not a fool. Hundreds of samurai in this city would gladly test a sword on a Portuguese neck to prove their loyalty to the shogun."

Hiro released the shuriken and withdrew his arm from his sleeve. He didn't trust Ozuru, but this particular conversation seemed unlikely to lead to mortal combat.

"I don't expect you to trust me," Ozuru said, as if reading Hiro's thoughts. "You know my loyalty lies with Koga. Still, my commander ordered me to treat you as an ally, and an ally deserves a warning when danger threatens. What you do with the information is up to you."

Unfortunately, Ozuru's words could hide a trap as well as an honest warning.

"Perhaps you can tell me," Hiro said, "does Hisahide plan to exterminate all of the Portuguese in Kyoto, or only the single merchant and the priest?"

"That, I do not know," Ozuru said. "Regrettably, Hisahide is a man of limited vision. I believe his time as shogun will be short."

"He is not shogun yet," Hiro said.

"He will be. Get your foreigners out of the city now."

"Thank you for the warning," Hiro said. "I will repay the favor, should the opportunity arise."

"Forget the favor," Ozuru said. "Just take your priest and the merchant and leave the city while you can."

CHAPTER 15

Hiro returned to the Jesuit's home to find Father Mateo sitting alone in the common room. A kettle hanging over the fire sent a curl of steam into the air.

The shinobi approached the hearth as Ana emerged from the kitchen bearing a tray with a teapot, a cup, and a plate of rice balls.

The housekeeper looked at Hiro. "Hm. I suppose you're hungry too."

"He can share my plate," Father Mateo said. "Please bring a second cup. That's all we need."

Ana set the tray in front of the priest. "The way he eats? You won't get a bite. I will make another plate."

Gato trotted in from the kitchen as Ana left the room. The tortoiseshell cat gave a trilling mew and bounded toward Hiro, tail high with excitement.

Hiro knelt and extended a fist. Gato butted his hand with her head, then whipped her face upward and bit the shinobi's knuckles.

"Hey!" Hiro pulled his hand away as Gato swatted it with her paw. She fell on her side and waved her legs in the air.

Hiro reached for the cat's white belly. Gato grasped his wrist with her paws, sank her teeth in his sleeve, and kicked at his arm. Her purr rose up through a mouthful of silk.

"Don't let Ana catch you," Father Mateo warned. "You'll never hear the end of it if Gato rips your robes."

Hiro scooped the cat into his arms. She tightened her grip on his sleeve and bit down harder.

"That's enough." He laughed and stroked the cat.

Gato kicked at his sleeve once more, released her grip, and sniffed in the direction of the food.

"Don't let her near the rice balls either," Father Mateo said. "She licked the last ones."

Hiro laughed again.

"Hm. That isn't funny." Ana returned with a second tray of rice balls and a cup for Hiro's tea. She set the tray down and took the cat from his arms.

Gato's purr increased in volume.

"I have something for you in the kitchen," Ana told the cat as she turned to leave. "A nice little fish. I'd rather you had it than Luis."

Father Mateo sneezed. As usual, Gato's presence made his nose turn red and his eyes water. Even so, the priest allowed the cat to stay. He seemed to like her, despite the discomfort she caused him.

"Did Jiro meet you as he promised?" Father Mateo asked.

Hiro nodded. His mouth was full of rice.

"I'm surprised," the Jesuit said, "but at least we know he's innocent."

Hiro swallowed. "Not at all. Running would prove he had something to hide. Talking gives him a chance to lie."

"Or tell the truth." Father Mateo lifted the steaming kettle off its chain and poured hot water into the teapot. "What did he tell you about the coin?"

"Nothing new." Hiro watched a tendril of scented steam rise up from the pot. "He claimed he hadn't seen it before and said he wouldn't have given it to a girl."

"Seems reasonable," the Jesuit said. "A golden coin is a rich man's bauble. To a poor man, it's a meal."

"If true, it suggests the girl had another patron," Hiro said, "or perhaps a client."

Father Mateo frowned at the implication—that Emi worked as a prostitute. "Or else that Satsu is correct, and the killer left the coin as a warning."

"Possibly," Hiro said, "though I find the other options more compelling. Still, I believe she knew her killer. She wouldn't let a stranger close enough to put a rope around her neck."

"That much matches Jiro's story." Father Mateo poured Hiro's tea and then his own. "He claimed he fell asleep on the bank and woke up to find Emi dead beside him. She wouldn't go willingly with a stranger, and even a man in a drunken slumber would have heard her scream."

"Why would the killer drag her back to Jiro?" Hiro asked. "No killer strangles a girl in the open, where passersby could see. Few enough would risk returning her to a spot so near the path."

"It seems to me the killer wanted Jiro to take the blame," the Jesuit said.

"Or Jiro is the killer," Hiro countered. "He might have dragged the body up the bank to throw suspicion off himself."

"Why would Jiro kill a girl and then lie down to sleep beside her body?" Father Mateo asked.

"We don't know that he did," Hiro said. "We have only his word that he fell asleep at all."

"This is impossible," Father Mateo said. "We don't even know where to start with a list of suspects."

"We have Jiro," Hiro said, "and Emi's sister, Chou, can tell us more about the people Emi knew."

Father Mateo sipped his tea. "She didn't say much this afternoon."

"She wouldn't, in front of her parents." Hiro raised his teacup and inhaled the fragrant steam. He sipped and paused to enjoy the delicate flavor of the tea.

Muffled barking outside the house announced the approach of someone in the street. Hiro loathed the neighbor's Akita, but, at least in this, the dog was useful.

The front door creaked, and heavy footsteps thumped across the entry.

"Good evening, Luis," Hiro said without turning.

"How do you always know it's me?" The merchant entered the common room.

"The rest of us are home already," Father Mateo said.

Hiro would have answered the question differently, but let it pass. Father Mateo wouldn't approve of him saying Luis had the grace of a drunken ox.

Luis leaned over Father Mateo's shoulder to inspect the tray of snacks. He straightened with an indignant sniff. "Rice balls again. I should have known. This country needs some decent food, like bread, and meat, and Portuguese wine."

Hiro considered the merchant's rounded belly and puffy face. For all Luis's complaining, the Japanese diet hadn't harmed his girth.

"I ate near the warehouse anyway." The merchant started toward his room. "Big day tomorrow. I have a shipment coming from Yokoseura."

"Yokoseura?" Hiro remembered Ozuru's warning. "You say it arrives tomorrow?"

Luis turned back. "Why do you care?"

"I don't," Hiro lied. "I was being polite."

"Oh." Luis scratched his stomach. "Well, since we're being polite, I'll answer. The shipment won't arrive for a couple of days, but I need to make room in the warehouse, which means a very long day tomorrow, supervising lazy peasants who'd rather nap in the corner than do the job I've paid them for.

"And now, I need my rest. Good night, Mateo."

Luis went into his room and closed the door.

CHAPTER 16

"What's going on?" Father Mateo looked suspicious. "You're never 'just polite' to Luis."

"Perhaps my character is improving." Hiro refilled the Jesuit's tea and poured himself another cup as well. As before, he raised the cup to inhale the fragrant steam.

Father Mateo didn't care for extravagant food or special teas, but Luis kept the Jesuit's pantry stocked with *ichibancha*—the most-expensive, first-picked leaves. Hiro's sensitive nose and tea-loving palate considered this a rare redeeming point in the merchant's favor.

"Right," the Jesuit said, "and I'm a Buddhist. What's the truth?"

Hiro closed his eyes and drew another lingering breath. He sipped the tea and felt the liquid roll across his tongue.

"Hiro," Father Mateo said expectantly.

Hiro sighed. A cultured man should not disrupt a special cup of tea with sour talk. He opened his eyes and lowered his cup.

"After I spoke with Jiro, I ran into a man from Koga." He spoke softly to ensure his voice wouldn't carry through the walls or across the rafters.

"A man . . . like you?" Father Mateo avoided the word "shinobi," even at home, because Luis and Ana didn't know the truth.

"He warned us to leave the city at once." Hiro considered how much of Ozuru's message to reveal. "Kyoto is no longer safe for you— or for Luis."

"I hope that God will prevent a war," Father Mateo said. "I pray for it every night and every morning."

"Your god may have the power to prevent a war in Portugal," Hiro said, "but the kami like a good war now and then."

"There is only one God, and he can prevent a war in Japan, if he chooses."

"And if he doesn't?" Hiro asked.

"Then I will trust him anyway."

Hiro shifted the conversation back to its original topic. "The man from Koga warned me that Hisahide has sent for a Portuguese merchant, a replacement for Luis."

"Replacement?" Father Mateo echoed. "Luis hasn't mentioned wanting to leave Kyoto. No more than usual, anyway, and he never truly means it."

"Hisahide does not forgive disloyalty," Hiro said.

"Do you mean Luis's sale of Portuguese firearms to the warlord— the Miyoshi daimyo?" Father Mateo asked. "That happened months ago—and he didn't follow through."

"Fish will spoil with age; revenge does not," Hiro said. "Hisahide will kill Luis, and perhaps you also, as soon as the other merchant reaches Kyoto."

"He has no authority to kill us," Father Mateo said. "Luis and I have an imperial pass. We are immune to punishment, unless we break the law."

"You speak of authority," Hiro said. "I speak of regrettable accidents. Mistaken identities. Bad translations. A samurai making a most unfortunate error. Apologies would be made, of course, and reparations paid to your king. But you and Luis Álvares will be dead."

"You're overreacting," Father Mateo said.

Hiro raised his cup but didn't drink. The tea was cold.

"What would you have me do? Leave the city?" Father Mateo asked. "I cannot abandon my congregation."

"You can, and you will, if preserving your life requires it." Hiro selected a rice ball from the plate. He expected the priest to argue, but Father Mateo did not respond.

Unfortunately, Hiro knew the Jesuit's silence did not constitute consent.

After a moment just long enough to permit a change of subject without rudeness, Father Mateo asked, "How will you persuade Chou to admit what she knows about Emi's trip to the river?"

Hiro smiled. "I'm not going to persuade her. You are."

The following morning, Hiro and Father Mateo left the house right after breakfast. The sky was a deep, autumnal blue, and a heavy scent of wood smoke permeated the chilly air. At Hiro's instruction, Father Mateo carried Emi's coin in his purse.

The guard at Marutamachi Bridge nodded but didn't stop them as they turned onto the path that paralleled the eastern side of the river.

"Do the samurai seem more relaxed to you?" Father Mateo asked.

"Relaxed?" Hiro resisted the urge to look over his shoulder at the bridge.

"Less nervous," Father Mateo said. "Is it possible that the emperor named Hisahide shogun without us knowing?"

"When the emperor names a shogun, it's no secret," Hiro said. "The guards have simply become complacent. No man can maintain vigilance forever."

"Do they believe the threat of rebellion has passed?"

"Quite the opposite," Hiro said. "The Ashikaga clan has lodged a formal objection to Hisahide's claim on the shogunate. They haven't begun an armed revolt, but only because they lack the strength, and numbers, to seize Kyoto. That could change if the proper claimant appeared at the city gates."

"The proper claimant...Shogun Ashikaga's brother?" Father Mateo asked.

Hiro nodded. "Rumors say he plans to claim the shogunate."

"Will the emperor honor his claim, now that Hisahide controls the city?"

Hiro shrugged. "That depends on the size of the army he brings with him."

CHAPTER 17

A thin boy crouched on the ground outside the building that housed the Yutoku-za. He looked no more than eight years old, with skinny limbs and a freshly shaven scalp. The razor had nicked the back of his head, but a crusty scab already covered the spot.

The boy squatted close to the ground and poked at something with a stick.

As Hiro drew closer, he realized the boy was steering a beetle away from the street. A horn projected several inches out from the beetle's face. The insect moved with caution, like an elderly samurai in spiky armor.

Every time the beetle tried to turn back toward the road, the child nudged it in the opposite direction. Slowly but surely, the beetle moved away from the crushing feet of passersby.

Hiro wondered if Father Mateo had saved such helpless creatures as a child. He decided the Jesuit probably had. In many ways, the priest resembled the squatting boy, determined to help the innocent things that could not help themselves.

The boy looked up as Hiro's shadow fell across the beetle's path. His curiosity faded to dismay at the sight of the samurai and the priest. He laid his palms in the dirt and bowed his forehead to the ground, taking care to shield the beetle in the space between his hands and knees.

"Good morning," Father Mateo said. "What is your name, young man?"

The child raised his face to the priest. "Please do not kill me, noble sir."

"Nobody's going to kill you," Father Mateo said. "I merely asked your name."

"Please, sir, I am Haru, son of Satsu." The child returned his face to the ground. "Forgive my impertinence for speaking in the presence of a samurai."

He spoke with unusual precision, rare in a child so young.

"Stand up, Haru, son of Satsu," Father Mateo said. "I don't like talking to the backs of people's heads."

The boy stood up, but continued to face the ground.

"That's a fine-looking beetle," Father Mateo said. "Is it yours?"

The beetle butted at the stick, which Haru had positioned to stop the insect from returning to the street.

"The *kabutomushi*?" Haru looked up. "No, sir. He belongs to himself. I'm only helping. I didn't want someone to step on him before he finds a mate. Of course, this late in the year, he might not find a lady beetle, but I think that he should have the chance to try."

"A noble sentiment," Father Mateo said. "Are you a Buddhist?"

"A Buddhist, sir?" Haru ran a hand across his scalp. "I'm not a monk, if that's what you mean. My mother shaved my hair for my sister. She died, and we're in mourning. That is, my sister died. My mother is alive."

"I am sorry to hear about your sister," Father Mateo said.

"I wanted to save the beetle because I couldn't save my sister." Haru's voice cracked, and he looked down at the kabutomushi.

"It isn't your fault she died." Father Mateo started to reach for the boy, but stopped before Haru noticed. Hiro approved. Men of samurai status did not touch commoners voluntarily.

"Thank you, sir," Haru said, with a pause that suggested he might have said more, had etiquette allowed it.

Hiro took over the conversation. "Is your father home this morning?"

Haru bowed. "I apologize, sir, but my father has gone to the temple, with my mother, to speak to the priests about Emi's funeral. I can fetch him for you, if you wish."

"We have only a minor question," Hiro said. "Perhaps your sister, Chou, is home to answer it for us?"

"Chou?" Haru sounded doubtful. "She doesn't know much of anything, except about Yuji." He said the last word in a dreamy tone, as if mimicking someone—it wasn't difficult to guess who.

Hiro squared his shoulders and glared at the boy. "You will tell your sister we've come." One advantage to samurai status was never having to ask, or explain himself, when speaking to commoners.

"Of course, sir." Haru bowed and used the gesture to scoop the beetle into his hand. "I will fetch her at once." He backed to the door of the house and slipped inside.

"You didn't have to frighten the child," Father Mateo said, "and we could have gone with him. He didn't have to call his sister to the street."

"Frightened children don't remember to take the beetle," Hiro said, "and we do need Chou to come to the street. She will not reveal Emi's secrets where others might overhear."

"Maybe they didn't have any secrets," Father Mateo said.

Hiro stared at the priest. "You don't know much about women, do you?"

Father Mateo frowned.

Before he could answer, Haru returned with Chou.

The girl stood shorter than average, with a sturdy build and a mottled complexion completely unlike her sister's silken skin. Her dark hair lacked the gleam so common in girls from wealthier families, and her features seemed to disagree about the proper proportions for her face.

"You lead the questioning," Hiro murmured to Father Mateo in Portuguese. "The girl won't fear a priest—not even a foreign one—as much as a samurai."

Father Mateo nodded, acknowledging Hiro's words and Chou's arrival simultaneously. As the young woman bowed, he said, "Good morning. Do you remember us from yesterday?"

Chou began to nod, then hastily added, "Yes, sir."

Hiro suspected Chou had little experience talking with men of higher rank.

"I am a priest of God," the Jesuit said. "This man is my interpreter, Matsui Hiro."

"But you don't need a translator," Haru objected. "You speak Japanese quite well."

Hiro stifled a smile. Most adults considered the Japanese language too nuanced for a foreigner to master. Children lacked that prejudice, which made them difficult to fool.

"I help him with our customs as well as the language," Hiro said.

Haru opened his mouth to speak, but Chou nudged him. "Enough." She bowed again. "I apologize for my brother. He is young and forgets his manners. How may I help you?"

Father Mateo reached into his purse. "Your father asked me to find the owner of the coin your sister wore the night she died."

He displayed the golden coin in his palm. The leather dangled toward the street.

Chou clutched the sides of her faded kimono. "I'm sorry, sir, I don't know where that came from. I saw it only yesterday morning, after we brought her home."

"Might a friend have given it to her?" Father Mateo asked.

Chou shook her head. "Emi didn't have any friends who could give a gift like that."

Father Mateo glanced at Hiro. The Jesuit seemed to have run out of questions.

"Your brother speaks well for his age," Hiro said. "Does he act on the stage?"

Haru straightened with obvious pride.

"He will make his debut as a *kokata* soon," Chou said.

"A child actor," Hiro translated for Father Mateo's benefit. "Some plays have special roles that are played by children."

"I will take the stage next month," Haru said.

"Will Yuji act in that performance also?" Hiro asked.

"Perhaps." Chou blushed and cast her eyes downward at the mention of Yuji's name.

"But not as shite," Haru added, "only in the lesser roles. When I am older, I will play the shite's roles, but Yuji never will." He spoke without arrogance, as if simply stating a fact that everyone took for truth.

"Do not say such things," Chou cried, with a hint of anger.

"I'm only repeating what Grandfather said." Haru raised his chin. "Yuji's flower does not advance as it should. He cannot handle the larger roles."

"Haru," Chou began as if to scold the boy, but her demeanor suddenly changed. "Did you notice the drummers warming up as we left the house?"

"No!" Haru said. "You promised to tell me when they started. I want to see the practice!"

Chou gestured toward the house. "You haven't missed it. . . ."

"Please excuse me." Haru bowed and hurried back inside.

Hiro admired the ease with which Chou diverted her brother's attention. He also hoped she had something useful to tell them, now that they were alone.

CHAPTER 18

"I apologize for Haru," Chou said as the door swung shut behind the boy. "Talented children in our art do not receive much discipline before the age of eight. Grandfather says that too much restriction distorts their natural talent."

"Is your father waiting for Yuji's skills to improve before you wed?" Hiro spoke too bluntly for a conversation between men, but samurai owed no subtlety to a woman.

Chou bowed her head. "Our parents wanted us to wed last New Year, after the festival, but Yuji's father died two days before the festival began. Now, we will marry as soon as our year of mourning is complete."

"Do you participate in the mourning also?" Father Mateo asked.

Chou nodded. "I will soon be Yuji's wife. It is proper that I share this duty."

"Had your parents found a husband for Emi also?" Hiro asked.

"No, sir." Chou paused as if deciding how much to say. At last she settled on, "My father couldn't find an appropriate match."

"Did Emi cause problems within the Yutoku-za?" Father Mateo asked.

"No, sir, quite the opposite. Father couldn't find a man he thought was good enough for Emi. Not with Yuji already betrothed to me. And despite what Haru said, my Yuji is a rising star. Grandfather simply thinks he needs more time for his talent to mature. No one is as handsome, or as skilled on the stage, as Yuji."

"You seem to know him well," Father Mateo said.

The comment made Hiro wonder whether the Jesuit had noticed

77

Chou's unusual use of the words, "my Yuji." Few unmarried women, and not even many wives, would speak of a man with such familiarity.

"We grew up together, in the za," Chou said. "Our parents always planned for us to marry. They arranged it before Emi was even born."

Hiro caught a hint of defensiveness in her tone. He wondered whether there was more to her possessiveness—and Emi's lack of a husband—than Chou revealed. He decided not to press the issue further. Not for the moment, anyway.

"Did Emi have a suitor your parents didn't know about?" Father Mateo asked. "Perhaps a man who gave her the coin as a pledge?"

"Impossible." Chou shook her head. "We shared a room, and shared our secrets. If she had a man . . . or a golden coin . . . I would have known."

"Then you believe, as your father does, that Emi acquired the coin the night she died?" the Jesuit asked.

Hiro gave the priest a disapproving look.

Chou didn't seem to notice. "That must be what happened. A thing like that, she certainly would have shown me."

"Do you know where your sister went that evening?" Father Mateo asked.

"Yes, sir." Chou gestured to the shrine across the road. "To Chugenji. She went there every evening, sometimes even when it rained."

"She prayed there?" Father Mateo sounded surprised as he turned to look at the little shrine. "Not at one of the larger temples?"

Chou shrugged. "She thought, because the shrine is small, the god would hear her prayers more clearly than the kami at the bigger temples."

"She went only to that shrine?" Hiro asked.

"As far as I know, sir. She would have mentioned another." After a pause, Chou added, "Emi often walked by the river after praying. She said it gave her space to think—'to think,' she would say . . . as if she was a man. I told her, girls like us don't need to think. We marry and our husbands do the thinking."

"Did Emi tell you what she thought about?" Father Mateo asked.

"No, sir." Chou looked at the ground. "She said I would not understand."

"Then how do you know she had no need to think?" Father Mateo asked.

Chou seemed to struggle between an honest answer and the pro-hibition on contradicting a man of samurai rank. At last she said, "Nice girls don't walk alone by the river at night, for any reason."

Hiro noted the nonresponsive answer. "Did your parents know that Emi walked by the river?"

Chou looked up with fear in her eyes. "Please, sir, do not speak to them of this. They would be angry. . . . Emi swore she never stopped or talked to anyone by the river. She told me she only went there alone— to think—and I believed her. . . ."

"Do you believe something different now?" Father Mateo asked.

Chou's nose turned red. Tears filled her eyes. "I do not know what I believe. Someone gave that coin to my sister. I don't know who, or why. Please . . . I don't want my parents to blame me for her death, because I didn't tell . . ."

"I see no reason to mention it, as long as you've told the truth," Hiro said.

"I've told you everything." Chou sounded desperate. "I promise."

"We appreciate your assistance," Father Mateo said.

"Perhaps you can help with another issue also," Hiro added. "Father Mateo wishes to learn as much as he can about Japan, but has yet to speak with an actor about his craft. Perhaps you would ask Yuji to share his knowledge of nō with the priest?"

Chou's face burst into a brilliant smile. "Of course!" She bowed to Hiro and then to Father Mateo. "My Yuji would be honored to help the foreigner. When would you like to speak with him?"

"Now, if possible," Hiro said. "We can wait for him here and go to a teahouse. We do not wish to disrupt your home."

Hopefully, the choice to conduct the conversation away from the house would keep Chou from returning along with Yuji. Even if she did, a woman was easily sent away when a group of men decided to visit a teahouse.

After Chou disappeared into the house, Father Mateo asked, "Do you think she will tell her parents that she spoke with us?"

"No chance of that." Hiro shook his head. "Especially since she lied."

"She did? Which part was a lie?"

"There's more to her relationship with Yuji than she shared, and I suspect she knows more about Emi's walks than she let on. I'm curious to see what Yuji tells us."

"Do you think he's involved in the murder?" For once, the Jesuit didn't sound surprised.

But Hiro was. "What makes you think he might be?"

"I'd like to believe that Chou's betrothed would not have made advances toward her sister. However, Emi was beautiful, Chou is not, and I doubt that fact escaped young Yuji's notice."

Hiro wondered how the priest understood the Japanese concept of beauty so well, when his own appearance diverged so widely from it. He tried to imagine a female version of Father Mateo's pale skin, enormous nose, and unusual height. He decided that Portuguese women must look like trolls.

"You don't agree?" Father Mateo asked. "You've got an odd look on your face."

"Do women in your country have noses like yours?" Hiro asked.

"What's wrong with my nose?" Father Mateo touched it gingerly. "In Portugal, this is considered a nice-looking nose."

"I'm sure it is," Hiro said. "I was trying to picture it on a woman's face."

"We don't all have the same noses," Father Mateo said. "If anything, we look even more different from one another than Japanese people do."

Hiro opened his mouth to reply, but closed it again as a middle-aged woman emerged from the Yutoku-za.

She wore a dark kimono and the purposeful look of someone on an errand. Her gaze settled on Hiro and Father Mateo, and she approached as if she knew them. The lines on her face suggested age, though her ebony hair revealed no trace of gray. Her clothing was cut in the latest style and embroidered with colorful leaves and flowers, but Hiro noted the silk itself was not of the finest quality.

The woman stopped in front of them and bowed. Although she waited for them to address her, as custom required, she carried herself with unusual boldness, and Hiro doubted she would permit rebuff.

CHAPTER 19

"Good morning." Father Mateo's tone suggested he didn't know the woman. "May we help you?"

"Good morning, sir. My name is Rika, and my son is Yuji, of the Yutoku-za." After a pause she continued, "I came to tell you my son is ill and cannot see visitors this morning. He sends his apologies."

"How considerate of you to come, instead of sending Chou to deliver the message," Hiro said.

Father Mateo tensed, as he often did when Hiro behaved more rudely than a situation warranted. However, Hiro considered his abruptness justified. Only a daring mother—or a guilty one—would intervene on her son's behalf.

"With respect, you do not need to interview Yuji about the murder," Rika said. "He barely knew Emi, and though her death was a tragedy, my son knows nothing of it."

"Who mentioned an interview?" Hiro asked.

"Chou claimed the foreign gentlemen has interest in nō," Rika said, "but—again, with respect—my future daughter-in-law is quick to believe any compliment given to Yuji. Samurai have no interest in river-bank people except when a crime occurs. You asked for my son. A girl is dead. An investigation is the reasonable inference."

Hiro decided to overlook the woman's lack of deference. He also respected her reasoning skills too much to persist in the lie. "Where was Yuji two nights ago?"

Rika didn't hesitate. "Home, with me."

"Can anyone else confirm that?" Hiro asked.

"As I mentioned, my son has been ill," Rika said. "He left his room for lessons with Master Botan, nothing more."

"Thank you for confirming Yuji's whereabouts," Father Mateo said, "and do not worry, we don't suspect him of the crime. We're trying to find the owner of this coin." He held it up. "Have you seen it before? Do you know who it belongs to?"

Rika shook her head. "I'm sorry. I might have seen it, but how would I know? It looks no different than any other."

"Does Yuji possess any golden coins?" Hiro asked.

"Not that you would find near Emi's body," Rika said. "My son is betrothed to Chou. He would not give a gift to another woman."

Hiro found it curious that Rika characterized the coin as a gift, and also that she knew where it had come from. "You're certain your son didn't leave the house two nights ago? Not even briefly?"

"Only to use the latrine." She started to say something more but stopped.

"What were you going to say?" Hiro asked.

"Nothing, sir." She shook her head.

"A person's lips don't part for nothing." Hiro affected a samurai scowl. "Tell me what you began to say."

"I apologize." Rika hung her head. "The comment was inappropriate."

"Women do not tell samurai what is and is not appropriate," Hiro growled.

The tone drew a disapproving glance from Father Mateo.

"A thousand apologies." Rika bowed and held the obeisance for several seconds. "I started to say that Yuji wanted nothing to do with Emi—alive or dead."

"How do you know this?" Father Mateo asked.

Rika straightened. "My husband and I chose Chou for Yuji many years ago. She is plain, but also steady of temper, patient, and hard-working. She will make an excellent wife."

"And Emi?" Father Mateo asked.

Rika's lips took on a pinched expression. "The girl had dreams beyond her station."

Hiro turned to the priest and spoke in Portuguese. "Few women want their sons to marry a beautiful, independent girl. A son who loves his wife too much is difficult for a mother to control." He switched to Japanese. "Did Yuji share your opinion of Emi?"

"Of course," Rika said. "No man wants to marry a girl with a bad reputation."

Hiro found Rika's openness surprising—and suspicious. Actors didn't behave like other commoners, but even they would normally show restraint in the presence of samurai. Rika clearly wanted them to believe in Yuji's innocence, and wanted it more than Hiro considered normal.

"Did Emi have a bad reputation?" Father Mateo asked.

"She would have, had anyone known the truth." Rika sniffed. "She met men by the river, at night, when her parents thought she had gone to the temple."

"How do you know this?" Father Mateo asked.

"Yuji told me," Rika said, "although he never saw her do it. Chou told him of her sister's behavior about a week ago. She was worried about Emi, alone on the riverbank at night."

The Jesuit frowned. "Why would Chou tell Yuji instead of her parents?"

Rika shrugged. "Young people do not always show good judgment. Chou didn't want to cause her sister trouble. She thought Yuji might persuade Emi to change her wanton ways."

"Did you tell Satsu and Nori about Emi?" Hiro asked.

"No, sir." Rika shook her head. "I wanted to, but Yuji said he would handle the situation himself. He promised to speak with Satsu, if Emi refused to cooperate."

"How kind of him," Hiro said with sufficient irony to contradict the words.

Rika raised her chin. "My son did not want Emi's behavior injuring the reputation of our troupe."

"But he didn't mind taking a prostitute's sister to wife?" Hiro countered.

"I never called Emi a prostitute," Rika said quickly. "I heard that she met and talked with men by the river. Nothing more."

"How dedicated was Yuji to stopping Emi?" Hiro asked.

"Sir, my son was home the night Emi died. In any case, Yuji had no need to soil his hands. Satsu would never have let his daughter get away with such wicked behavior."

Hiro wondered whether Rika realized she'd just admitted Yuji—as well as Satsu—had a motive for wanting Emi dead.

"Thank you for telling us what you know about the incident," Father Mateo said.

"I know nothing about the incident." Rika paused. "And my son doesn't either."

Hiro made a dismissive gesture. "You may go."

"Thank you." Rika bowed. "Please excuse me, I will attend to my shopping."

She scurried off toward the Kamo River.

"Do you have to behave so much like a samurai?" Father Mateo asked.

Hiro raised an eyebrow at the priest. "I am a samurai."

Father Mateo sighed. "No point talking with Yuji now. He'll only repeat his mother's story."

"Maybe." Hiro started toward the Yutoku-za.

"Where are you going?" Father Mateo asked. "Satsu isn't home and Yuji's sick."

Hiro paused in front of the door. "Making this the perfect time to see Botan."

CHAPTER 20

The door swung open the moment Hiro knocked.

An elderly woman stood in the doorway. Her unadorned kimono and simple braid suggested a servant. She bowed. "Good morning, gentlemen. Welcome to the Yutoku-za. How may I help you?"

"We have come to speak with Botan," Hiro said.

She bowed her head. "I apologize, sir, but the master has gone to the tailor this morning. He is not at home."

"Which tailor does he use?" Hiro asked.

"Today he has gone to Shigeru's shop on Sanjō Road, just north of Pontochō."

Hiro frowned. "Shigeru sews kimono for entertainers."

The woman nodded. "The master has gone to obtain kimono for use in female roles."

Hiro turned to leave.

"Thank you for your assistance," Father Mateo said.

The woman blinked, surprised by the unexpected courtesy. She bowed. "Of course. I am sorry the master could not see you."

Father Mateo followed Hiro away from the house as the woman closed the door.

"What now?" the Jesuit asked.

"We pay a visit to Shigeru," Hiro said.

"Now?"

Hiro shrugged. "If we wait until later, Botan will have left."

Hiro and Father Mateo crossed the Kamo River at Shijō Road. Near the entrance to Pontochō, an indigo noren in front of a building read "SHIGERU: TAILOR, SPECIALIZING IN WOMEN'S KIMONO."

The shop sat east of the pleasure district, on the south side of the street.

"I'd never noticed this shop before," Father Mateo said.

"No reason you should have," Hiro replied. "Your taste in kimono doesn't run to embroidered flowers and butterflies."

Father Mateo smiled. "As far as you know."

The noren parted, revealing a middle-aged woman in the entrance. "Good morning, gentlemen." She bowed. "How may I help you?"

"We seek an actor named Botan," Hiro said. "We were told we might find him here."

"One moment, please." The woman ducked back through the entrance.

Before they could follow, a high-pitched voice inside the shop said, "I need daylight to check the color."

The noren flew aside, and a willowy woman emerged into the street. She wore a lavender kimono under a violet surcoat embroidered with giant chrysanthemums in startling shades of orange. Silver embroidery at the collar accentuated her slender neck, and the flowing sleeves hung almost to the ground.

She tilted her head appraisingly as she noticed Hiro and Father Mateo. "Good morning," she said with a graceful bow.

"Good morning. I am Father Mateo Ávila de Santos." The Jesuit gestured to Hiro. "My translator, Matsui Hiro."

"I am called Aki." The woman gave Father Mateo a special smile. "Have you business with Shigeru? He is the best tailor in all of Kyoto."

"W-we have come to speak with a customer," Father Mateo stammered, "an actor named Botan."

Hiro found it amusing that the Jesuit grew tongue-tied in the presence of attractive women—especially since, despite the kimono and feminine mannerisms, Aki was not female.

"With Master Botan?" Aki seemed surprised.

"Yes," Father Mateo said, "about a private matter."

"Botan doesn't hire out for . . . private matters." Aki's appraising gaze ran the length of Father Mateo's kimono. "But I do, and would gladly offer you a special price." The gaze shifted to Hiro. "Slightly higher if I entertain you both."

Father Mateo's patient expression turned to one of horror as he realized what Aki thought he meant by "private matter."

"Thank you," Hiro said, "but we will wait and speak with Botan."

Aki waved a dismissive hand that failed to conceal his disappointment. "As you wish, but if you change your mind, you can find me at the Yutoku-za."

He twisted to examine his robe, nodded acceptance, and disappeared back through the noren.

"Did she . . . was she offering . . ." Father Mateo trailed off, unable to complete the sentence.

"A special, and truly private, performance," Hiro confirmed.

"I am a priest!" Father Mateo protested. "I don't hire women for that kind of private performance. I took vows!"

"Japanese priests take different vows." Hiro could no longer stifle his amusement. "And, I should probably add—Aki was not a woman."

Father Mateo's horror deepened. "What?"

"Women cannot perform on the stage. In nō, the female roles are played by men." Hiro gestured toward the tailor's shop. "Aki is an actor in female dress."

"Are you certain?" Father Mateo peered at the noren.

Hiro touched the lump in his throat that only males possessed. "You didn't look in the proper place. Aki is most assuredly male, though he emulates a woman almost perfectly."

"He's not onstage at the moment," the Jesuit said. "Why try to fool us?"

"I don't think he intended to," Hiro said. "Any Japanese person would have known him for a man."

The noren parted yet again, revealing a man whose eyes still held a youthful sparkle, though his hair had turned more white than gray. The lines on his face seemed far too few for the snowdrift covering his head, and he moved with graceful steps and measured gestures that did not betray his real age.

He bowed to Hiro and then to Father Mateo, holding the gesture in deference to his lesser status. "I am Botan, of the Yutoku-za. Have you come from the police or from the shogun?"

"Which do you think?" Hiro asked.

"With apologies, I do not know." Botan straightened with a hesitant smile. "I've paid my taxes and caused no trouble."

"The way we heard it, someone caused you trouble," Hiro said.

Botan's smile froze. "I apologize. I don't know what you mean."

"How much gold did you give the samurai who tried to extort you?" Hiro hoped the question would bypass the actor's reserve and startle him into an honest answer.

Botan's mouth dropped open in shock. "Who told you about the samurai?"

CHAPTER 21

Hiro ignored Botan's question. "Do you recognize this coin?"

He gestured to Father Mateo, who held up the golden coin on its leather thong.

Botan drew back as if the gold was poisoned. "Yes, I know it."

"Because you used it to bribe a samurai?" Hiro demanded.

"No." The actor's voice grew cold. "Because it hung around my dead granddaughter's neck. Satsu told me about the coin and that he asked some men to help him. I assume you are the ones of whom he spoke." Botan paused. "And, to answer your question, I did not bribe a samurai."

"Paying for silence sounds like a bribe to me," Hiro said.

"With respect, sir, he accused me of harboring spies within the Yutoku-za. He demanded that I pay him or face the magistrate." Botan raised his hands, palms up. "I have no spies within my troupe, but how could I persuade a magistrate? I paid the samurai only to make the problem go away."

"Can you prove this isn't a coin you gave him?" Hiro asked.

"You already know that I cannot. I wish I could." Botan kept his gaze on Hiro and didn't look at the coin again. "The golden ones look pretty much the same."

"Perhaps the actors in your troupe could help identify it," Hiro said.

"Unfortunately, they cannot," Botan replied. "I spoke with the samurai alone. I told only Satsu and my brother, Tani, about the threat. However, it wouldn't surprise me to learn that coin is one I gave him."

Hiro hadn't expected that. "Why not?"

"I didn't have the entire amount he wanted," Botan said. "I gave him only half the demanded sum. He said I'd regret my stinginess, but I explained I had no more—he could take what I offered or nothing. I believed he would accept the lesser sum and find someone else to harass for the rest. . . ."

"But instead he killed Emi and left the coin as a message," Father Mateo finished.

"Don't give him ideas," Hiro hissed in Portuguese.

"Please put the coin away." The actor closed his eyes. "I cannot bear to see it."

Father Mateo tucked the coin into his purse.

When Botan opened his eyes, they were filled with tears. "It is my fault my granddaughter died. If only I had been able to pay the full amount . . ."

"Do you know the man who bribed you?" Hiro asked.

"He wore a mask across his nose and mouth. I didn't recognize his voice."

"Can you remember anything else about him?" Father Mateo asked.

Botan looked upward and thought for a moment. "He stood about the average height, and his body was neither fat nor thin. He wore a pair of swords and fixed his hair in a samurai knot." The actor shrugged. "I'm sorry. He looked like any one of a thousand samurai in Kyoto."

"Except for the mask," Hiro said.

Botan nodded. "I admit, that was unusual."

"Did you pay this samurai immediately?" Hiro asked. "Or did you make him wait to receive his money?"

"I had to retrieve the gold from the storehouse," Botan said. "I do not keep it at the Yutoku-za. The samurai said he would return the following morning, at dawn. That is when I paid him."

"No one saw you do it?" Hiro asked.

Botan shook his head. "No one knew I went to the storehouse, and the actors usually sleep late. I did tell Satsu and Tani, but only because they handle the accounting and would have noticed the money missing."

Hiro considered it interesting that Botan trusted Satsu enough to let him handle the finances of the troupe. "How would the samurai have known that Emi was your relative?"

"Everyone in the theater district knows the Yutoku-za. Anyone could have pointed out my family." Botan wiped a tear from his eye. "I never thought he would hurt them. I truly believed he was bluffing."

"Would you recognize this samurai if you saw him?" Father Mateo asked.

"I do not know." Botan paused. "I doubt it."

"Why don't you want this samurai brought to justice?" Hiro asked.

"Forgive me," Botan said, "but only samurai have the luxury of justice. Even if you find the man, the magistrate will let him go and punish me for paying a bribe. That's how it works, when men of my station accuse a samurai."

"We can help you," Father Mateo offered.

"Please . . ." Botan sighed. "I mean no disrespect, and I know my son-in-law requested your assistance, but you will help my family best by leaving us alone."

Father Mateo opened his mouth to speak, but Hiro caught the Jesuit's eye and shook his head.

"We have no further questions," Hiro said. "You may return to your business."

"We appreciate your cooperation," Father Mateo added.

Botan bowed and returned to the tailor's shop, pausing in the doorway long enough to add, "Good day, gentlemen, and thank you."

"Did he really just ask us to let his granddaughter's killer get away?" Father Mateo shook his head in disbelief as he followed Hiro away from the tailor's shop.

Hiro shrugged. "At times, a man must accept the unacceptable in order to avoid a greater harm. If a samurai murdered Emi, and learned about our investigation, he might return to kill Chou and Haru too."

"Or"—Hiro glanced at the priest—"Botan might want us to drop the matter because he killed his granddaughter himself."

"Botan?" Father Mateo sounded shocked. "Why would he kill Emi?"

"A man's first duty is keeping his family safe," Hiro said, "and Botan's family is the Yutoku-za. By meeting men at the river, Emi risked not only her own reputation, but that of the theater troupe as well."

Father Mateo seemed confused. "How could she have hurt the troupe if women can't act on the stage?"

"Groups like the Yutoku-za earn money by performing at the request of wealthy samurai," Hiro said. "Noblemen only want to hire the troupes with the best reputations, and 'reputation' includes professionalism as well as skill. That's probably why Botan disapproves of the 'private performances' Aki thought we wanted."

Father Mateo blushed. "You didn't have to bring that up again."

Hiro gave him a sideways look. "It appears your taste in kimono doesn't run to chrysanthemums after all."

When they reached the Kamo River, Father Mateo paused to ask, "Do we have to stop the investigation, since Botan asked us to leave his family alone?"

"Not for a moment." Hiro started across the bridge. "Samurai give orders to commoners, not the other way around."

Father Mateo followed. "Where are we going?"

"Botan might not want us to find the samurai who bribed him," Hiro said, "but hopefully Satsu knows enough to help identify a suspect."

CHAPTER 22

"How could Satsu help us find the man who threatened Botan?" Father Mateo asked. "He wasn't there. The samurai could be anyone in Kyoto."

"It isn't me," Hiro said, "or you, or Luis. That's three men off the suspect list already."

"That hardly leaves a manageable number," Father Mateo replied. "You can't throw a stone in Kyoto without hitting a samurai."

Hiro glanced at the priest. "Then may I suggest not throwing stones."

Chou emerged from the Yutoku-za as Hiro and Father Mateo approached. She closed the door behind her, turned, and startled.

"Good morning," she said as she bowed to Hiro and the priest. "I didn't expect to see you back so soon."

"Has your father returned?" Hiro asked.

"I am sorry, he has not." Chou glanced at the house. "My mother returned a few minutes ago and sent Haru back to the temple. Father teaches some of my brother's lessons there."

"Where, precisely?" Hiro asked.

"They use an open patch of lawn, just inside the entrance to Kenninji." Chou's eyes grew red. "Sometimes, Emi and I would walk in the gardens while Father taught Haru. That is, before . . ."

"I am sorry about your sister," Father Mateo said.

"No," Chou replied with another bow. "*I* am sorry. Earlier . . . I did not tell the entire truth."

Before the men could react, she continued, "Please forgive me. The truth is, Father hadn't found a husband for Emi because she refused

94

to marry. She didn't want to be a wife or a mother. She planned to become an entertainer in one of the high-class houses. Not the ones in Pontochō—the expensive ones on this side of the river.

"Father refused to allow it. I don't know why. Actors are entertainers, too, even if girls can't act on the stage, and a talented girl can make a lot of money in a teahouse."

"Was Emi talented?" Hiro asked.

Chou nodded. "She sang beautifully. Everyone said so. When Father refused to help her find a place, Emi visited some of the houses on her own. She told the owners she was an orphan and asked to become an apprentice, but no one would take her. They told her she was too old for training. One of them suggested she check with the brothels in Pontochō."

"But she didn't," Father Mateo said.

"Of course not." Chou sounded offended on Emi's behalf. "She was furious with the teahouse women for even suggesting such a thing. She said she would find another way—even buy her own house, if she had to."

"Buy her own teahouse?" Hiro asked.

"That's what she said." Chou nodded. "Impossible, I know, but that's what she said."

"Impossible?" Father Mateo repeated. "Why?"

"The cost is unthinkable," Hiro said. "Kimono for the entertainers cost even more than the house itself, and when you add all the other expenses of running a high-end house . . . most women 'purchase' their teahouses from retiring mentors, paying only a fraction of their value. A girl like Emi wouldn't stand a chance of raising the funds required, even if she found a house for sale."

"I told her that too," Chou said, "but she wouldn't listen. Girls like us . . . the best we can do is marry well and raise successful sons. Dreams of anything more lead only to sorrow."

A woman walked past with a toddler in tow. The child stopped to stare at Father Mateo's foreign face. His mother took his wrist and pulled him away, while keeping her own face toward the ground, as if doing so made her invisible.

Chou watched the woman and her child continue up the street.

"How did your sister intend to raise the money for her teahouse?" Hiro asked.

Chou shifted her weight from one foot to the other. "I'm sorry, sir, I do not know."

"I think you do," Hiro said, "and you can either tell us now, or explain in front of your parents. I suspect they would want to hear how much you knew about your sister's plans."

Chou clasped her hands together and straightened her back as if steeling herself to tell the truth. To her credit, she did not flinch or beg. "Emi said she had found a man to help her. She wouldn't tell me who he was, or where they met, or why he offered to do it—though anyone can guess that part. Men only spend money on girls like us for one reason."

"Did she tell you his name?" Hiro asked.

"No, sir." Chou shook her head. "She refused to tell me. I tried to persuade her not to sell herself for a man's assistance, but she wouldn't listen. She told me it was her life, not mine and not Father's, and that if I tried to stop her she would tell them I was lying."

Chou sniffled as her eyes turned red. "I didn't tell my parents. They would not have believed me anyway."

"Why do you think your parents wouldn't believe you?" Father Mateo asked.

"Emi never did anything wrong." Chou started to cry. "She was always the perfect daughter. Father never knew she talked with teahouse owners behind his back. She told him she had changed her mind, decided to become a nun. That's why she spent her evenings at the shrine.

"Besides"—Chou sniffed again, more loudly—"Emi was my closest friend. I didn't want to get her in trouble. I know it was wrong, but if she really had found a man with the money to buy her a teahouse, or even a place in one . . . I'm getting my dream, with Yuji. He's everything I ever wanted. Why shouldn't my sister have the chance to see her dream come true?"

"Can you remember anything more about this man?" Father Mateo asked. "Anything at all might help us find him."

Chou wiped her eyes as she shook her head. "I'm sorry, Emi wouldn't tell me anything. At the time, I was glad she refused. I didn't want to know enough to get in trouble too, if she got caught."

Father Mateo retrieved the golden coin from his purse. "Did he give her this?"

"I do not know," Chou said. "I told you the truth about that. I never saw it before she died."

"Is it possible she had it and concealed it from you?" Hiro asked.

"No." Chou sounded adamant. "If Emi had a golden coin, she would have shown me."

"One last question," Hiro said. "If you didn't want to cause trouble for Emi, why did you tell Yuji about the man—or was it *men*—she met by the river?"

The bluff worked. Chou's eyes grew wide.

"Answer me!" Hiro demanded. "And tell the truth. I have no patience for your lies."

"I-it was only one man, that I knew of, and I-I had to tell Yuji," Chou stammered. "He saw them—Emi and the man—by the river, about a week ago. He asked me why my parents let her meet him all alone. I had to tell. I begged him to keep it a secret, but he threatened to get my father involved. He didn't want Emi hurting his reputation—the troupe's reputation—with bad behavior."

The story didn't match Rika's. One—or both—of the women was telling lies.

"You lied to us earlier." Hiro glared. "Why should we believe you now?"

Chou looked at her hands, which started trembling. "I'm sorry, sir, I was afraid. I thought you would think that Yuji killed Emi, to stop her from shaming the Yutoku-za. But he didn't. Yuji would never hurt my sister."

"Do not lie to us again." Hiro laid a hand on the hilt of his sword, though he had no intention of harming the girl. "No father should lose a second daughter before he finishes mourning for the first."

Chou bowed. "I beg you, please forgive me."

"Of course we forgive you," Father Mateo said quickly with a warning look at Hiro. "You showed great courage, telling the truth. Now, if you will excuse us, we have business to attend to."

She bowed again, and Father Mateo started up the road toward Kenninji.

A frustrated Hiro followed in his wake.

CHAPTER 23

"In Japan, a man does not excuse himself to a woman of common birth," Hiro said when they had left the house behind them.

"A man of honor never demeans one, either," Father Mateo said. "Interrogating a samurai woman is one thing. Chou is only a common girl, who recently suffered a tragedy. You have no cause to treat her like a criminal."

"She is a liar," Hiro said.

"She is a child—and your cousin, even though she does not know it." Father Mateo's tone conveyed his disapproval. "Of course she lied—she's terrified of you."

"And of you also," Hiro said. "However, I will minimize my threats in the future, if you will remember to treat her as a commoner, not an equal."

"All people are equal in the eyes of God," the Jesuit said, "but I will try to respect the Japanese way."

Hiro nodded. He could ask no more.

"Do you intend to tell Satsu what Chou revealed to us just now?" Father Mateo asked. "I worry that he might hurt her if we do."

"I'm not the one who usually reveals the damaging facts to suspects."

"Then we agree," the Jesuit said, completely missing Hiro's point.

At the entrance to Kenninji, the samurai on guard returned Hiro's nod, but didn't speak.

"How do you plan to find Satsu?" Father Mateo asked as they passed through the massive gate and onto the temple grounds.

Hiro nodded toward a pair of teenage monks who stood a little way down the path. They had their backs to the entrance, watching something on the grassy lawn beyond. "If you want to find an actor, follow the crowd."

Satsu stood on the grass just past the monks. Nearby, Haru walked around on the lawn with his feet in the air and his hands where his feet should be. The boy seemed thoroughly comfortable upside down.

"Over and up, like a monkey," Satsu said.

Haru flipped himself upright with a single fluid motion and instantly squatted on his haunches, hands drawn close to his chest like a resting monkey. He glanced at his father, ignoring the monks' appreciative noises.

Satsu nodded approval. "That was better." He noticed Hiro. "All right, enough for today."

The monks followed Satsu's gaze. At the sight of Father Mateo, they scurried away with guilty expressions on their blushing faces.

Father Mateo watched them go. "Did they leave because of me?"

"Indirectly," Hiro said. "They must have mistaken you for a senior monk, at least at first, and suddenly remembered they have duties— which do not include an hour wasted watching actors' lessons."

"May I go home?" Haru asked.

"Only if you promise not to interrupt the actors," Satsu said.

Haru frowned. "But they make mistakes—"

"—and correcting them is Botan's job, not yours." Satsu's voice held a warning edge.

"It will be mine," Haru said, "when I'm the master."

"Until which time, you learn by silent observation." Satsu nodded. "Very well, you may watch the lessons if Botan permits, but do not interrupt."

Haru bowed. "Yes, Father."

Satsu made a gesture of dismissal, and Haru ran off toward the temple gate.

The actor turned and bowed to the other men. "Haru mentioned you wanted to see me. I planned to look for you when his lesson finished."

"Your son is a talented acrobat," Father Mateo said. "I didn't realize nō performances featured acrobatics."

"They don't," Satsu replied, "but some of the *kyogen* interludes, between the plays, have roles for acrobats. I started training Haru for kyogen several years ago, in case he lacked the skills to act in nō. I needn't have worried. Botan has decided that Haru has the skills to be shite."

"We heard about his upcoming debut," Father Mateo said.

"The role is small and played by a child to keep the focus on the adult actors," Satsu said. "But even simple roles help children learn the rules of nō."

"Why continue to train him in acrobatics?" Hiro asked.

"You are thinking that handsprings and balancing skills would serve a shinobi's needs as well as an actor's." Satsu didn't wait for affirmation. "These lessons provide a diversion for Haru, something else to absorb his time. Otherwise, he spends every waking moment watching actors and correcting their mistakes. He has memorized all the plays in our current repertoire, and has a flawless memory. Unfortunately, he is not good at holding his tongue when others err."

"Do actors' children have more freedom to speak than samurai boys?" the Jesuit asked.

"Noble children learn etiquette before they learn to walk, but actors avoid restricting children before they reach the age for formal training," Satsu said. "However, I do expect my son to demonstrate self-control."

"Do you expect the same from your daughters?" Hiro asked.

Satsu frowned. "What makes you ask?"

Hiro saw no point in subtlety. Satsu was trained to recognize subterfuge. "Did you know your daughter was meeting a man by the river before she died?"

"Emi?" Satsu shook his head. "No, though when you mentioned a 'friend' had told you about her death, I suspected something of the kind. The river is the only place she could have met him without being noticed."

"We have reason to believe she met him regularly," Hiro said, "including the night she died. We also suspect there may have been more than one man."

Emotion flickered through Satsu's features, but disappeared before Hiro could identify it.

"I did not know this," the actor said, "but I will not deny it could have happened."

Hiro waited for him to continue.

"I'm not a fool," Satsu said. "My daughter wanted independence. Specifically, she dreamed of entertaining in a teahouse. She was too old to enter a high-end establishment, and I wouldn't allow her to go to a house where patrons expect a girl to do more than sing. She didn't understand why I refused, and disagreed with me, but children often fail to appreciate the reasons why their parents make decisions.

"She and I had reached an impasse. Emi refused to bend her will to conform to mine, or anyone else's. She threatened to run away, and I believed her.

"Then, about a week ago, she told me she had changed her mind and wanted to become a nun instead. I found that surprising, and also strange. I wondered what caused the decision, but in my relief I didn't demand a reason. I realize, now, I did not know my daughter nearly as well as I believed."

"You don't seem very surprised to learn that Emi met with a man without you knowing," Father Mateo said.

"My daughter is dead," Satsu replied. "Not much can surprise me about her anymore. Emi often went to the temple at night, to Chugenji or, sometimes, Kenninji. She told us she prayed and came directly home. I wish I had not trusted her at her word."

"When did you learn she wanted to become an entertainer?" Hiro asked.

"Emi sang before she spoke and danced as soon as she learned to walk." Satsu's eyes took on the glaze of memory. "She had a difficult time accepting that she could not act in nō. She would have made a fine shite, if she hadn't been born a female.

"I never realized how strongly she felt about it until we announced Chou's betrothal to Yuji. That's when Emi told me she did not ever intend to marry. At first, I thought she was jealous of Chou, but Emi explained that she had no desire to become a wife or a mother. She said no man would own her, that her life belonged to her alone."

"Perhaps she had a preference for women." Had Satsu not been an Iga shinobi, Hiro would not have made the comment. Polite conversation precluded direct discussion of such private topics.

"Not that I knew or suspected," Satsu said, "and if she did meet men by the river, it suggests she enjoyed their attention. I think she simply wanted to control her life in ways no woman has a right to claim."

"Shinobi women can claim it," Hiro said.

"I am forbidden to speak that truth to my family." Satsu's voice took on a bitter edge. "Even had I realized her inclination soon enough, that way was barred to her."

CHAPTER 24

"You learned of Emi's refusal to marry the day that Chou was betrothed to Yuji?" Hiro asked.

"The day we announced it," Satsu said. "Yuji's father and I arranged the betrothal shortly after Chou was born. I was looking for an arrangement for Emi, too, but she threatened to hang herself on her wedding night if we forced the issue. I believed that she would do it. As I mentioned, she also threatened to run away."

"You let your daughter refuse a marriage?" Hiro asked.

Satsu shrugged. "I hoped she would change her mind, in time, when she realized no high-class house would have her. She was young. I thought, when she saw her sister happily married to Yuji...I was wrong."

"When did she mention becoming a nun?" Hiro asked.

"A week ago," Satsu said. "One evening, she didn't come home before dark. I found her at the Shijō Bridge, tossing pebbles into the river."

"The samurai on guard didn't stop her?" Father Mateo asked.

"He normally stands on the opposite side of the river—closer to Pontochō—in hopes of spotting a teahouse flower out for an evening stroll. He doesn't care about this side, unless someone crosses the bridge after dark."

"What about Emi's decision to join a monastery?" Hiro asked.

"The night I saw her at the bridge, she confessed to visiting teahouses, hoping to become an entertainer over my objections," Satsu said. "She told me they all refused her, and some of the owners recommended she become a prostitute. She asked me not to speak of it to anyone. I haven't, until now. Not even to Nori. Emi said, if she couldn't become an entertainer, she would become a nun."

"Wouldn't a nun have less independence than a married woman?" Father Mateo asked.

"That depends on how you define independence," Satsu said.

"Dedicating your life to a kami is not the same as answering to a man," Hiro added.

Father Mateo nodded. "But if she wished to become a nun, why would she meet a man by the river?"

"She wouldn't," Satsu said, "which means she lied—to the man by the river, or to me."

"Or both," Hiro said.

Satsu's face flushed red. "You've had two days to investigate. Is this all you've learned about the coin and Emi's killer?"

"Public anger does not suit an actor speaking with samurai." Hiro spoke politely, in recognition of Satsu's status as his uncle. "If you had known about Emi meeting men by the river, would you have stopped her?"

After a pause, Satsu recovered his composure. "I wouldn't have killed her, and don't pretend that isn't what you're thinking."

A cold voice behind them said, "Matsui Hiro—you will come with me."

Hiro turned to see Yoriki Hosokawa, flanked by the usual pair of scruffy dōshin.

Hiro pulled a silver coin from his purse and handed it to Satsu. "Thank you for taking the time to teach the foreigner about your art."

The actor accepted the coin with a bow and knelt before the yoriki.

"What are you doing here?" Yoriki Hosokawa demanded.

"This man is an actor," Father Mateo said.

The yoriki's scowl deepened. "Yes, and I ordered you to leave him alone! This is the man whose daughter we found on the riverbank two days ago."

"The same man?" Father Mateo squinted at Satsu. "Are you certain?"

"Do not play the ignorant foreigner with me!" the yoriki thundered. "You are under arrest, and so is your translator!"

The dōshin brandished their hooked jitte as if eager to use them on the foreign priest.

Hiro stepped between Father Mateo and the dōshin. "This priest has committed no crime, and neither have I."

"You disobeyed an order from an assistant magistrate," the yoriki snarled.

"Your order?" Hiro asked. "The last time I checked, your words do not carry the weight of law."

He fought the urge to lay a hand on the hilt of his katana. Aggressive action would lead to a fight, and though he longed to shame the assistant magistrate in combat, Hiro knew better than to pick a fight with the Kyoto police.

In public, anyway.

"I don't think I've seen this man before." Father Mateo bent down and looked at Satsu from the side.

"Lies will not help you," the yoriki said. "You can tell one Japanese face from another, and even if you failed to recognize this man at once, your ronin interpreter would have known him."

"Drop the falsehood," Hiro muttered in Portuguese. "You're making it worse. I'll handle this."

Hiro turned to the yoriki, bowed, and switched to Japanese. "Forgive me. Though we have met several times, we have not formally exchanged our names. I am Matsui Hiro, son of—"

The yoriki raised a dismissive hand. "You may call me Yoriki Hosokawa. I will not have my given name soiled by your filthy ronin tongue."

"Very well, Hosokawa-*san*." Hiro deliberately dropped the title. "I repeat, this man has committed no offense. You ordered us not to investigate the death of the actor's daughter. However, you never prohibited the foreigner learning about the art of nō. Has the shogun instituted a law against curiosity?"

Yoriki Hosokawa scowled. "Curious men have a way of finding trouble."

Hiro shrugged just rudely enough to cause offense.

Yoriki Hosokawa turned on Satsu. "You! Get out of here—and understand, I'll have you whipped if you ever speak to this foreigner again!"

Satsu nodded, jumped to his feet, and scurried away.

"And you"—the yoriki turned to Hiro and Father Mateo—"will come with me."

"What charge do you bring against us?" Hiro kept himself between the priest and the other men.

"That is for the magistrate to tell you." The yoriki smiled. "Unless you resist, in which case I will gladly arrest you for refusing to obey the magistrate's summons."

"The magistrate wants to see us now?" Father Mateo glanced at the sun. "He won't be hearing cases at this hour."

"He said to bring you immediately, before the afternoon audience."

"How did you find us?" the Jesuit asked.

"Quit stalling! And never question my competence!" Yoriki Hosokawa's hand started toward the hilt of his sword.

"Why does he want to see us?" Father Mateo asked with a vacant tone that Hiro recognized as intentional foolishness.

The dōshin stepped forward.

"I am finished explaining," Yoriki Hosokawa said. "You can follow me now, of your own accord, or we can drag you in by force. I assure you, either choice is fine with me."

CHAPTER 25

The samurai guarding the magistrate's compound stepped aside as Yoriki Hosokawa approached with Hiro and Father Mateo. The yoriki swaggered through the gates with his chin in the air and his hand on his hip. Hiro resisted the urge to step on the arrogant samurai's sandal from behind and send him sprawling.

The magistrate's compound had already filled with people awaiting the start of the afternoon session. Men and women thronged the yard. A line of dōshin stood near the wooden dais, watching over a cluster of prisoners bound with ropes. As Hiro and Father Mateo followed the yoriki toward the magistrate's house, the scruffy dōshin disappeared into the crowd.

Yoriki Hosokawa marched across the graveled yard with the air of a man who expected absolute deference. Commoners scrambled out of his way like a troop of monkeys fleeing a wrathful tiger.

When they reached the wooden veranda that surrounded the magistrate's home and office, Yoriki Hosokawa left his sandals beside the door and entered the building. Hiro and Father Mateo did the same. Inside, the yoriki led them into a large, tatami-covered room with a bed of white sand and a dais on one end.

Hiro recognized the magistrate's office. He and Father Mateo had been here a little over a year ago, while investigating the murder of Akechi Hideyoshi, a retired general and an ally of the Ashikaga clan.

This time, they didn't have to wait for the magistrate to appear. Magistrate Ishimaki already knelt on the wooden dais. His jet-black robes absorbed the light from the brazier in the corner, creating the momentary illusion of a balding, disembodied head presiding over the room.

"Approach the magistrate!" Yoriki Hosokawa ordered.

Magistrate Ishimaki's aging features settled into a look of concern as Hiro and Father Mateo approached the dais.

Hiro stopped a couple of feet behind the white sand bed and noted with approval that Father Mateo did as well. The *shirazu* symbolized justice and purity. Criminals knelt there for sentencing. It was not a place for innocent men to stand.

Magistrate Ishimaki nodded to Yoriki Hosokawa. "You may go."

The yoriki opened his mouth as if to protest.

Magistrate Ishimaki raised a hand and repeated, "You may go."

Yoriki Hosokawa scowled at Hiro and left the room. He slid the paneled door shut behind him with just enough rattle to demonstrate frustration.

Hiro waited for the magistrate to speak. To his relief, Father Mateo also held his tongue.

Magistrate Ishimaki sighed. "It seems you make a habit of investigating murders."

Father Mateo took half a step forward, right to the edge of the sand. "My faith requires me to help the innocent."

Hiro wondered whether the Jesuit realized just how cleverly he had answered, with a response that neither admitted nor denied the allegation.

"I appreciate your generosity," Magistrate Ishimaki said. "Your skills brought General Akechi justice, and I enjoyed your contribution to the brewer's trial some weeks ago."

Father Mateo bowed. "It honors us to serve your office."

"However," the magistrate continued, "not everyone appreciates your efforts. Earlier today, I received a complaint."

"A complaint?" Father Mateo repeated.

Magistrate Ishimaki nodded. "Regrettably, I must insist you cease your current investigation."

"There has been a mistake," Hiro said. "We have no investigation at the moment."

"I'm glad to hear it," the magistrate said, "since Hosokawa-*san* forbade one. Had you admitted to an investigation, I would have had to arrest you."

"May we inquire who lodged the complaint?" Hiro asked.

"You may not," the magistrate said. "That is, you may ask, but I cannot tell you. The petitioner requested that I keep his identity secret."

Father Mateo spread his hands. "My religion requires that you tell us. The Christian faith prohibits conviction except on the testimony of two or more witnesses."

Magistrate Ishimaki smiled. "Fortunately for your religion, you do not stand convicted."

Hiro resisted the urge to smile. Father Mateo argued well, but Magistrate Ishimaki had years of experience handling logical men.

"However"—the magistrate raised a finger—"I understand that your religion also requires priests to keep a secret even unto death. Is this correct?"

"Sometimes," Father Mateo said. "A priest cannot reveal a confession a person makes to God."

"Then I confess—to your god, of course—that Yoriki Hosokawa presented me a complaint from a rice merchant named Basho. The merchant objects to you questioning his apprentice about the death of a riverbank girl." Magistrate Ishimaki looked from Father Mateo to Hiro, as if judging their reactions to his words.

Hiro didn't believe in the Christian religion, but knew the rules for confessions did not apply unless the speaker was also a Christian—which the magistrate most certainly was not.

"Yoriki Hosokawa brought the complaint?" Father Mateo asked.

The magistrate nodded. "He spoke with Basho this morning. The merchant did not wish to present his petition personally. He hoped to avoid the humiliation of public association with a crime."

Hiro wondered whether Basho approached the yoriki first or whether Yoriki Hosokawa planted the fear of humiliation in order to prompt a complaint. He also wondered why Hosokawa-*san* seemed so determined to block the investigation—and whether the reason went beyond frustration at their involvement in solving the brewery murder.

"We never accused Basho's apprentice of killing anyone," Father Mateo said.

Technically, that misstated the truth, but Father Mateo had not been present when Hiro spoke with Jiro the night before.

"You made him fear arrest was imminent," Magistrate Ishimaki said. "Basho objected strenuously to your insensitive treatment of his nephew, particularly after the yoriki reassured him that no crime had been committed."

"No crime?" Father Mateo shook his head. "A girl was murdered. How can the yoriki say there was no crime?"

"I do not know the laws in your country," Magistrate Ishimaki said, "but, in Japan, not every death is a crime."

"Is this what you call justice?" Father Mateo asked. "Ignoring the death of an innocent girl, but calling righteous men to task when a merchant lifts a finger in complaint?"

"I did not summon you here for a debate about the nature of justice." The magistrate frowned.

"Clearly not." Father Mateo's voice held an equal edge. "A man who cared about justice would not sacrifice it for a merchant's happiness."

Magistrate Ishimaki leaned forward and shifted his gaze to Hiro. "I choose to believe this foreigner has an imperfect grasp of our language, and that he does not understand the words he speaks."

Hiro bowed to give himself time to think.

"Indeed," he said as he straightened. "I believe the priest intended to express his deep regret at this unfortunate mistake. We never intended Basho or his apprentice harm. We only sought to return an object found on the dead girl's body. We believed—mistakenly—that it belonged to the apprentice."

Magistrate Ishimaki's frown softened to curiosity. "What is this object of which you speak?"

Hiro nodded to Father Mateo, who held up the leather strip and golden coin.

"This gold was found on the girl?" Magistrate Ishimaki's forehead wrinkled in concern. "It was not hers?"

"Her family claims they do not know its origin," Hiro said.

Magistrate Ishimaki thought for a moment and shook his head. "Even so, your search must end today. Return the coin to the family, with instructions to keep it safe in case the owner returns to claim it."

"But—" Father Mateo began.

The magistrate spoke over him. "Wise men do not tread on a stranger's melon field. My yoriki says no crime was committed. His words, and mine, are law."

Father Mateo switched to Portuguese. "What do melons have to do with murder?"

Hiro replied in kind. "A man in another man's melon patch may be accused of trespassing . . . or stealing. He is warning us against an innocent act that might cause trouble."

Magistrate Ishimaki looked at Hiro. "Does he understand?"

Hiro bowed. "I will ensure he does."

"I understand your words," the Jesuit said, "but I respectfully disagree. The killer deserves to answer for his crime."

"While I appreciate your love of justice, this investigation ends today." Magistrate Ishimaki glanced past Hiro at the sliding door. "The shogun ordered me to respect the merchants, to ensure they remain in Kyoto and pay their taxes without complaint."

"You're doing this because the shogun wants the merchants coddled?" Father Mateo's voice revealed disbelief . . . and anger.

"No man resists the shogun." Magistrate Ishimaki rose to his feet. "The blade of grass that stands the tallest is the first to be cut down."

Hiro spoke quickly to keep the Jesuit silent. "Yes, we understand."

It didn't work. "Respectfully, I—"

Hiro spoke over Father Mateo. "Forgive the foreigner's lack of comprehension. I assure you, we will cause no further trouble."

Magistrate Ishimaki gestured to the doors behind them. "You may go."

Hiro heard a rustling in the corridor as he approached the doors, but when he slid it open the space was empty.

Father Mateo followed Hiro from the room without complaint, but with a scowl that promised the discussion was not over.

CHAPTER 26

"How can a magistrate turn his back on justice?" Father Mateo demanded as he turned onto Marutamachi Road.

Hiro eyed the priest. "Impressive. You held that back for ten whole minutes."

The Jesuit opened his mouth to argue, but Hiro continued, "He had no choice. If Matsunaga Hisahide ordered the merchants coddled, it must be done. Even so, the magistrate showed us favor. He could have arrested us instead of issuing a warning."

"Finding Emi's murderer outweighs Basho's embarrassment." Father Mateo's voice grew calm, a sign of building fury. "A woman's life is worth far more than a merchant's reputation."

"Why do you care so much about this murder?" Hiro asked.

"You know I care about every life and every person's soul."

"Not enough to lose your self-control." Hiro gauged the priest's expression. "Is it because this victim was a girl?"

Father Mateo clenched his jaw and drew a deep breath. "I do not care what the magistrate says or whether or not you agree with him. I will find Emi's killer, with you or without you."

"I never said you would have to do it without me," Hiro countered, "but we must beware the magistrate, and also Yoriki Hosokawa. He has already set his dōshin on our trail."

Father Mateo stopped walking and turned around. Half a block behind them, a scruffy samurai ducked into an open storefront.

"Did he follow us from the magistrate's compound?" Father Mateo asked.

Hiro nodded. "He accosted me near Ginjiro's last night also.

I believe that meeting was accidental, but today he's trailing us intentionally."

"Why does the yoriki care so much about our investigation?" Father Mateo paused. "Perhaps he's involved in the crime."

"More likely, he simply holds a grudge. He looked foolish when we solved the brewery murder without his help." Hiro turned back toward the river and started walking. "However, we cannot eliminate any possibility at this point. I wonder how much he had to do with Jiro telling Basho about the girl."

"I wondered about that also." Father Mateo matched Hiro's pace. "Do you think he intends to follow us all the way home?"

"The dōshin?" Hiro asked. "He's no trouble, as long as he keeps his distance."

"And if he follows us later?"

Hiro shrugged. "A problem we can handle if it arises."

"How can we solve the murder with him watching?"

"I thought you didn't worry about the magistrate." Hiro suppressed a smile.

"I don't," the Jesuit said, "but we weren't being followed when I said it."

"Actually, we were." Hiro smiled. "I don't consider that dōshin much of a threat. We'll simply have to be careful and watch our backs."

Father Mateo lowered his voice. "We need a list of suspects to investigate."

"We have suspects"—Hiro counted them off on his fingers— "Botan, Satsu, Yuji, and Jiro, as well as the unknown samurai who threatened the Yutoku-za."

"Could *that* be the reason Yoriki Hosokawa wants to block the investigation? Maybe he's the mysterious samurai."

"Possible, but doubtful," Hiro said. "Surely Botan would have recognized his voice."

Father Mateo looked disappointed. "True. I hadn't thought of that. We have to find that samurai. I don't think Jiro is guilty, or Botan, and why would Satsu ask us to investigate if he's the one who killed her?"

Hiro adjusted his sword, using the gesture to cover a backward glance. The dōshin was over half a block behind them, out of earshot.

"Shinobi specialize in diversions," Hiro said. "Satsu might be using us to blame the crime on someone else."

"Why would he need to?" the Jesuit asked. "The yoriki didn't investigate. The magistrate doesn't care."

"The magistrate's opinion is not the only one that matters," Hiro said. "Satsu needs to persuade his family as well."

The conversation stalled until they reached the Kamo River. At the western end of the bridge, Hiro paused. "Wait here."

Before the priest could answer, Hiro marched back up the street toward the dōshin. Near the river, private houses lined the road, leaving the startled samurai nowhere to hide. He scowled as Hiro approached.

"Thank you for the escort," Hiro said without a bow. "We appreciate your master's concern for our safety."

The dōshin's lip curled into a sneer. "Your safety is not his concern—but it should be yours."

Hiro raised his chin. "You have no authority to threaten the emperor's honored foreign guest. Magistrate Ishimaki set us free without restriction."

"He ordered you to cease your investigation," the dōshin growled. "Yoriki Hosokawa will ensure that you obey."

"We have obeyed." Hiro gestured toward the bridge. "Even a child could see we are walking home."

The dōshin took a hostile step forward. "Do not tell me what I see."

"Very well, I'll tell you what I see." Hiro did not back away. "A common bully, who threatens men without legitimate cause."

"I could kill you for that!" the dōshin snarled.

"If you intended to act on those words, you would have drawn your sword already."

"I wouldn't soil my blade with your ronin blood," the dōshin said. "Go follow your master home, like the dog you are."

"Tread carefully near dogs," Hiro warned. "They bite when provoked. And, lest you lack the intelligence to understand a subtle word—stop following us, or I will report this harassment to the magistrate."

He turned and walked away before the dōshin could reply, but listened carefully in case the dōshin struck him from behind.

The attack never came.

The samurai guarding Marutamachi Bridge stepped forward as Hiro and Father Mateo approached. "Is there a problem?"

Hiro glanced over his shoulder.

The dōshin stood where Hiro had left him, watching.

Hiro bowed to the samurai guard. "Merely a misunderstanding, nothing more."

After a moment that lasted too long for comfort, the samurai stepped away.

Hiro did not speak again until they passed the *torii* gate at the entrance to Okazaki Shrine. "As soon as we identify Emi's killer, we're leaving Kyoto."

"I will not run away from my work and home," Father Mateo said, "and I'm surprised that you even think I might. I'm not a child and not afraid of danger."

"Even a child knows not to tempt a tiger," Hiro said.

"I refuse to leave the city. I will not argue this point again."

Hiro saw no point in arguing, either. When the time came, the priest would leave, even if Hiro had to drag him out of Kyoto against his will.

CHAPTER 27

Gato lay on the porch of the Jesuit's house, flicking her tail from side to side. As Hiro and Father Mateo approached, she jumped to her feet and trotted toward her master.

Hiro scooped the cat into his arms as he followed the Jesuit into the house. Just before the door swung closed, he heard a horse approaching on the road.

Father Mateo continued into the common room, but Hiro set Gato down and peered back out into the street. Nervous tension rose in his stomach, but dissipated as he recognized Luis Álvares approaching on a small brown horse. He closed the door and joined the Jesuit in the common room.

Father Mateo frowned. "Is someone out there?"

"Only Luis, home early," Hiro said.

Father Mateo nodded and changed the subject. "We need to talk with Yuji."

"I had planned to go this evening," Hiro said. "At sunset, or a bit before."

"Why sunset?" Father Mateo asked.

Hiro smiled. "It is the hour when women prepare the evening meal. I would prefer to speak with Yuji when his mother is occupied."

Luis Álvares stormed through the doorway, face bright red and hands in fists. The lace on his dark green doublet shook like a plum tree's leaves in a thunderstorm.

"Backstabbing vipers!" the merchant bellowed as he started toward his room.

"Trouble with the samurai?" Father Mateo asked.

Luis whirled and glared at the priest. "This time, it's our countrymen I speak of!"

"Word from Portugal?" Father Mateo sounded excited.

"No! Another merchant coming here to take my business!" Luis stomped across the room. "Bad enough that half of Lisbon flooded into Yokoseura, stealing all the sales outside the capital—now that snake, Simão Duarte, is coming here to steal from beneath my nose!"

Hiro heard Ozuru's warning echo through his memory. *Your merchant will suffer a most unfortunate accident soon thereafter. . . .*

"What are you talking about, Luis?" Father Mateo asked.

"Simão Duarte, from Lisbon." Luis walked in a circle, gesturing wildly. "He arrived in Japan last year and set up a warehouse at Yokoseura. Now the shogun has issued him a license to open one in Kyoto—directly next to mine!"

"When did he reach the city?" Hiro asked.

Luis pulled a crumpled paper from his doublet. "His letter just arrived today, by messenger. It says he'll arrive by the end of the week, along with a load of firearms that he wants to store in my warehouse while he gets his cleaned and ready for business!"

The merchant flung the letter toward the hearth, but the parchment merely fluttered to the ground beside his boot.

Luis stomped on it.

Hiro stared at the missive. The time had come to force the issue. Father Mateo had to leave Kyoto.

The Jesuit looked at the letter. "What does it say, precisely?"

"Simão brags that Shogun Matsunaga issued a license for him to sell firearms in the capital. He gives the address of his warehouse—next to mine." Luis glared at Hiro. "You claim Hisahide isn't really the shogun. Is there any way to block this license?"

Without waiting for an answer, Luis scooped the letter from the floor and waved the page in the air. "Simão Duarte. That self-important windbag!"

Hiro noted the irony, but kept his expression neutral.

"Does the letter explain why Hisahide issued a second license?" the Jesuit asked.

"To meet the demands of war." Luis glanced at the letter and made a scornful sound. "I've never missed a deadline, despite his unreasonable demands. I procured the weapons he needed to seize Kyoto. I didn't know why he needed them, but even so, I met the need. And now he repays me by bringing Simão Duarte to kill my profits?"

"He plans to kill more than your profits," Hiro said.

Luis turned to face the shinobi. "What do you mean?"

"Some weeks ago, Hisahide accused you of treason," Hiro began.

"A ridiculous charge," Luis interrupted. "Completely without foundation."

"Perhaps," Hiro said, "but Hisahide interprets the incident differently."

"You think he plans to revoke my license?" Luis demanded.

"No," Hiro said. "I think he intends to kill you."

"And risk a war with Portugal as well as the Miyoshi?" Luis snorted. "Not a chance."

"No king starts a war to avenge a single merchant," Hiro said. "Especially the king of a faraway land."

Father Mateo frowned. "We cannot let Hisahide harm Luis."

"We cannot stop him," Hiro said. "The only way to guarantee safety—Luis's as well as yours—is to leave the city."

"This has nothing to do with Mateo," Luis said. "I'll take a trip to Yokoseura and pick up a shipment of firearms. Once there, I'll find a reason to stay until you send word that the danger has passed."

Hiro found it curious, but not a surprise, that Luis agreed to leave so readily; Hiro had always considered the man a coward. "If you escape to Yokoseura, Hisahide's anger will fall on those you leave behind." He turned to Father Mateo. "You need to leave the city too, and quickly."

The Jesuit started toward his room.

Hiro raised his voice. "This conversation is not over."

Father Mateo paused with a hand on his door. "I did not say it was."

"Then where are you going?" Hiro conquered his frustration and lowered his voice to a normal level.

Father Mateo bowed his head. "To pray for guidance in this decision."

"I've already given you all the guidance any man requires," Hiro said. "Surely your god wouldn't want you to stay and die?"

Father Mateo looked back over his shoulder. "The God I serve can deliver me from Matsunaga Hisahide. But whether or not he does so, I will serve him anyway."

The Jesuit entered his room and closed the door.

Luis shook his head. "Priests. Almost as stubborn as samurai." He looked at Hiro. "He's not a fool. If danger comes, he'll leave."

Hiro disagreed with that assessment. If Father Mateo truly believed his god preferred him to stay in Kyoto, no power on earth would make him leave the city voluntarily.

Fortunately, Hiro had no problem moving the priest by deception, or even by force. He had sworn an oath to keep Father Mateo alive, and Hiro's own life would be forfeit if he failed.

Hiro had never failed a mission, and he had no intention of failing now.

CHAPTER 28

An hour before sunset, Hiro fastened his swords through his obi and prepared to leave the house. He left his room and discovered Father Mateo waiting in the common room.

"Time to go?" the Jesuit asked.

Hiro wondered, but didn't ask, if the foreign god had answered Father Mateo's prayers for guidance. In Hiro's experience, gods didn't bother with people very much. He didn't blame them. Prayers sounded more like whining than worship, at least to Hiro's ears. If he had created the universe—as Father Mateo claimed his god had done—he wouldn't listen to human petitions either.

The two men left the house and headed west on Marutamachi Road. Afternoon sunbeams lit the wooden houses with a crimson glow. Today, the color reminded Hiro of war, not beauty.

He didn't distract himself with abstract thoughts about the city, and whether or not he would miss it in days to come. Distractions, like assumptions, did not end well.

Father Mateo wore a contented expression that made Hiro wonder whether the priest was praying or simply enjoying the lovely evening. He didn't ask. He felt no need to fill the silent, peaceful spaces in a friendship.

When they reached the Kamo River, the samurai on guard approached and said, "Good evening. Heading to the city?"

"Yes," Hiro said, "but not to the center. Only on the east side of the river."

The samurai nodded. "Don't stay long. The shogun issued new

orders today—no one passes the bridges late at night. Rumor has it, enemy spies have infiltrated the capital."

"Thank you for the warning," Hiro said. "We won't be late."

Hiro and Father Mateo reached the Yutoku-za as the sun disappeared below the horizon, leaving only smears of pink against the purples and blues of the evening sky.

The door to the house stood open.

Hiro entered without knocking. After a pause, Father Mateo followed. They passed through the entry and into the giant common room beyond.

Braziers burned in every corner, illuminating the space. A paneled screen blocked off one edge of the room. Hiro didn't remember seeing it during his previous visit.

A trio of men stood opposite the screen. The oldest looked about sixty and carried an hourglass-shaped *ōtsuzumi* at his side. Each of the younger men held a similar drum.

"Do actors also play music?" Father Mateo asked in Portuguese.

"Drums and flutes accompany nō performances," Hiro said. "The musicians may, or may not, be members of the acting troupe."

The older man turned at Hiro's voice. Before he spoke, Yuji emerged from behind the paneled screen.

The actor wore a gold surcoat atop an elaborate, patterned kimono. A pair of pleated pants peeked out beneath the kimono's lower hem, and though the young man wore no mask he moved with the practiced sliding step of a shite entering the stage.

"I thought the actors wore masks," the Jesuit whispered.

"Not to practice." Hiro shook his head.

Yuji dropped out of character at the sight of Hiro and the priest. "What are you doing here?"

The elderly drummer gave Yuji a look of dismay and started across the floor. When he reached an appropriate distance, he bowed to Hiro and then the priest.

"Good evening, gentlemen," he said. "I apologize for the inappropriate welcome. How may we serve you?"

"We have come to speak with Yuji." Hiro looked past the older man.

Yuji glanced at the other musicians, who suddenly seemed completely absorbed in their instruments. His gaze returned to Hiro, and he bowed. "Of course. Please give me a moment to change my clothes. I would be honored to buy you a flask of sake at the restaurant up the street. I would not dare dishonor you by asking you to remain in a house of mourning."

Hiro considered a comment about the actor's rapid recovery from illness, but decided not to harass the youth as long as he cooperated. "You may go and change."

Yuji bowed and disappeared through a sliding door at the back of the room.

The elderly drummer turned to the young musicians. "Continue your practice in the garden. I will join you shortly."

"But, Master Tani," one of them said, "the evening air will wet the drums. . . ."

"No more than it will in two days' time, when you perform outside at the temple." The old man made a dismissive gesture. "Light the lanterns. I will join you soon."

The drummers bowed and left the room.

Tani turned to Hiro and bowed again. "Forgive my presumption, but are you the men investigating the death of my grandniece, Emi?"

"The magistrate has forbidden investigation," Hiro said. "The yoriki declared there was no crime."

"Of course, sir. Please forgive my error." Tani nodded deeply. "I would never question a yoriki's word."

Something in the old man's tone made Hiro ask, "If we did have an interest in certain events by the river, two nights past . . . would you have information to provide?"

"I am only an elderly man, granduncle to a beautiful girl who died far younger than she should." Tani lowered his gaze to the ground. "What could I know?"

"Something you'd rather your students did not hear," Hiro countered. "Otherwise, you would not have sent them into the evening air, where the dew might wet the ōtsuzumi skins."

Tani looked up. "Do you play the instrument, sir?"

"I know the sound will suffer if the skin gets damp." Hiro paused. "What do you know about Emi's murder?"

"Nothing about the killing," Tani said, "but a man who wanted to learn the truth might ask if anything else of value disappeared from this place the night that Emi died—or the night before."

"Something of value," Father Mateo said. "Like golden coins?"

"Gold?" The old man shook his head. "Perhaps, to a priest, that seems a treasure. Sir, I speak of something irreplaceable—a mask. A sacred mask for nō, bestowed by the kami on the Yutoku-za as a sign of special favor."

"The mask disappeared—it was stolen?" Father Mateo asked.

"Unless the kami took it back." Irony weighted Tani's words. "Or, possibly, someone sold it."

"Sold it? For what purpose?" Father Mateo seemed confused.

Tani looked over his shoulder, as if to ensure the room was empty. "A mask so important that only the head of the za is allowed to touch it? Sir, an object so important to us would never disappear, unless its owner needed the money for something . . . vital."

A *shoji* at the back of the room rustled open, revealing Yuji. The actor now wore a light blue tunic and gray striped pants beneath a patterned kimono. He hadn't bothered to bind his hair, which flowed down his back like a waterfall.

Hiro silently cursed the young man's timing. He wanted to learn more about the mask.

Yuji approached and bowed. "I apologize for keeping you waiting. If you please?" He gestured toward the exit and offered them a nervous smile.

Hiro nodded farewell to Tani and turned to Yuji. "Lead the way."

CHAPTER 29

As they left the Yutoku-za, Hiro glanced across the street and through the gate of Chugenji. An elderly woman bowed before the shrine, in fervent prayer. Hanging lanterns illuminated her face and shoulders, rendering her features clearly visible.

Hiro spoke in Portuguese. "See the woman standing by the shrine?"

Father Mateo turned. "I do not know her."

"Neither do I," Hiro said in the Jesuit's language. "I merely find it interesting that we can distinguish her features at this distance and after dark."

"You think the . . . man who took the gold . . . might have seen the victim praying." Father Mateo took care to use words that Yuji would not recognize.

Hiro nodded. "And that might have made the girl a target."

The teahouse sat just half a block from the Yutoku-za. Its narrow, unassuming entrance featured an indigo noren painted with simple characters: "TEA" on one panel, "SAKE" on the other. Wooden slats covered the single window that faced the street, and the flickering light seeping out through the noren suggested a dim interior.

Hiro paused in the doorway and removed his sandals. The teahouse smelled of grilling fish, the tang of sake, and the overly grassy scent of decent, but not high-quality, tea. To his relief, he didn't notice the stench of urine and stale food so common in lower-end establishments.

He looked at Yuji and nodded consent. With a bow, the actor led the way inside.

Past the narrow entry, the teahouse opened into a nine-mat room with wood-paneled walls and medium-grade tatami on the floor. A sliding door in the opposite wall led off to an unseen room beyond.

A pair of braziers flickered in the corners, filling the room with gentle light.

The mats on the floor gave off a feeble scent of drying grass, suggesting age, but Hiro saw no visible stains or crumbs of food.

The door across from the entrance opened, revealing an aging man in a striped kimono and pleated trousers.

"Good evening, Yuji." He bowed, with the extra-welcoming smile that shopkeepers offered the first guests of the evening. "May I bring tea and food for your party?"

Yuji nodded. "Thank you."

The teahouse owner bowed again and disappeared back through the door as Yuji led Hiro and Father Mateo to the corner with the best view of the entry. The actor knelt with his back to the wall and faced the entrance.

Hiro's opinion of Yuji, not high to begin with, dropped even further.

"Do not reprimand him," Father Mateo murmured in Portuguese, with a gesture to the brazier as if discussing the decor.

Hiro forced a smile. "He should have offered you that seat."

"We want his cooperation." The Jesuit knelt to Yuji's right, with his back to the entrance.

Hiro knelt to the actor's left and angled his body to watch the entry as well as the sliding door at the back of the room.

Father Mateo switched to Japanese. "This is a pleasant teahouse. Thank you for showing it to us."

Yuji nodded. "Of course. The honor is mine."

The teahouse owner returned with a tray that carried a steaming teapot, a trio of cups, and several plates of food. He set the tray before Yuji, bowed, and disappeared back through the sliding door.

The steam that rose from the teapot smelled too sharply grassy for Hiro's taste, but he hadn't expected a delicate tea in a business of this stature. Fortunately, the cups seemed clean, and the snacks looked good enough to excuse the less-than-average tea.

One of the plates held fried tofu, the second, thin-sliced fish, and the third, a pile of *umeboshi*. Hiro suppressed a smile. Father Mateo hated pickled plums. The priest had never acquired a taste for the salty, sour treat.

"May I pour you tea?" Yuji reached for the pot. "Please help your-selves to the delicacies."

Hiro accepted a cup of tea and selected a pickled plum. He liked them, and the flavor would take the edge off the bitter drink.

After filling the teacups, Yuji said, "Thank you for agreeing to speak with me away from the house."

Hiro nodded but did not answer.

Father Mateo had already started to drink his tea, so Yuji con-tinued, "I admit, it surprised me to see you, since the yoriki forbade an investigation of Emi's death." He shook his head. "Regrettable, but also understandable, under the circumstances."

"Which circumstances are those?" Hiro asked.

"May I speak freely?" Yuji asked. "Without consideration of social status?"

Father Mateo lowered his teacup. "No one objects to honesty." He glanced at Hiro. "And no one will punish you for it."

Yuji nodded. "Thank you, sir. The circumstances of which I speak relate to Emi's behavior before her death. Women who act improperly often come to violent ends. Her death, though unfortunate, did result from her own inappropriate choices. No one else should have to bear the blame."

"How, precisely, do 'improper' choices justify a woman's death?" Father Mateo's voice held a warning edge.

Hiro cleared his throat and switched to Portuguese. "Need I remind you of your recommendation not to provoke the suspect?"

Father Mateo frowned but nodded.

Hiro turned to Yuji. "The priest does not understand what you meant by 'inappropriate choices.'"

"A woman who spoils her virtue has no value," Yuji said. "A girl who meets men by the river deserves her fate."

"Did Emi engage in such behavior?" Father Mateo asked.

"My mother said she spoke with you this morning." Yuji selected a slice of fish. "Regrettably, I know nothing more than she has shared already."

"We would like to hear it from you," Hiro said.

"With respect, I cannot see why it matters, since there will be no investigation." Yuji wore the arrogant expression of a man who believed he had made a critical point.

"We seek to return a valuable item found at the scene of Emi's death." Hiro helped himself to another plum. "The girl's behavior may offer a clue to the object's owner."

Yuji lowered his teacup. "What kind of object?"

"Are you missing something of value?" Hiro asked.

"Of course not." Yuji leaned back as if offended. "I merely wanted to know."

"Unless the item belongs to you, its nature does not concern you," Hiro said. "Now, tell us what you know of Emi and the men she met by the river."

He duplicated Yuji's use of the plural—men—even though Chou had mentioned only one.

CHAPTER 30

Yuji refilled the teacups—a delay that, Hiro noted, gave him time to formulate an answer.

"I learned about the situation a little over a week ago," the actor said as he set the teapot down. "Chou came to me, worried about her sister meeting men by the river in the evenings. She didn't believe that Emi had become a prostitute—not yet—but worried she might, in order to earn the money she needed to buy a place in a teahouse."

The story didn't match Chou's precisely, but Hiro accepted the differences for the moment.

Father Mateo didn't. "Are girls required to purchase positions in a teahouse?"

"Quite the opposite," Yuji said. "A teahouse normally pays the parents of girls who become apprentices there. Emi misunderstood how the system works, or else she lied. Speaking freely, and in confidence, I think she wanted to become a prostitute. Chou mentioned some of the teahouse owners suggested it."

"Why would Emi make that decision?" Father Mateo asked.

"I could not tell you," Yuji said, "but Emi didn't want the things that other girls desire. She wanted to make decisions for herself. As one might expect from a woman's decisions, many of them were ill-advised."

"Did you speak with anyone else about Emi's behavior?" Hiro asked.

"Aside from Chou?" Yuji shook his head. "Only Mother. I did not want to interfere. I did, however, tell Chou to speak with her father at once, before Emi caused us trouble with the police."

"The police?" Father Mateo asked.

Hiro selected a third umeboshi. They tasted uncommonly good.

"Prostitutes cannot legally ply their trade on the riverbank," Yuji said. "If the dōshin caught Emi doing so, they would arrest her. The magistrate would expose her connection to the Yutoku-za at her trial, and that would ruin our reputation as a legitimate theater troupe."

After a pause, he added, "I am a rising star on the stage. I cannot have people whispering that my troupe allows its women to prostitute themselves by the river."

Or that you married a prostitute's sister, Hiro thought. Aloud, he said, "That would indeed be most unfortunate."

Yuji gave him a grateful look. "Thank you, sir, I knew you would understand. Like samurai, we actors must avoid disgrace and public humiliation at all costs. My talent will make me a great shite. I can lead the Yutoku-za to fame. But a scandal involving my future sister"—he shook his head—"such a thing would ruin my reputation at this critical point in my career. I could end up relegated to the chorus, without a chance of securing the roles my skills deserve."

He took a sip of tea. "Emi's death is regrettable, but prevented a greater tragedy. The less attention it receives, the better."

"The death of a child is *never* a fortunate event," the priest said sternly.

"Even when it saves two families permanent disgrace? Prevents the financial ruin of a guild?" Yuji met the Jesuit's stare without repentance. "I humbly apologize, but we must differ on that point."

Hiro shifted the conversation before the priest could argue. "Do you know whether Chou discussed Emi's actions with Satsu?"

"She did," Yuji said. "I told her to do it, and, unlike Emi, Chou does as she's told."

"Are you certain?" Father Mateo asked, brow furrowed in disapproval.

"Do you ask because Emi didn't stop meeting men by the river?" Yuji shrugged. "With respect, unruly women find ways of straying, no matter what men do."

"One last question," Hiro said, "and then we really must leave. If

Emi's behavior hadn't stopped, would you have broken your betrothal to Chou?"

"I do not have that option." Yuji's voice held unexpected bitterness. "When Botan retires, or dies, control of the Yutoku-za will pass to the eldest eligible male in the troupe. Satsu is an outsider and not sufficiently talented to lead. I have the skills, and looks, required, but without Chou I lack the proper connections. Only a fool would surrender the chance to marry Botan's granddaughter and inherit control of the troupe."

"Assuming he chooses you and not another," Father Mateo said.

Hiro hoped the Jesuit wouldn't mention their conversation with Chou and Haru.

"There is no other candidate." Yuji smirked. "The day I marry Chou, it is decided."

Father Mateo opened his mouth, but Hiro cut him off. "You are certain you know nothing more of Emi's male companions?"

Yuji shifted his gaze to Hiro. "If I did, Matsui-*san*, I would tell you, though I assure you we are all better off with her gone."

Father Mateo stood up. "That is enough." He looked at Hiro. "Time to go."

Yuji bowed from a seated position as Hiro followed the Jesuit from the teahouse. For the first time in Hiro's memory, Father Mateo did not bow, or say farewell, before departing.

"He killed Emi," Father Mateo whispered as they put on their sandals and returned to the street.

"Yuji?" Hiro glanced back at the noren hanging in the teahouse entrance. "I don't think so."

"He did," the priest insisted. "He wanted her dead, and he had a motive to kill her. Weren't you listening?"

Hiro started toward the Yutoku-za. "Yuji is a pathetic, self-centered fool, but not a killer."

"He said we were all better off with Emi dead," the priest objected.

"I do not argue that he had a motive." Hiro paused, remembering Yuji's interest in the unnamed object found with Emi's body. "But he doesn't seem the type to soil his hands. Especially since the coin and the killing might not be related after all."

Father Mateo looked confused. "Not related? Why do you say so?"

"What if Emi saw the samurai who extorted money from Botan?"

"He concealed his face," the priest protested.

"Yes," Hiro said, "but he would have removed the mask when leaving the Yutoku-za, to avoid attracting attention in the street. Emi might have seen him from the shrine, and we now know it's possible that he could have recognized her as well."

"The murder didn't happen the night the samurai demanded money, or even the morning that Botan gave it to him." Father Mateo paused and raised his head as if remembering something. "But the mask disappeared the night before she died."

"Precisely," Hiro said. "Do you know how much that mask would sell for?"

"Enough to prevent a samurai from killing Botan's family, I presume. Also, Botan didn't mention giving the mask away."

"He wouldn't," Hiro said. "The shame would be too great to bear."

"But was it stolen, or sold, or paid to the samurai with the gold?" the Jesuit asked.

"I think I know who can tell us." Hiro paused outside the Yutoku-za. "The question is whether or not he will."

As Hiro knocked on the door, the priest said, "Satsu may not know the mask is missing."

"He knows," Hiro said, "and I also think he's the reason Botan had the mask in the first place."

Father Mateo looked confused, but the door swung open before he could ask a question.

CHAPTER 31

Satsu answered the door himself, and quickly enough that Hiro suspected the actor had seen them coming.

"Good evening." Satsu bowed. "How may I help you?"

Hiro smiled. "The weather is mild and pleasant. We hoped you would join us and walk by the river."

Satsu looked at the darkened sky and then at Hiro. "I sense a chill. However, I must be mistaken. I would not presume to contradict a samurai."

He stepped outside and closed the door behind him.

They walked toward the river, but no one spoke until they reached the bridge. As usual, the armored samurai stood on the opposite side, with his back to the river and his face toward Pontochō.

"Shall we cross?" Satsu asked with a nod.

"No need." Hiro started south along the road that paralleled the river.

"Why this direction?" Father Mateo asked in Portuguese.

"To take us out of Yoriki Hosokawa's jurisdiction. The ward ends two blocks south of Shijō Bridge." Hiro answered in Japanese. Satsu would have recognized the names and guessed the topic anyway.

They continued south until Hiro knew the guard could no longer see them from the bridge. A breeze fluttered the leaves of the cherry trees along the path. It carried the odor of grilling fish, along with drying leaves and the tang of the river.

Hiro's stomach rumbled. Umeboshi and tea didn't pass for a meal.

"I'm going no farther." With no one around to hear him, Satsu let his voice take on a suspicious edge. "What news do you bear that can't be said where other ears might hear?"

Father Mateo stiffened, but Hiro took no offense from the actor's words. Despite his assumed identity, Satsu ranked as Hiro's senior within the Iga ryu.

"What do you know about the missing mask?" the priest demanded.

"Less than subtle," Hiro remarked in Portuguese, though he didn't mind. Satsu would expect politeness. Unexpected accusations might provoke an honest answer—or, at least, a useful one.

"What mask?" Satsu turned to Hiro, his face in shadow. "What does he mean?"

Father Mateo stepped forward. "The one that disappeared from the Yutoku-za the night before Emi died."

"Who told you about the mask?" Satsu demanded. "Botan wouldn't, and I didn't . . ."

He trailed off, as if expecting Father Mateo to answer. When no one spoke, the actor said, "It must have been Tani." He sighed. "You are correct, a mask was stolen the night before Emi died."

"Stolen?" Father Mateo asked, "or sold to pay a samurai bribe?"

"Sold—" The frustrated edge left Satsu's voice. "Did someone admit to selling it, or is this just conjecture?"

"Botan has not confirmed the theory," Father Mateo admitted.

Satsu shook his head. "Then it did not happen. Botan would never sell that mask."

"Why not?" Hiro asked.

At the same time, Father Mateo said, "Not even to save Emi's life?"

"The mask was sacred to the Yutoku-za," Satsu replied, "our most important and divine possession. It once belonged to a famous actor—a master, revered within our art. Botan valued the mask so much that he kept it locked away in his personal office. Only he—as head of the troupe—ever touched it or wore it on the stage."

"Which means no one would notice it missing if Botan didn't want the troupe to learn about the samurai's demand," Hiro said.

"Botan would never sell that mask or give it to anyone, let alone a thieving samurai." Satsu paused. "Botan acquired that mask from me. I brought it to Kyoto in order to purchase a place in an acting family."

"I suspected as much," Hiro said. "No outsider marries a shite's daughter unless he has something exceptional to offer—and you mentioned that your skills did not suffice."

"How would its origin stop Botan from selling it?" Father Mateo asked.

"Botan believed the kami sent him the mask, through me, as a sign of favor," Satsu said. "However, the Yutoku-za has fallen on hard times in recent months. After Shogun Ashikaga's death, our wealthiest samurai patrons left the city. Without them to hire us, Botan depends even more on the kami's favor to see us through.

"In dire circumstances, Botan might sell a mask to pay our debts— or even to pay a samurai's demand. However, he would never sell that particular mask for any reason. No, I am convinced the mask was stolen."

"If he did want to sell a mask, who would buy it?" Father Mateo asked.

"Any theater troupe in Kyoto would want that mask," Satsu replied, "and samurai collectors would buy it also. Special masks of proven provenance are valuable and difficult to find."

"I still think Botan sold it," Father Mateo said, "or gave it to the samurai."

"Either way"—Satsu looked from the priest to Hiro—"I do not understand why you needed to bring me out in the dark to discuss it now."

"We need to find the samurai who threatened Botan," Hiro said. "We think you know his name."

"If I knew it, I would tell you." Satsu shook his head. "I never saw him. No one saw him. Botan said he wore a mask."

"Do bandits normally steal from actors' families?" Hiro asked.

"No—and generally speaking, bandits are not samurai."

"Any man can wear a pair of swords," Father Mateo said.

"Robbing a man with a dagger is just as effective," Satsu answered, "and it carries far less risk of beheading if a samurai catches you in the street."

"If you want us to find the person who killed your daughter," Hiro said, "you must make Botan tell you more about the samurai who threatened him."

"We have to find that samurai in order to identify Emi's killer," Father Mateo added.

Satsu bowed. "I owe you both an apology. When I asked you to find my daughter's killer, I did not realize the danger you would have to face. The yoriki will not tolerate you asking further questions. I could tell when he tried to arrest you at the temple. I cannot have your arrest—or worse—on my conscience. Although I appreciate your efforts, I release you from your pledge to find the killer."

Hiro stared at the actor, momentarily at a loss for words.

"Do you still have the golden coin?" Satsu asked. "I would like it back, if you do."

"We do not have it with us," Hiro lied, "but we can return it tomorrow morning, if you wish."

"Thank you." Satsu bowed again. "No coin can repay my daughter's blood, but it was hers—and the Yutoku-za does need the gold. Tomorrow morning I must attend a dress rehearsal at Fushimi Inari Shrine, to the south of the city. If you don't mind, perhaps you could bring the coin to me there. I would rather my wife did not have to see it again."

A samurai's shadowed form appeared on the path.

"You there!" a familiar voice called. "Stop! By order of Yoriki Hosokawa!"

Satsu dropped to his knees and bent his forehead to the ground.

"Run," Hiro whispered.

"He's already seen us," Satsu whispered back. "I cannot risk it."

CHAPTER 32

As the samurai approached, Hiro recognized the scruffy dōshin who followed them from the magistrate's office earlier in the afternoon. He wondered how the samurai had found them, since he hadn't noticed anyone following since they left the Jesuit's house.

"The two of you are under arrest," the dōshin snarled, "and this commoner's life is forfeit."

Father Mateo stepped forward. "You have no cause to take his life."

The dōshin grasped the hilt of his sword. "A samurai needs no cause."

"Only an honorless coward would kill a man without a reason." Father Mateo spoke in a voice as calm as the burbling river, but firm as a mountain.

"His family told me he left the house with a foreigner and a ronin." The dōshin spat out the final word as if it tasted foul on his tongue. "Yoriki Hosokawa told him what would happen if he spoke with you again."

"He threatened whipping, not execution," Father Mateo countered. "I was there—and you have no business harassing innocent people outside your jurisdiction."

The dōshin ignored the Jesuit's words. He crossed to Satsu and drew his sword with a motion that would have severed the actor's neck—but at the final moment Satsu ducked and rolled away.

The dōshin's blade swished harmlessly through the air.

"How dare you!" The samurai started for Satsu, but Hiro stepped between them.

"The foreigner is correct," Hiro said. "I will not let you kill this man."

"Then you condemn yourself and the priest as well." The dōshin raised his sword.

Satsu lunged for the samurai with unexpected speed. A dagger glinted in his hand.

The dōshin leaped away, avoiding Satsu's blade by inches.

"You filth!" The dōshin swung his sword, but once again the actor dodged.

"Kneel and accept your punishment," the dōshin ordered, "or your entire family will die!"

"Sheathe your sword and forget this happened," Father Mateo said.

Hiro shook his head. "Too late for that."

The dōshin raised his sword and leaped toward Satsu. This time, Hiro's katana blocked the strike.

The dōshin slashed at Hiro, but the shinobi avoided the blade. As Hiro counterattacked, the policeman grunted, but not enough to confirm a successful strike. Hiro jumped away, suspecting a trick—and felt a wave of air on his face as the dōshin's sword passed by.

He circled sideways, into the shadow of an overhanging branch. The dōshin countered Hiro's movement, maintaining the space between them. Lanterns along the path cast flickering spots of light and shadow over the samurai's scowling features.

Hiro froze, awaiting an opening.

The dōshin swayed from side to side, weaving like a snake. He stamped his foot, but Hiro did not flinch or jump to attack.

A moment passed. Hiro drew a silent breath and felt his senses sharpen.

Overhead, the cherry branches rustled with a breeze. The river burbled past within its banks.

The dōshin stamped his foot again and lunged.

This time, Hiro stepped aside and countered with a sideways strike. He felt the blade slice through the air. He missed.

He spun to avoid the counterstrike, which came more quickly than expected.

Hiro traded blows with the dōshin. Some passed harmlessly through the air. Others ended with a clash of steel on steel. Despite his loathing for the dōshin, Hiro admired his opponent's skill with a sword.

"You fight well," Hiro said when the combat paused. "It is unfortunate that you must die."

The dōshin lunged and swung his sword. As Hiro jumped away, he spun and aimed a lethal strike across the dōshin's neck. This time, Hiro felt his blade strike home.

The dōshin's grunt became a cough, and then a ragged gasp. He dropped his sword and clutched his throat. Blood pattered down on the earthen path with a sound like falling raindrops.

Hiro stepped to the side and raised his katana. "Your skill has earned you a rapid death."

In a single motion, he cut off the dōshin's head.

Before Hiro could sheathe his katana, Satsu ran forward and grasped the dead man's hands. "We have to get him off the road."

He dragged the body into the shadows beneath a cherry tree.

Hiro picked up the dōshin's head and followed.

"You killed him," Father Mateo said. "What are we going to do?"

"Dispose of the body," Hiro replied. "And quickly."

"You killed him," Father Mateo repeated.

Hiro nodded. "An established fact."

Father Mateo stared at the body. "We have no way to bury him."

"And the river's too shallow and slow at this location," Satsu added. "However, I know a place. There is a bathhouse around the corner—it closed about an hour ago."

"You want to leave the body in a bathhouse?" Father Mateo asked.

"Trust me." Satsu looked at Hiro. "My *other* work in Kyoto involves the disappearance of unwanted people—alive *and* dead."

"Very well," Hiro said. "Let's go."

"I don't understand." Father Mateo looked from one man to the other. "It doesn't seem appropriate to hide a samurai's body in a bathhouse."

"I'll explain when we get there," Satsu said. "Let's go—and don't forget his head."

The bathhouse sat just east of the river, on a street whose businesses were closed and shuttered at this time of night. Despite the lack of passersby, Hiro and Satsu remained in the shadows as they carried the dōshin's body between them. Father Mateo followed with the head, holding it as far away from his body as he could manage.

"This way." Satsu turned into a narrow passage between the bathhouse and the business next door.

A double line of trees separated the back of the building from the open common space at the center of the block. In daylight the trees offered privacy and enhanced the lovely setting for bathhouse patrons. In the darkness, they provided perfect cover for three men and a samurai's headless corpse.

Satsu paused in front of the undersized door that led to the bathhouse boiler room. "Set him down for a minute."

Hiro helped the actor lower the body to the ground.

"What's going on?" Father Mateo whispered as Satsu opened the little door and ducked inside. "Isn't that where they . . ."

A rustling came from the boiler room, followed by a metallic creak. Sparks flared to life in the house's wood-burning oven as Satsu stirred the coals with a poker. The actor's silhouette blocked the glow as he tossed a handful of kindling into the oven. The sparks grew into flames.

Father Mateo's mouth fell open in horror. He shook his head, the motion barely visible in the shadows.

Satsu returned to the yard. The orange glow of tiny flames emerged from the darkened room beyond.

"As I hoped, the fire was banked but came to life at once with a little kindling." Satsu extended his hands to the priest. "We'll start with the head."

Father Mateo backed away.

"This isn't the time for argument," Hiro whispered. "We have no choice."

"The bathhouse owners will find him in the morning!" Father Mateo sounded close to panic. "The flames may burn his flesh, but not the bones."

"The owners will bury the bones and ask no questions," Satsu said. "Now hand it over."

Father Mateo turned his face away and handed the dōshin's head to Satsu. When the burden left his hands, he made the sign of the cross and bowed his head to pray.

Satsu ducked into the boiler room and tossed the head into the fire. He added another handful of kindling; moments later the air was filled with the odors of scorching hair and burning flesh.

Father Mateo coughed and retched.

"The smell will attract attention," Hiro said.

"Fortunately, this bath is known for its scented waters." Satsu grabbed a fresh pine bough from a pile beside the boiler room. He tossed it onto the fire, and though the smoke that rose from the oven didn't completely hide the acrid, fatty smells of burning samurai, it did reduce the stench to a level that wouldn't raise alarm.

"One more problem," Hiro said. "The body won't fit in the oven in this condition."

Satsu reached inside his tunic and withdrew a wicked-looking dagger. "That's a problem I can solve. It's time for you to take the foreigner home."

Father Mateo raised his head. "We cannot leave you here alone."

"With respect, you also cannot stay." Satsu turned to the priest. "One of my duties in Kyoto is handling inconvenient corpses. This is not my first dead samurai. I am better trained, and better able, to address this problem. I appreciate your sense of honor, but I promise your concern is quite misplaced.

"Please bring my daughter's coin to Fushimi Inari tomorrow morning. After that, we must not ever speak again."

CHAPTER 33

Hiro and Father Mateo returned to the river and walked along the bank in silence. Discomfort dripped from the priest like heavy rain from a temple's eaves. Even so, Hiro did not speak. No words can change the things a man has seen.

Just before they reached the bridge at Marutamachi Road, Father Mateo said, "I do not blame you for killing him."

"Blame me?" Hiro asked, surprised. "He would have killed us all."

"I know that." Father Mateo nodded. "I cannot thank you for taking a life, but I deeply appreciate you saving Satsu."

"And you also."

"I do not want you to kill on my behalf," Father Mateo said.

"You know that's why I came to Kyoto: to guard your life at any cost."

"Now that I have seen you kill, the cost is far too high."

"It will happen again," Hiro said, "and more than once, unless you leave the city."

Father Mateo struggled for words. "Perhaps it is you who should leave. Alone."

"That, I cannot and will not do. The oath I took can be broken only by death—either yours or mine."

"An oath you made to a man we do not know, whose motives I cannot understand." The Jesuit shook his head. "I release you from that oath."

"Only death can release me," Hiro said. "Once given, this oath cannot be retracted."

"Doesn't it bother you? Pledging your life at the request of a man you do not know?"

"On behalf of a man I have come to know quite well." Hiro paused. "But, to answer your question, no. Hattori Hanzo trusted your benefactor enough to accept the contract and to honor his request for anonymity. I accepted Hanzo's judgment on the matter—this is not the first such contract I've fulfilled."

The question that followed was not what Hiro expected.

"Why did you lie to Satsu about the coin? You know I have it with me."

Hiro found the Jesuit's change of subject interesting. Samurai used the tactic to avoid a fight with important family members or lifelong friends.

He honored the priest's decision to leave the previous topic at an impasse. "I found it strange, and also suspicious, that Satsu asked us to stop the investigation. I wanted time to think before I had to return the coin."

The samurai on guard at the bridge stood halfway across the span, in order to watch both sides of the river effectively. He nodded, but did not approach, as Hiro and Father Mateo turned onto Marutamachi Road.

The wind sent a cluster of fallen leaves swirling across the road like tiny specters. In the distance, a dog began to bark.

Hiro and Father Mateo walked in silence until they reached Okazaki Shrine.

There, a priestess stood beside the torii. She held a basket of amulets, and nearby braziers cast their flickering light across her face. The priestess bowed. "Good evening."

"And to you." Father Mateo nodded as he passed.

Hiro wondered if the Jesuit knew the woman's name. They passed her at the gate quite often, but the priest had never stopped to talk.

After they left the shrine behind them, Father Mateo said, "Yuji must have killed her."

"Emi?" Hiro asked.

"Yes, it must be him. He worried that Emi would damage his reputation and career, but he also couldn't break his betrothal to Chou. I think he went to the river and took care of the problem . . . personally."

"How do the coin and the missing mask fit into that scenario?" Hiro asked.

"Unrelated," Father Mateo said. "I think Botan sold the mask to pay the samurai's demand, or gave it to him as a partial payment. I don't know how the coin fits in—or doesn't, as the case may be—but Yuji had the motive, and the chance, to kill the girl."

"That doesn't make him a murderer," Hiro said. "He's an actor—and a selfish fool—but a crime like this is probably beyond him."

"You don't know much about actors, do you?" Father Mateo asked.

Hiro wasn't used to hearing his own expressions turned against him. "And you do?"

"As it happens, yes."

"How does a priest know anything about actors?"

Father Mateo glanced at Hiro. "Because I almost became one."

CHAPTER 34

"An actor?" Hiro couldn't believe it. "You planned to become an actor?"

Questions flooded Hiro's mind, making him realize just how little he knew about Father Mateo. He had never considered the priest as anything more, or less, than his current self.

"We were speaking of Yuji," the Jesuit said.

"Not anymore. What changed your mind about acting?"

Father Mateo shrugged. "Things happened, and I chose another path." His tone suggested he had no intention of answering further questions. "Now, about Yuji."

Hiro put the Jesuit's past aside for the moment. "I agree that he had a motive to murder Emi. However, that answer seems too simple."

"Murder doesn't have to be complicated," Father Mateo said.

"It usually isn't," Hiro agreed, "but your solution doesn't account for the mask or the coin. Even a simple explanation must incorporate all of the relevant facts."

"Unless the coin and mask are not connected to the crime," the Jesuit said.

"True." Hiro nodded. "We're missing too many facts to know for certain."

"What if Emi saw the samurai leave the Yutoku-za with the mask, and he saw her too, and followed her to the river. When she ran into Jiro, the samurai waited until the boy fell asleep and then approached her."

"She wouldn't have gone with him," Hiro said. "Why would she walk away from Jiro with someone she didn't trust? Especially if she saw him taking something of value from her home?"

"Maybe she knew him," Father Mateo suggested.

"Actors' daughters do not follow samurai so quickly. Also, Emi would have gone with the killer only if she knew that Jiro wouldn't object to seeing them together. Otherwise, she would not risk him waking . . ."

"Those facts point to Yuji as the killer," Father Mateo said. "She knew him, and Jiro could hardly object to Emi speaking with her sister's betrothed."

"Those facts condemn the entire Yutoku-za—except for Haru, who lacked the physical strength to kill his sister," Hiro said.

"We can eliminate the women, also." Father Mateo seemed annoyed.

"Perhaps the older ones," Hiro said. "But all of this means nothing. We must leave the city—now—before the yoriki learns about the dōshin's disappearance and before that merchant comes to replace Luis."

"Satsu is family." Father Mateo sounded disappointed. "How can you turn your back on his distress?"

"He released us," Hiro said, "and even if he hadn't, duty supersedes a family obligation. As you so recently pointed out, I swore an oath to keep you alive, and I hold it just as sacred as you hold the vows you make to your god."

Father Mateo had drawn a breath, but released it without speaking.

Hiro pressed his advantage. "Would your god have sent me to guard you if he wanted you to die? Strategic retreat is not surrender. Sometimes it offers the only path to victory."

"Yes, but—"

Hiro raised a hand for silence. With the other, he pointed down the darkened road.

Across the street from the Jesuit's home, the neighbor's Akita barked with a fury far too great for wind or shadows.

Father Mateo whispered, "Is something wrong?"

"The dog started barking when we made the turn from the river road." Hiro strained his eyes, but saw no movement in the shadows. "It hasn't stopped."

"Most likely just the wind and fallen leaves," Father Mateo said.

"That doesn't explain it barking so intensely for so long." Hiro stopped walking. "We should turn back."

"It's probably nothing," the Jesuit said, "and if it's not, we can't abandon Ana and Luis."

Luis, I could leave, Hiro thought. Aloud, he added, "I cannot let you walk into danger."

"I am neither an invalid nor a child," Father Mateo said, "and only a coward runs away from danger."

Hiro scowled. "If you were any other man, that insult would have cost your life."

"If you were any other man, I would have held my tongue." Father Mateo took a step forward. "I'm going to check on Ana. You can come with me, or not, as it suits you."

He continued toward home at a rapid walk.

Hiro followed with an angry sigh. As he caught up, he laid a hand on the Jesuit's arm. "Please stop."

To his surprise, Father Mateo obeyed.

Hiro drew his katana and handed the longsword to the priest. "Take this. It seems you've forgotten to bring your own."

"Keep it," Father Mateo said.

"Only a child or an invalid goes into a fight unarmed." Hiro drew his *wakizashi*. "I can defend myself well enough with the shorter one." *Along with the weapons in my sleeve*—though Hiro kept the last part to himself.

Father Mateo held the sword with an awkward, double-handed grip.

Hiro shook his head. "Try not to stab yourself—or me."

"No promises."

As they approached the house, the Akita released another stream of furious, snarling barks.

"He's barking at us," the Jesuit whispered.

"Quiet," Hiro whispered back. "If we're attacked, keep your back to mine. Don't let them separate us or get behind you."

Father Mateo nodded.

Hiro pushed the front door open and paused to listen. He heard no movement and smelled no foreign scents. Orange light glowed through the paneled walls between the entry and the common room—a fire still burned in the Jesuit's hearth.

Hiro crossed the entry using a special step that silenced his movements on the wooden floor. He slipped his free hand into his sleeve and retrieved a hidden shuriken. He hoped he wouldn't need it, but felt better with a weapon in each hand.

When he reached the doorway, Hiro drew a breath and peered into the common room.

CHAPTER 35

Gato lay on her side by the hearth, enjoying the warmth of the dying fire. Otherwise, the room looked empty.

Hiro stepped through the doorway and gestured for Father Mateo to follow. They paused by the hearth. Hiro raised a finger for silence. Father Mateo nodded.

The paper panels that led to the rooms belonging to Hiro, Father Mateo, and Luis were dark, but pale light flickered on the opposite side of the kitchen door.

Hiro started toward the kitchen, motioning for the priest to stay behind him.

Father Mateo touched Hiro's arm and pointed to Luis's room. The shinobi shook his head. If the merchant was home, he was sleeping . . . or dead. Not worth disturbing, either way.

As they reached the kitchen door, they heard a rustling from the other side. A shadow flickered across the panels. It grew in size and clarity as the figure approached the door.

The shadowed person wielded a staff.

Hiro drew a breath to calm his heart.

On the other side of the sliding door, a shadowed hand reached for the paneled frame.

Hiro raised his sword as the door slid open—and jumped away with a startled noise.

Ana stood before him with a poker in her hands.

The metal pole had cast a shadow like a fighting staff.

The housekeeper shrieked and swung the poker. Hiro ducked, avoiding the strike by inches.

"Ana!" Father Mateo called. "It's us—just me and Hiro!"

"*Ai!*" Ana shrieked. "Why are you sneaking around like a pair of thieves?" She glared at Father Mateo and then at Hiro, fury etched in every wrinkle of her face.

"The neighbor's dog was barking," Father Mateo said.

"It barks at everything . . . and nothing." Ana scowled. "I might have killed you."

"But you didn't," the Jesuit said.

Hiro straightened and looked around, half expecting a real attack. A good assassin took advantage of the enemy's confusion.

"Why were you prowling around like a pair of shinobi?" Ana demanded.

"We wanted to save you." Father Mateo sounded like a child caught with forbidden sweets.

"Hm. Only thing I need saving from is you." Ana waggled the poker at Hiro. "This was probably your idea."

Hiro felt his cheeks grow warm. Ana blamed him for everything, but this time it was warranted.

The housekeeper turned toward the stove and lowered the poker. "Wait by the hearth. I'll bring you a meal." She glanced at Hiro. "You too, though you don't deserve it."

After eating, Hiro returned to his room and changed into a dark-colored tunic and trousers. He slid the veranda door open and knelt in the doorway, enjoying the cool air as he prepared for his evening meditation.

Gato gave a happy trill and trotted past him into the night.

Hiro closed his eyes and attuned his senses to the sounds and scents around him. A breeze rustled the dying leaves of the cherry tree near the garden wall. The koi made sucking sounds and little splashes in the pond. Wood smoke gave the air a heavy quality, enhanced by the underlying odors of decaying leaves and dying grasses.

The murmur of Father Mateo's prayers rose and fell in the next room over.

The neighbor's Akita barked, and continued barking.

Hiro opened his eyes and listened for hooves or footsteps, but heard only the furious snarling of the dog. He stood up and closed the door behind him. Grasping the edge of an eave, he pulled himself onto the sloping roof and crawled up the thatch on his hands and knees, staying low to avoid detection. When he reached the long, thick beam that formed the ridge of the roof, he threw a leg across it and shimmied forward until he saw the street below.

The waning moon had not yet risen, leaving the road in shadow. Across the way, the dog kept barking. Hiro scanned the street for movement, wishing his eyes could penetrate the darkness like a dog's.

The Akita's barking slowed. It flopped to the ground with a malcontented thump.

The dog had no sooner settled than hoofbeats echoed on the road. A horse appeared from the shadows, lit by the tiny metal lantern the rider held. The faint light caught the horseman's face, and Hiro recognized Luis Álvares.

The Akita's barking resumed with a vengeance, as if the dog took special umbrage at the merchant's appearance.

Hiro felt a spark of compassion for the canine on that point.

The horse turned off the road and trotted along the side of the house to the stable.

Hiro wondered what had kept Luis so late. The merchant normally closed his warehouse down at dusk, like most Kyoto shops. Luis did not like Japanese food and had no friends in Kyoto, so he didn't stay out late to socialize.

Hiro kept his gaze on the street. He wondered what had upset the dog before the merchant arrived. Father Mateo and Ana might think the Akita barked at leaves and wind, but Hiro believed that something else explained the beast's unusual agitation.

East of the house, shadows moved in the street. The Akita leaped to its feet, still barking, but now with a strangled edge, as the massive dog lunged at the end of its tether. Hiro wished the rope would break, as it had the previous summer. A dog wouldn't stop a trained assassin, but Hiro wanted to know if he faced a shinobi or a common thief.

The shadows moved closer, and Hiro's heartbeat quickened as he realized two people angled toward the Jesuit's home.

He reached up his sleeve and retrieved a pair of shuriken. Ranged attacks were not his strength, but flying metal stars would buy him time to reach the ground.

Across the street, a door swung open.

"Who's out there?" The neighbor appeared on his porch with a lantern.

Light spilled into the road, illuminating a young man with a woman by his side. Shadows hid their faces, but the youth wore a commoner's striped kimono, the girl the pale robes of a temple maiden. They flinched and ducked their heads as if ashamed to face the light.

The man put a protective arm around the woman's shoulders. She flinched away, then changed her mind and accepted the shelter of his embrace.

"Go home before the samurai catch you," the neighbor called. "It's dangerous on the street this time of night."

The youth and the maiden hurried off toward Okazaki Shrine. Given the samurai guards on the bridge, the couple couldn't have crossed the river after dark. The boy must live in the neighborhood, and the girl resembled a temple maiden from the shrine. The couple had either lost track of time or wanted the privacy darkness offered. Either way, their presence explained the barking dog, both now and earlier in the evening.

Hiro thought of Emi and Jiro walking by the river. Like this couple, and so many others, they needed the darkness and quiet streets to hide the emotions society's rules forbade them from expressing. Young people thought they knew the truth, yet youth and the heart made unreliable compasses.

Hiro straightened with the shock of sudden realization. He'd focused too much on the older suspects and not enough on the younger people's words. Despite the danger, it might not be too late to find the killer after all.

He could not risk the Jesuit's life by staying in the capital much longer. Even so, Hiro wanted to learn the truth before they left the city. Father Mateo considered the murder important because of Hiro's family ties, but Hiro suspected his uncle might be playing them for fools. The more he reflected on Satsu's behavior, the more he believed that Satsu had something else at stake in addition to finding Emi's killer. As a shinobi, that was almost certainly true.

Hiro intended to discover Satsu's real motivation for requesting— and then stopping—the investigation. If he learned that his uncle had murdered Emi, for any reason, not even their common blood would protect the actor from Hiro's wrath. It wasn't the killing that bothered him most, though he certainly didn't approve of murdering family. What angered Hiro enough to require vengeance was the thought that Satsu might have murdered his own child and preyed on Hiro's trust to escape from justice.

CHAPTER 36

The neighbor's Akita fell silent as the couple disappeared up the street. A few minutes later, Luis emerged from the stable and entered the house. The dog barked as he passed, but not for long. The earlier excitement had worn it out.

Hiro remained on the roof for several hours. No one passed on the road, and the Akita didn't bark again. A crispness in the air suggested colder days approaching.

Midnight arrived. The waning moon appeared on the horizon. Hiro started down from the roof. He wondered whether Father Mateo might agree to visit Iga—assuming Hiro could obtain permission for a foreigner to enter the shinobi stronghold. To Hiro's knowledge, Hattori Hanzo had never allowed a foreign person visit Iga village. Not many Japanese had seen it, either.

Hiro decided to risk the request. Few places in Japan were safer than Iga—at least for those who entered with permission. If Hanzo refused, they would head to the Portuguese settlement at Yokoseura. Hiro didn't like the thought of living among foreigners, especially if most of them behaved like Luis Álvares, but he would make that sacrifice to save his charge—and friend—from mortal danger.

At dawn Hiro rose and dressed in his gray kimono.

Father Mateo's rhythmic prayers floated over the open rafters from the adjacent room. Hiro decided not to interrupt. He didn't believe that any god would answer human prayers, but also knew that Father Mateo would not leave Kyoto without time to ask his deity's direction.

Hiro left the house through the garden. At the gate he heard a voice, and also horses, in the road. He peered through an opening in the fence.

A glossy black stallion stood in the street outside the Jesuit's home. It wore a leather saddle and a bridle of foreign make, and it dwarfed the Japanese horse and robe-clad acolyte beside it.

Hiro knew the stallion. It belonged to Father Vilela, the priest who ran the Jesuit mission and its church within Kyoto proper. The Jesuits' primary mission focused on the samurai, who would have disapproved of Father Mateo's work among the common classes. For that reason, Father Mateo had special permission to live and work apart from the other priests. The senior Jesuit rarely visited Father Mateo's home. In fact, he had done so only once before.

That visit had not brought good news.

Hiro doubted this one would be better.

He returned to the house just as Ana led the senior Jesuit into the common room.

Father Vilela dressed, and wore his hair, in samurai style. Japanese swords hung from his obi, and even his beard and mustache were carefully trimmed. Except for his foreign features and the wooden cross around his neck, Father Vilela could easily pass for samurai.

Hiro bowed to the foreign priest. In truth, he outranked the Jesuit, but like everyone else, Father Vilela believed that Hiro was merely a humble ronin.

Father Vilela nodded to Hiro and bowed to Father Mateo, who had just emerged from his room.

"Good morning," Father Mateo said. "I am honored by your visit. Would you like tea?"

"Regrettably, I cannot stay for refreshments." Father Vilela crossed to the hearth and knelt in the place reserved for guests.

Hiro stood beside his door as Father Mateo joined the senior Jesuit by the fire. Custom did not permit a ronin translator to act as his master's equal.

"Does your congregation keep you busy, Mateo?" Father Vilela asked.

The innocuous question put Hiro on alert. Samurai often opened unpleasant conversations with innocent inquiries.

Father Mateo smiled. "Japan has become my home, and the Japanese people, my people. Attending to their needs is not a burden."

"Indeed." Father Vilela nodded. "Yet I wonder, perhaps, if you have become a bit too attached to these people."

"No more than the Lord whose example I follow," Father Mateo said. "He commanded us to love without reservation."

"And also to respect authority," Father Vilela added.

"Who have I offended this time?" Father Mateo's question shattered the subtle Japanese tone of the conversation.

Though Portuguese by birth, Father Vilela showed a samurai's discomfort at the question. "Mateo . . ."

"You said you had no time for a social visit," Father Mateo said. "With respect, let's drop the charade and get to the point. You come here only when someone complains. I simply wish to know whose dog I kicked."

Hiro appreciated the choice of words. Most of the samurai in Kyoto were sworn retainers of various daimyo, so calling them dogs was not far off the mark.

"As you wish." Father Vilela nodded slowly. "Yesterday afternoon I had a message from the magistrate, Ishimaki. He asked me to inform you that the Kyoto police have sole authority over crimes in the capital. Your investigative assistance is not required and will no longer be tolerated."

"I spoke with the magistrate yesterday, myself," Father Mateo said. "I assured him I would let the matter drop."

"This is not about a single matter." Father Vilela sighed. "Mateo, I care for the Japanese people as much as you do. Had I not, I wouldn't have granted permission for you to establish this ministry and preach God's Word to the common classes. But you have exceeded your mandate. You have no authority to investigate crimes or bring killers to justice. Leave those matters to the authorities."

"The authorities do not care—"

Father Vilela held up a hand for silence. "For three years, I have supported you, defended you when samurai took offense. I allowed you to hire a translator and to finance your work through the efforts of Luis Álvares, in order to give you more freedom than the Church could formally approve."

The senior Jesuit folded his hands and laid them in his lap. "Now, the situation has changed. I do not have the ear, or the friendship, of Shogun Matsunaga. He keeps his distance in ways that make me fear for the Church's future in Japan. We must not anger him, or the magistrate, at this crucial time."

"Are you ordering me to turn a blind eye to injustice?" Father Mateo's voice revealed frustration.

"I am warning you," Father Vilela said, "that I cannot protect you any longer."

"Protect me?" Father Mateo repeated.

"I have reason to believe that Matsunaga Hisahide intends to expel the Jesuits from Kyoto," Father Vilela said, "and that he will do it before the Miyoshi reach the city."

"You know about the Miyoshi army?" Father Mateo asked.

"The samurai speak of little else. Most of my congregants pray for the chance to distinguish themselves in the coming war." Father Vilela smiled sadly. "I tell them, time and again, that those who live by the sword will die by its blade. . . ."

"Yet samurai aspire to such an end," Father Mateo finished.

"Indeed. But that is not my mission here today. You will promise not to involve yourself in any more investigations." Father Vilela looked at Hiro. "Both of you will make this promise."

Hiro raised his chin and didn't answer. He rarely appreciated orders, especially from men without authority to command him.

Father Vilela frowned. "If you refuse to give your word, then I must ask you both to leave Kyoto."

CHAPTER 37

Hiro could hardly believe his luck.

"Leave the city?" Father Mateo protested. "But my work is here."

"Not if Shogun Matsunaga bans our order from Kyoto," Father Vilela said, "and if he does, our lives will be in danger. I am sending the younger acolytes into the countryside to keep them safe. I think it wise for you to leave as well."

"Matsunaga Hisahide cannot ban us from Kyoto," Father Mateo argued. "The emperor granted us permission to live and work in the capital, and he outranks the shogun."

"In name, perhaps, but not in power," Father Vilela said. "My assistant, Izumo, received a warning that Hisahide does not want us in the city. He will not tell me how he knows this, but I trust his sources and his instincts."

Hiro wondered which of the shinobi clans had warned Izumo, and whether the trusted acolyte was also a shinobi in disguise. If so, he must belong to the Koga ryu.

Father Vilela turned to Hiro. "You do not come from Kyoto."

Hiro nodded agreement. "My family lives in Iga."

Relief washed over the senior Jesuit's face. "The shogun does not control that province. Would you take Mateo for a visit to your family home?"

Hiro paused in surprise before answering. "This is a most unusual request."

But a welcome one.

"Pardon me," Father Mateo said, "but I would prefer to remain in Kyoto. I will not abandon my congregation."

Father Vilela turned back to the hearth. "Do not become a fool for the sake of pride."

"This has nothing to do with pride." Father Mateo stood up. "I will not abandon my work because a warlord threatens exile. I will wait until I have no other choice."

"Then wait no longer." Father Vilela rose to his feet, as calm as a pond on a summer evening. "Under the authority vested in me by the Holy Catholic Church, I hereby order you to leave Kyoto no later than sunset tomorrow. You may not return until I rescind this order."

"Tomorrow?" Father Mateo sounded shocked. "Impossible. I need more time—"

"You have until the barricades close tomorrow evening." Father Vilela brushed an invisible speck of dirt from his kimono. "Luis Álvares may remain to watch the house and run his business. If he chooses to leave along with you, the Church will care for the property in your absence. I will also arrange for a Japanese priest to lead your congregation. Prepare a list of your gathering times and Masses. Leave it here for him when you go."

Father Mateo looked horrified, but Hiro felt relieved. He only hoped Luis's replacement didn't reach the city ahead of schedule.

Father Vilela bowed. "I am sorry it came to this. Goodbye, Mateo. *Dominus vobiscum.*"

Father Mateo bowed in return. "And may the Lord be with thy spirit also."

Father Vilela nodded and left the house.

"How can I leave my congregation?" Father Mateo turned to Hiro. "Not to mention abandoning the search for Emi's killer?"

"Can you refuse to obey him?" Hiro asked.

"Not without risking expulsion from the Church," Father Mateo said.

"Then it appears you have no choice." Hiro shrugged. "As for finding the murderer, we have today and tomorrow."

Father Mateo frowned. "Last night you'd given up. What changed?"

"A man who takes advantage of blood deserves to have it spilled," Hiro said.

"Satsu?" Father Mateo asked. "Did you solve the murder in the night?"

"Not exactly, but I strongly suspect there's more to this killing than just a girl who wanted her independence. Also, I don't understand what Satsu hoped to gain from our investigation or what changed to make him call it off last night."

"Perhaps he really is worried about your safety," Father Mateo suggested. "He is your uncle, after all."

Hiro shook his head. "That's not our way. Do you have the coin?"

Father Mateo looked surprised. "You want to return it?"

"I want you to bring it," Hiro said, "but don't admit to having it with you, unless I tell you otherwise."

It took well over an hour for Hiro and Father Mateo to reach Fushimi Inari Shrine, which lay southeast of the city proper and east of the Kamo River.

Hiro approached a bald-headed monk at the enormous torii gate that marked the entrance to the shrine. "Good morning. Can you direct us to the stage where the nō rehearsal is taking place?"

"With respect, you've come too early," the monk replied. "The performance won't take place until tomorrow."

"Forgive me." Hiro bowed. "We did not come to watch the show. The foreign priest is curious. He hoped to see the actors in rehearsal."

"Ah." The monk nodded. "Forgive my error. They finished setting up the stage this morning. The actors should be starting practice now." He turned and gestured to the east. "If you follow the path in that direction, around the base of the mountain, you will find them. Or, if you prefer, I can escort you."

"Thank you," Hiro said, "but we can find the way ourselves."

The monk bowed. "Of course, sir. As you wish."

Hiro and Father Mateo walked along the tree-lined path. The golden beams of the rising sun filtered through the branches as the scents of dust and pine perfumed the air.

Father Mateo looked at the pine trees towering overhead. "What a lovely place."

"Inari is one of the most important kami," Hiro said.

"The god of foxes, unless I'm mistaken," Father Mateo replied.

"As well as rice, and tea, and sake," Hiro added, "and other things."

"I wonder why the Yutoku-za is performing here, instead of in a private home."

"Most likely, the samurai wanted to garner favor with Inari *Ōkami* as well as friends and family," Hiro said. "That, or he lacked the space to host a performance in his home."

A wailing chant echoed through the trees from somewhere up ahead.

"I am a courtier in the service of Emperor Shujaku. You must know that the prime minister's daughter, Princess Aoi, has fallen sick . . ."

Father Mateo stopped walking. "What is that?"

Hiro smiled. "Rehearsal has begun."

They continued along the path until they emerged from the trees and entered a clearing large enough to hold at least a hundred people. On the opposite side of the clearing, a trio of drummers knelt across the back of a large, raised platform, which served as a stage. A line of men in matching blue kimono knelt along the right side of the stage, facing inward toward the platform's center. A masked performer wearing a white outer tunic knelt in front of the group. His face tilted downward, toward a folded gold kimono that lay near the front and center of the stage.

Yuji stood near the back of the stage, wearing a patterned surcoat over white hakama. He held a fan and wore a courtier's tall, cylindrical hat atop his head.

"Stop here," Hiro murmured. "We don't want to interrupt."

CHAPTER 38

Yuji continued his warbling chant as Hiro and Father Mateo watched.

"What play is this?" Father Mateo whispered. "Do you know it?"

Hiro nodded, still watching the stage. "*Aoi no Ue*. It's based on *The Tale of Genji*. Do you know the work?"

Father Mateo shook his head.

Hiro glanced at the priest and whispered, "Yuji is playing the role of the courtier, who narrates this part of the play. The actor in the mask is playing the role of Priestess Teruhi, who has come to exorcise the demon plaguing Lady Aoi."

"Where's Lady Aoi?" Father Mateo whispered back.

Hiro nodded toward the stage. "The *kosode*."

"You mean, the kimono with no one in it?" Father Mateo asked.

Hiro nodded again and whispered, "Yes. It represents Lady Aoi."

"Will Haru play that role in the performance?"

Hiro looked at the priest. "Lady Aoi *is* the kimono."

"Yes—but who wears it?"

Hiro shook his head. "No one. It just lies there."

"How is that Lady Aoi?"

"A painting of a mountain is not a mountain," Hiro said, "and yet you recognize the image as a mountain. In similar fashion, that kimono represents the Lady Aoi."

"So, no one wears it."

"Watch for a moment," Hiro whispered. "You will understand."

Yuji finished his opening speech, and the actor playing the priestess began to chant.

"Pure above; pure below. Pure without; pure within. Pure in eyes, ears, heart, and tongue . . ."

"I don't understand what he's saying," Father Mateo whispered.

Hiro continued watching the stage. "It's a chant of exorcism, calling the demon out of Lady Aoi."

"So it's a *possessed* kimono . . ."

Hiro shot the priest a disapproving look but did not reply.

The drummers beat a measured cadence as another actor stepped up onto a narrow walkway that connected to the left side of the stage. He wore a red kimono and an obi adorned with a scaled pattern, along with a mask that looked like a woman with golden teeth and eyes. He carried a fan and moved with a shuffling walk that barely raised his feet.

As the actor moved along the walkway toward the stage, he chanted, *"In the Three Coaches that travel the Road of Law, I drove out of the Burning House. Is there no way to banish the broken coach that stands at Yugao's door?*

"This world is like the wheels of the little ox-cart; round and round they go, till vengeance comes . . ."

"What's happening?" Father Mateo asked. "I'm lost."

Hiro nodded toward the actor on the walkway. "That is Botan."

"I recognized his voice," the Jesuit said, "but the chant doesn't make any sense."

"It does, if you know the story. He's playing the shite's role—the lead—the angry ghost of Lady Rokujo."

"Let me guess . . . she's the one possessing Lady Aoi."

Hiro nodded.

"Will the words make sense later on?" the Jesuit asked.

Hiro sighed. "You have to know the story and how it's told. Lady Rokujo's vengeful spirit is sad because Genji—her lover—shunned her in favor of his wife, the Lady Aoi. Lady Rokujo's jealousy became an evil spirit that drove out Lady Aoi's soul, resulting in this illness."

"The one the kimono is suffering."

"I don't have to continue," Hiro said.

"I apologize. Please, go on."

"In the second half of the play, the family calls upon a priest, who prays to restore the soul of Lady Aoi," Hiro said. "At that point, Lady Rokujo's jealousy takes on the form of a female ogre—the actor uses a different mask—and the ogre attacks both Lady Aoi and the priest, who then invokes the kami to ward off the ogre. In the end, the priest is victorious, and Lady Rokujo's spirit becomes a Buddha."

Botan had reached the stage. He stood at the back, beside the drummers, as the actor playing the priestess began to chant.

"I see a fine lady I do not know, riding in a broken coach. She clutches the shafts, from which the oxen have been unyoked.

"In the second coach sits a lady who appears to be a new wife. The lady in the broken coach is weeping, weeping. A piteous sight."

"This is the part where they identify the demon as Lady Rokujo," Hiro said.

"What's all the talk of coaches?" Father Mateo asked.

"Lady Rokujo intends to confront Genji at a festival, but her carriage is pushed aside and broken. The wife in the unbroken carriage is Lady Aoi."

"How does the audience know all this?" Father Mateo asked. "It's quite confusing."

Before Hiro could answer, Haru approached. When he reached a respectful distance, he stopped and bowed.

"Good morning," Haru said quietly. "My father told me to watch for you and receive the coin on his behalf. He offers his apologies, but he's busy on the stage."

"Is your father playing the priestess?" Father Mateo asked.

Haru grinned, as if he found the comment funny. "No, sir. Father sings in the chorus."

On the stage, Botan was chanting, *"Long ago I lived in the world. I sat at flower-feasts among the clouds..."*

"Should I give him the coin?" Father Mateo asked in Portuguese.

"No," Hiro said in the Jesuit's language. "Let me handle the conversation. As it happens, I'd hoped to speak with the boy."

He turned to Haru. "Is there a noodle cart in the area?"

Haru's forehead wrinkled. "Father said you were coming to leave a coin."

"But I am hungry." Hiro knew the child could not refuse a samurai's request. It wasn't an original trick, but it was an effective one—and he *was* hungry.

Hiro glanced at Father Mateo. The Jesuit didn't like udon, but Hiro needed an excuse to speak with the child away from the rehearsal.

Haru thought for a moment. "I saw a vendor just outside the shrine."

"Show us," Hiro said, "and I will buy you a bowl as well."

"I've never eaten noodles with a samurai." Haru led them back along the path. "Or a foreigner."

Haru's memory proved correct. The vendor's cart sat just outside the shrine. Hiro ordered three bowls of noodles and watched the vendor ladle dark, rich broth across the piles of steaming udon. After adding a sprinkling of scallions and several slices of fish that bore the lines of a charcoal grill, the vendor handed the bowls to Hiro and the others one by one.

The savory scents of noodles, fish, and salty sauce set Hiro's mouth to watering. He led the others several steps away to eat their meal.

Haru devoured his udon with obvious relish. He finished his bowl and slurped the broth from the bottom in startling time.

For a moment, Hiro felt sorry he couldn't acknowledge they were cousins.

"Thank you for the noodles." Haru bowed. "They're my favorite, and I don't get them often."

"Your father mentioned the troupe had fallen on difficult times of late," Hiro said.

Haru nodded. "Most of the samurai cancelled performances after the shogun died. We hope, when the emperor names a new shogun, the work will come back as well."

"How does your troupe earn money when samurai do not have performances?" Hiro asked.

"I don't know." Haru shrugged. "We were lucky Hosokawa-*sama* hired us for this one."

CHAPTER 39

"The Hosokawa clan arranged this performance?" Hiro asked.

The words had no sooner left his lips when a voice shouted, "You! What are you doing here?"

Yoriki Hosokawa hurried toward them, scowling.

"What if he recognizes the boy?" Father Mateo whispered in Portuguese as the yoriki approached.

"He won't," Hiro replied in kind. "Samurai rarely notice commoners' children, and the boy has not appeared on the stage."

As he finished speaking, he realized that Haru had disappeared.

Hiro turned to Yoriki Hosokawa and raised his empty bowl. "Until a moment ago, we were eating noodles. Now, we are having a conversation—or were, until you interrupted."

The yoriki narrowed his eyes. "You have no reason to be here. I should arrest you!"

"I believe Fushimi Inari lies outside your jurisdiction," Hiro said. "In addition to which, we've committed no crime. I merely brought the priest for a bowl of noodles and a tour of the shrine."

"The shrine is closed to you today," the yoriki growled, "and tomorrow also. My father arranged a private performance here, to honor the shogun."

"A performance?" Hiro asked. "What kind of performance?"

"None of your business," the yoriki snapped, "but important people are coming to see it, and I don't want you anywhere near this shrine, today or tomorrow. Understand?"

"Is this not a public shrine?" Hiro asked.

"Do not provoke me, ronin." Yoriki Hosokawa lowered his voice. "My father has been planning this event for over a month, and I will not allow you and your foreign master to ruin it. If you haven't left this place when I return, in no more than ten minutes, I will arrest you both and throw you in prison. Is that clear?"

Father Mateo bowed. "We apologize for our inconvenient presence."

Yoriki Hosokawa looked surprised. "It seems the foreigner has learned some manners overnight." He raised his chin. "Finish your noodles and be gone."

He turned his back and entered the shrine.

A movement at Hiro's side announced Haru's return.

"Where did you go?" Hiro asked.

Haru nodded in the direction of the shrine. "That's Yoriki Hosokawa. He likes to yell, and he hits people too. Father told me to stay away from him."

"Is he the man who hired your troupe to perform at the shrine tomorrow?" Hiro asked.

Haru shook his head. "No—that was his father, Hosokawa Takeshi. Grandfather introduced me to him when he came to arrange the performance. Later, I overheard Grandfather telling Father that the event was strange because the Hosokawa clan is allied with the Ashikaga. He took the job because we needed the money, but he doesn't understand why the Hosokawa would offer a public show of support for Shogun Matsunaga."

"Indeed, that is most curious," Hiro said. "Almost as strange as your sister, Emi, walking alone by the river at night."

"That wasn't strange. She did it all the time." Haru looked at Hiro. "But it was a secret—I overheard her telling Chou, the day that Chou accused her of stealing Yuji."

"Really?" Hiro asked. "Did they argue often?"

Haru nodded. "That day was the worst. Emi called Chou an idiot. She also called Yuji a no-talent fake and said he'd never be head of the za." Haru's expression turned earnest. "She was right about that. Grandfather already picked his successor. It isn't Yuji—it's me."

"Does Yuji know this?" Hiro asked.

Haru shook his head. "It's still a secret. I heard Grandfather telling Father. They don't want anyone to know until I'm old enough for bigger roles."

"Did Emi know about Botan's decision?" Hiro asked.

"I don't think so," Haru said. "Chou didn't believe her when she said it, either."

"When did this argument happen?"

Haru thought for a moment. "Over and over, all the time. Chou thought Emi liked Yuji, and wanted to steal him for herself. But Emi said she would never get married, especially not to an actor."

The boy seemed pleased to have such a willing audience for his secrets.

"Why didn't Chou believe her?" Hiro asked.

"About a week ago, she said"—Haru bit his lower lip and paused, as if trying to recall the words—"she said that Emi *seduced* him by the river. What does that word mean, anyway? Father said it means talking to someone, but that's not what it sounded like to me."

"Don't question your father." Hiro had no intention of helping with that particular definition.

Haru bowed his head in assent.

The precious minutes had slipped away far faster than Hiro liked. "We should be going, but thank you for showing us the udon."

He took the empty bowl from Haru and Father Mateo's full one, and returned them to the vendor.

Haru followed. "Are you afraid of that yoriki?"

Hiro turned to the boy. "I am not afraid of anyone."

"I didn't think so." Haru grinned. "You're not like the other samurai."

"Are you afraid of the yoriki?" Father Mateo asked.

Haru shook his head. "I'm not afraid of anyone, either." He bowed. "Thank you for buying me noodles."

Hiro nodded. "You may return to your rehearsal."

"Thank you." Haru bowed again and ran away up the path to the shrine.

Hiro smiled. As he hoped, the boy had forgotten the coin completely.

He turned to Father Mateo. "Come on. We haven't got much time."

As they started toward home, the Jesuit said, "I find it a strange coincidence that Emi was murdered just before her family performs for the Hosokawa clan."

"Indeed," Hiro said, "but, like everything else, we do not know if that is coincidental, or something more."

"This case has far too many coincidences. Speaking of which, how did you know to ask Haru about Emi and the river?"

"Satsu told us he was always listening," Hiro said. "Late last night, I realized the child had probably memorized more than plays."

"We should have asked him about the samurai who threatened Botan."

"That happened later at night," Hiro said. "Most likely after the boy was asleep. More importantly, Haru would mention that kind of question. If we'd asked about the extortion, and Haru didn't know it happened, he would ask Satsu about it later on. As it is, if Haru mentions anything, it will be eating noodles with a samurai."

"So the udon was a ruse."

"I always want udon," Hiro said, "but now, I also want to speak with Chou."

CHAPTER 40

The elderly female servant who answered Hiro's knock invited them inside the Yutoku-za. Rhythmic chanting echoed through the house from the rooms beyond. The monks had commenced the mourning rituals for Emi's soul.

"No," Hiro said. "We prefer to speak to her here."

Chou arrived at the door in moments. "Good morning." She bowed. "I apologize, but my father has left for rehearsal."

"We came to speak with you," Hiro said, "about Emi and Yuji."

Chou glanced over her shoulder, stepped outside, and closed the door. "I apologize for not inviting you in, but visitors would interrupt the prayers for my sister's spirit. Would you be willing to talk at Chugenji?"

"I prefer to walk by the river." Hiro turned west, toward Sanjō Bridge.

Chou walked alongside him, face cast down. Every few steps, she glanced at Hiro as if wishing she could ask a question.

After the third such glance, Hiro snapped, "Speak up, if you have something to say."

"I apologize." Chou bowed her head. "I am afraid. Has something happened to Yuji?"

"Lying to a samurai is as foolish as hitching a stallion with rotten rope," Hiro said. "The rope will break, and the horse will turn against you."

He expected Chou to react with confusion. Instead she stopped and bowed.

"I beg you, please don't kill me."

"Give me a single reason why I should not." Hiro laid a hand on his sword.

Chou remained bent forward, face to the ground. "I feared you would blame Yuji for Emi's death, if you knew the truth."

"Because he killed her, and you helped him," Hiro bluffed.

"No"—she fell to her knees in the road—"he did not kill her. I did not help him. I swear this is the truth."

Her reaction seemed honest, but Hiro continued to push. "You have lied to me twice. Now you will tell your story to the magistrate."

"Please . . . no." Chou's voice caught. "He won't believe me."

"I do not believe you either!" Hiro glanced at Father Mateo, but saw no concern on the Jesuit's face. He frowned. Normally, Father Mateo objected to aggressive treatment of a woman.

Father Mateo nodded in Chou's direction as if to say, *"Get on with it."*

"Please . . ." Chou gestured to Father Mateo. "You are a priest. Show mercy."

"Trusting a liar is the same as handing a sword to a child," Father Mateo looked at Hiro. "I believe that is the Japanese proverb."

"Close enough." The priest conflated a pair of sayings, but Hiro found it impressive that the Jesuit remembered them at all.

Chou clasped her hands together. "Please, I beg you, hear my explanation."

Hiro looked at Father Mateo. The Jesuit looked away.

"Not even the foreigner believes your lies," Hiro said. "Continue at your peril."

"Yuji was only one of the men my sister met by the river. I know there were others, but not their names. She wouldn't tell me who they were.

"I didn't tell Father because I didn't want Yuji marrying Emi instead of me. I was afraid that if Father found out he would cancel my betrothal and make Yuji marry Emi. I couldn't risk it. Yuji means everything to me."

"Why would you want to marry a man who dallied with your sister?" Father Mateo asked.

"You are not a woman," Chou said, "so maybe you cannot understand. Yuji is handsome, and he will be famous. Every woman wants him. I am not pretty, or special, but Yuji wanted to marry me, and for that I would overlook his . . . indiscretions. Actors are often unfaithful to their wives. It is their way."

"You would overlook his behavior, but not Emi's," Hiro said.

Chou looked up, forehead wrinkled in confusion. "I am sorry . . . what do you mean?"

"You argued with Emi—repeatedly—about Yuji," Hiro said.

"I told her to leave him alone. This was her fault. She approached him first—Yuji said she seduced him, but only once, and he promised it would never happen again."

"Did Emi agree to leave Yuji alone?" Father Mateo asked.

Chou nodded. "She denied seducing him, even though I know she did. She said she didn't care for Yuji and only met him by the river because he threatened to hurt me if she refused.

"When I told her what Yuji said, her story changed. Then she claimed she seduced him to test his loyalty, to prove he was an unfaithful liar. She said I should thank her for revealing his faults before we married. She called him a no-talent actor who would never lead the Yutoku-za. She said"—Chou's voice caught—"'The crow who mimics the cormorant gets drowned.'"

"What do birds have to do with acting?" Father Mateo asked in Portuguese.

"Please!" Chou's eyes went wide with terror at the sound of the foreign words. "I'm telling the truth. I swear it. May a thousand demons haunt me if I lie!"

She prostrated herself on the ground.

Hiro decided to let her worry and answered the priest in Portuguese. "The expression means that a man who tries to rise beyond his abilities will fail, and also come to no good end."

"Wise words," the Jesuit replied in kind, "and often true."

"Please don't take me to the magistrate," Chou pleaded. "Every word I've said today is true."

"Get up." Hiro gestured. "It strains my neck to watch you on the ground."

Chou complied without a word.

"Can you prove that Yuji did not kill your sister?" Hiro asked. "Lovers' quarrels often end in violence."

"He did not kill her," Chou repeated. "I told him the terrible things Emi said, but he just laughed and called them the empty words of a jealous woman. He said I had nothing at all to fear."

"When did this conversation happen?" Hiro asked.

"At sunset, on the day she died. He came to me, looking for Emi, and I told him what she said because I wanted him to hate her."

"What happened then?" Father Mateo asked.

"He called her a liar and said he wanted nothing to do with her anymore. That's when he said she seduced him, but only once. He promised to find her and tell her it was over between them, once and for all."

"And your sister was murdered that very night," Hiro added.

"That is why I lied to you," Chou said. "I knew I shouldn't, but I was afraid. Yuji swore that he didn't kill her. He said he went to the river, but only to tell her it was over. He promised that when he left, she was alive—and I believe him."

"I do not care what you believe," Hiro growled.

A breeze spiraled a handful of fallen leaves across the road. One of them caught on the hem of Chou's kimono. She looked down. "Yuji made a mistake, but he would not—did not—kill my sister."

Chou raised her face as if remembering something. "I *can* prove it. The killer gave Emi a golden coin, but Yuji has no gold. He spends his money as soon as he earns it. He never has more than coppers in his pocket."

"Perhaps he found another source of coins," Hiro said.

Father Mateo nodded. "Such as stealing a mask from the Yutoku-za."

CHAPTER 41

Hiro inwardly cringed that Father Mateo had revealed the missing mask.

"Yuji would never steal from us." A flush of anger colored Chou's cheeks, though she struggled to keep her tone respectful. "All of the masks will belong to him when he becomes the leader. Only a fool would steal what he already owns—or will inherit. Besides, the masks are sacred. Yuji would never diminish the guild by taking them away."

The reaction suggested Chou was unaware of the missing mask. Had she known, she would have accused someone else, or at least acknowledged its disappearance.

Hiro had no intention of allowing the priest to reveal any more. "Tell us what you know about the other men your sister met by the river."

"I promise I know nothing more." Chou clasped her hands together. "Emi said that one of the men was going to get her a place in a teahouse. Maybe that man gave her the coin."

"He said he would get her a place . . . or buy her one?" Hiro asked.

"Is there a difference?" Chou replied. "It seems the same to me."

"Not necessarily. Which word did your sister use?"

Chou shook her head. "She might have used them both—or something else. I don't remember."

"You remember nothing more?" Hiro asked.

"Nothing," Chou repeated. "I have told the entire truth."

"Make sure you have," Hiro threatened. "Next time, you will not escape the magistrate."

"I understand—and thank you." Chou bowed deeply.

Hiro continued toward the river. After a moment's hesitation,

Father Mateo followed. When he drew alongside Hiro, the Jesuit said, "I suppose we need to talk with Yuji."

"I doubt it will help. He won't admit to anything, and we should not approach the actors again if we can avoid it. Yoriki Hosokawa will be watching."

At the bridge, they started north along the river road.

"Why do you suddenly care what the yoriki thinks?" Father Mateo asked.

"The magistrate spoke to Father Vilela," Hiro said. "In Japan, the message that sends is very clear. I cannot protect you if you are in prison. Especially if I am imprisoned also."

A voice behind them shouted, "Halt!"

Hiro knew the voice before he turned. "Good morning again, Yoriki Hosokawa."

The yoriki stood directly behind them, flanked by a single, scruffy dōshin. He didn't return the greeting.

"What were you doing in the theater ward?" he demanded. "Don't deny it. We saw you make the turn from Shijō Road."

Hiro heard footsteps approaching from behind. A thin young man stepped off the path and hurried around them, keeping well away from the confrontation. He gave the yoriki a nervous glance as he scurried past.

The young man's face seemed vaguely familiar, but Hiro didn't have time to search his memory. The youth had already disappeared behind the Shijō Bridge.

Hiro wished that he and Father Mateo could do the same.

"My business takes me to every ward in Kyoto," Father Mateo said. "Just now, I spoke with a girl who needs my help."

The yoriki narrowed his eyes at the priest. "You'd better be referring to your religion, not investigating crimes."

"Do not worry," Father Mateo said. "If I was any less involved in solving crimes, I would qualify to join the Kyoto police."

Hiro stared at Father Mateo, unable to believe the priest had just insulted the yoriki again.

"How dare you!" The yoriki's cheeks flushed red. He reached for his sword.

Hiro stepped forward and laid a hand on the hilt of his own katana. "Think before you draw that blade. The emperor considers the foreign priests his personal guests. This one has committed no crime. He is unarmed, and he is my employer. If you draw that sword, you fight with me."

Yoriki Hosokawa gave Father Mateo a calculating look. "What is it worth to you to stay out of trouble?"

"Pardon me?" Father Mateo asked.

Hiro could hardly believe what he was hearing.

"Give me the coin you received from the dead girl's family," the yoriki said, "and perhaps I will forget I saw you here."

"What are you talking about? What coin?" Hiro spoke quickly to keep the priest from answering.

"The one you showed to the magistrate yesterday. I want it now."

"I don't know what you're talking about," Hiro said.

"Liar. I heard you showing a coin to the magistrate." Yoriki Hosokawa's hand tightened on the hilt of his sword.

"Then you also know he told us to return it." Hiro remembered the rustling noise outside the magistrate's office as they left.

Yoriki Hosokawa nodded at Father Mateo. "For his sake, I hope you didn't."

"We have not returned the coin," the priest confirmed.

"But we don't have it," Hiro added quickly.

Yoriki Hosokawa turned on Hiro. "Where is the coin?"

"I dropped it in the river." Hiro gestured toward the bridge. "A most regrettable accident."

"Then give me something else," the yoriki said, "or I will arrest the priest."

"You have no grounds to arrest me," Father Mateo protested.

"I saw you investigating a crime, against the magistrate's orders." Yoriki Hosokawa turned to the dōshin. "You saw him, didn't you?"

The dōshin nodded.

Father Mateo opened his mouth to object—as an explosion rocked the bridge at Shijō Road.

CHAPTER 42

The explosion sent a plume of thick, dark smoke into the air. It seemed to originate under the pilings close to the eastern bank. Fortunately, the bridge did not collapse.

The samurai guarding the structure ran away up the opposite bank with a cry of terror.

Yoriki Hosokawa turned to the dōshin. "Go investigate!"

As the underling ran for the bridge, the yoriki glared at Hiro. "I expect a payment, if you want your foreign friend to avoid arrest."

He hurried after the dōshin without awaiting a response.

Hiro started up the path toward home. "Let's go—and hurry."

"Shouldn't we get to shelter?" Father Mateo looked back at the bridge. "The city is under attack."

"Home is safer than sheltering here," Hiro said. "That explosion was a distraction. Whatever it's trying to cover may not be over."

"How do you know?" Father Mateo matched Hiro's rapid pace.

"Do you see any enemy soldiers?" Hiro gestured along the river. "Any fighting? Any other sign of an attack?"

Father Mateo looked around. "Now that you mention it, no."

"A thin young man walked past us while we talked with Yoriki Hosokawa. He seemed familiar, though I couldn't place him."

"I remember," Father Mateo said. "The yoriki's presence seemed to make him nervous."

"As it would, if he was planning an explosion. The bridge didn't burn, or collapse, which indicates a shinobi charge designed to create a distraction."

"You think that young man set the charge?"

"He disappeared under the bridge a couple of minutes before the explosion," Hiro said. "He set the charge. The question is why. He's also too young to be working alone, which means there's another shinobi in the area—possibly more than one."

"Is that why we're leaving in such a hurry?" Father Mateo asked.

Hiro nodded. "I have no intention of getting us involved in whatever they're planning. Also, when the enemy gets distracted at an opportune moment, wise men do not wait to leave the scene."

Hiro didn't slow his pace until they turned onto Marutamachi Road.

"We're going home?" Father Mateo sounded disappointed.

"I told you home was the safest place, at least until we know for sure the explosion wasn't the start of a larger attack."

"You said it was just a distraction," the priest objected.

"I didn't want you panicking and running into danger," Hiro said.

"I wouldn't have panicked." Father Mateo turned petulant. "I don't want to go home. We only have one more day to find the killer."

At least he seemed to have accepted the need to leave the city.

"We've made good progress," Hiro said. "We identified the samurai who bribed the Yutoku-za."

"The one who demanded money from Botan?" The Jesuit seemed confused, but then a realization lit his features. "Yoriki Hosokawa! But wouldn't Botan have recognized his voice?"

"He could have disguised it," Hiro said. "Before, that seemed unlikely, but now that we know his family hired the troupe to perform in Hisahide's honor ... space at Fushimi Inari does not come cheap. The yoriki would know how much his father paid Botan, though he could not have known the guild had debts."

"So he assumed they would have the money to pay him, because of the gold they received from his father," the Jesuit said.

"We still need evidence to prove it, but yes, the pieces fell into place when he threatened us a few minutes ago."

Father Mateo stopped walking. "Something else—Emi would have left Jiro to follow a yoriki. She had no legal right to refuse his order."

Hiro nodded. "Keep moving. We need to get inside."

Father Mateo shook his head. "And here I'd been thinking Yuji did it."

"He easily could have," Hiro said. "We cannot rule him out without more evidence. Satsu remains a suspect also. Walk."

Father Mateo raised a placating hand and continued walking. "What about Botan? He seems less likely than the others, given the evidence."

"True." Hiro nodded agreement and glanced over his shoulder. The road was empty.

Father Mateo sighed with exasperation. "We're out of time. We need more evidence, and quickly."

Hiro shared the priest's frustration. He hated the thought of the killer getting away. "We'll have to risk a talk with Botan. If he identifies Yoriki Hosokawa as the samurai, at least we can tell the magistrate that truth before we go."

"We should report Hosokawa-*san* anyway," Father Mateo said. "He tried to steal from us just now."

Hiro shook his head. "Without a neutral witness, or real proof, he'll claim we only accused him to avoid arrest or that we offered him a bribe. We would end up in prison, or worse, and he would suffer no consequence."

"I wish we knew what happened to that mask. If we could prove that Botan gave it to the yoriki, or sold it to pay him, we would have the proof we needed."

"That only solves the extortion, not the murder," Hiro said. "Unless we can find a critical clue, we may fail to find the real killer."

When they reached the Jesuit's yard, Hiro paused. "We're going in through the garden gate, and I want you to wait outside while I check the house."

They entered the yard and closed the gate behind them.

Hiro lowered his voice. "Wait here. If you hear me yell, walk straight to the city gates and do not stop for anyone. Proceed to the inn at Ōtsu and wait for me there."

"I will not run away." Father Mateo frowned. "I do not fear death, if I die in the service of God."

"If foolish bravery serves your god, then he is no different from Japanese kami, who care nothing for the lives of men."

"That is not true," the Jesuit said.

"No?" Hiro asked. "Because you sound exactly like a Buddhist samurai."

"Fine, I will go," Father Mateo said, "but only if you promise to save Ana and Luis as well."

Hiro nodded. "If I can." He started toward the house.

CHAPTER 43

To Hiro's relief, the house was empty except for Ana and Gato, and the housekeeper reported no visitors since Father Vilela left. Hiro retrieved the priest from the yard, and they entered the house together.

"Why make me wait outside?" the Jesuit asked.

"Shinobi don't blow up bridges without a reason," Hiro said. "I had to make sure whatever they're doing didn't include an attack on the foreign priests."

Father Mateo nodded. "That makes sense. Do you think it's safe to visit Botan this evening?"

"No," Hiro said, "but we have to risk it if we want to solve the crime. Between now and then, I suggest you start packing for tomorrow's trip."

Father Mateo sighed. "I suppose I should, though I won't take much. I don't intend to stay away for long. Which raises another question—where will we go?"

"Father Vilela suggested Iga." Hiro smiled. "Home is pleasant in the autumn, if a little cold."

Someone pounded on the priest's front door.

The pounding continued as Father Mateo hurried through the common room, into the entry. Hiro followed.

Ana's footsteps entered the common room behind them, but stopped as the housekeeper realized Father Mateo had reached the door. She often reminded the priest that men of rank did not open the door themselves, but also wouldn't embarrass him in front of a guest by following him to the entry.

Father Mateo opened the door. "May I help . . ."

He trailed off at the sight of Yoriki Hosokawa.

Hiro glanced up the street but saw no sign of the scruffy dōshin. The yoriki must have ordered him to continue investigating near the bridge, or created another excuse to leave him behind. Either way, it did not bode well that Yoriki Hosokawa came alone.

"I want my money," the yoriki said.

"I'm sorry?" Father Mateo looked confused. "I do not understand."

The yoriki looked at Hiro. "Translate. Either the foreigner gives me gold or I will tell the magistrate that he—and you—are the ones who killed the girl by the river. I'll claim that you faked the investigation in order to blame the crime on someone else."

Hiro translated the threat into Portuguese to stall for time. At the end he added, "Pretend you're angry, so we can discuss this further without him understanding what we say."

"I don't have to pretend," Father Mateo replied in Portuguese. "Why didn't he do this when we investigated the brewery murder?"

"What's the problem?" the yoriki snapped.

Hiro bowed. "I apologize. The foreigner does not understand. In his country, the police are honest men."

"You lie." Yoriki Hosokawa looked at Father Mateo and shifted to simple Japanese. "You give me money or I hurt you badly."

Father Mateo feigned surprise. "Why would you hurt me? What have I done?"

"You see?" Hiro said. "He doesn't understand."

"He understands, and your lies will get you nowhere," the yoriki growled. "I need gold, for armor and weapons, to enlist in the shogun's army, and this foreigner is going to make that happen."

"I will try to explain." Hiro shifted to Portuguese. "Now I know why he didn't try this during the other investigation. The shogun recently offered honor and status to any man who volunteers for the army before the war begins."

"But he already has a government position," Father Mateo replied.

"A dead-end post in a low-ranking part of the government," Hiro said. "This is his chance to elevate his status."

"If he took money from the actors—and, presumably, from others too—why doesn't he have the gold he needs already?" Father Mateo asked.

"Armor and weapons are expensive," Hiro said. "With the shogun raising taxes, people haven't much gold to give. He probably believes you're wealthy."

"He's got a rude surprise in store." Father Mateo switched to Japanese. "I have no gold. In my religion, priests must live in poverty. We take a vow."

"Again, you lie." The yoriki glanced at the roof above the veranda. "You own a house, and there's a stable around the back."

Father Mateo made an expansive gesture. "These things belong to the church and to the merchant who shares this house, not me."

"It would be most unfortunate if this lovely dwelling burned to the ground while you were in prison awaiting execution," the yoriki said.

Hiro had an idea. "We'll get the gold, but we need time—a couple of days, at least."

"You have until tomorrow at sunset, not a minute longer." The yoriki paused. "And in return for my generosity, I want twenty golden coins. If you do not pay, I'll arrest you both for killing the girl. If you run, I will hunt you down and kill you."

Father Mateo drew a breath, but the yoriki barked, "No argument! I have spoken. And I warn you, my dōshin will swear they saw the priest attack the girl."

"Both of them?" Father Mateo asked.

"Both of them," Yoriki Hosokawa affirmed. A moment later he narrowed his eyes. "Why do you ask that question?"

"I merely wondered if all policemen were as corrupt as you," the Jesuit said.

"I could kill you right now!" the yoriki yelled. "Do not disrespect me again!"

"If you kill me, you will get nothing," the priest said calmly. "And calling you corrupt is a statement of fact, not disrespect. A man who steals from the poor does not deserve to be called a samurai."

"You know nothing of samurai," Yoriki Hosokawa hissed. "Get the gold, or your life is forfeit—and I will take pleasure in killing you." He turned and walked away.

Father Mateo stood in the doorway and watched the yoriki stride away up the street. "Did he really just extort us—and threaten to kill me?"

"Desperate men resort to desperate measures," Hiro said as they went inside. "It was foolish of you to mention the missing dōshin."

"I was trying to find out if they had found him."

"By asking a question that suggests he's missing?" Hiro asked. "He could have killed you—would have killed you—if the body had been found."

"But he didn't," Father Mateo said, "so now we know they haven't found the body."

"What body?" Ana emerged from the kitchen. "Are you investigating another murder?"

"No," the two men said together.

"Hm." Ana turned and went back into the kitchen.

Father Mateo drew the golden coin from his purse and examined it. "Why would he ask for gold? Most people in Kyoto trade in silver."

"Gold has higher value," Hiro said. "It's easier to carry and conceal."

Father Mateo returned the coin to his purse. "I hope Luis has the coins we need, or sufficient silver to trade for them."

"Don't worry about the gold," Hiro said. "By the time the yoriki comes for it, we'll be out of Kyoto and far beyond his reach."

"What about Ana and Luis?" Father Mateo frowned. "He threatened to burn the house—"

"He will not bother Ana. She has no gold. The part about the house was an empty threat."

At least, he hoped so.

"Maybe," Father Mateo said, "but we need to be certain. Later tonight, we're going to see Botan. And now we don't need to worry about the yoriki. He won't arrest us before he gets his money."

"Not unless he connects us with the missing dōshin."

"Even then, he won't arrest us," Father Mateo said. "He'll kill us."

"Yes, but, as you already noted, not until he gets his gold."

CHAPTER 44

After leaving Father Mateo to sort through his few belongings, Hiro went to the Jesuit's garden and meditated. The yoriki's threats had left him unsettled and angry. Worse, Hiro detested failure, and leaving the mystery unresolved felt like letting Emi's killer win.

He pushed his frustrations away and closed his eyes. His breathing stilled, and his heartbeat slowed. He listened to the breeze in the branches, the water in Father Mateo's pond, and the myriad other sounds that floated through the Jesuit's garden.

Something rustled the trees by the garden wall.

Hiro opened his eyes as a large black crow peered down from its perch in a cherry tree. The glossy corvid cocked its head and looked at Hiro without a trace of fear.

"If you've come from the kami," Hiro said, "go back and tell them I didn't need an omen."

The crow tipped its head in the other direction, as if listening to the words.

"Go on." Hiro waved his hand. "I'm not superstitious."

The bird just stared.

A black-and-orange shadow wiggled through the grass at the base of the tree. Gato's tail flicked with anticipation as she stalked the crow. She made a chittering noise, and the bird looked down.

Gato leaped for the trunk and climbed the tree in a series of scrabbling jumps. Before she reached the lowest branch, the crow extended its wings and flew away. Gato looked at Hiro and mewed.

"You couldn't have fought him anyway," Hiro said.

Gato leaped to the ground and walked away, tail lashing in frustration.

Hiro looked at the leaves on the tree the cat and crow had vacated. Some were green, but many had taken on the gold-and-orange hues of autumn.

Summer had passed, and the weather was turning.

Time to leave Kyoto.

Hiro had known this day would come from the night Hisahide claimed control of Kyoto. A hundred years of Ashikaga rule had come to an end, and the Japanese soil would drink of samurai blood before the land saw peace again.

They needed to find a way to leave the city without attracting attention. Since Father Mateo shared a travel pass with Luis Álvares, they had to leave together or one's departure would trap the other within the capital. Hiro didn't like Luis, but he had no intention of leaving the Portuguese merchant at Hisahide's mercy.

The door to the Jesuit's room rattled open. Father Mateo stepped outside and knelt beside Hiro on the porch. He smiled, but his eyes held only sorrow.

"I will miss this house," the Jesuit said, "especially the koi. I still wish we could find some way to stay."

"Only a fool attempts to fight a battle he cannot win."

"Only a coward flees from those who need him," the Jesuit countered.

Hiro watched as another breeze fluttered the trees by the garden wall. "A man cannot help anyone from a grave."

"We have to take Ana with us. And Luis." The Jesuit spoke with quiet determination.

"A group attracts more attention than a pair of pilgrims on the road."

"I will not leave without them," Father Mateo said.

Hiro nodded. "Then we will find a way."

"And I want to solve Emi's murder before we go," the Jesuit added.

Knocking echoed through the house.

Father Mateo looked over his shoulder. "Again? Could Yoriki Hosokawa have returned?"

Hiro was already on his feet. "Stay here," he said, though he knew the Jesuit wouldn't.

The two men entered the house as Ana's voice carried through from the entry.

"May I help you?" she asked.

"I have come to see the foreign priest."

To Hiro's surprise, the voice belonged to Yuji.

Father Mateo gave Hiro a look of surprise. They entered the common room together, as Ana showed the actor through from the entry.

"Good afternoon," the Jesuit said to Yuji. "Ana, brew some tea."

The housekeeper bowed and left for the kitchen.

Father Mateo knelt by the hearth and motioned for Yuji to join him there.

Hiro crossed to the hearth and knelt, reinforcing the visitor's lack of status.

Yuji didn't seem to notice. He did appear to have trouble settling and fidgeted nervously with his robe.

"Welcome to my home." Father Mateo opened with the pleasantries he offered every guest.

Yuji took a shallow breath, as if trying to force himself to respond in kind. At last he blurted, "I came to confess. The coin is mine—but I did not kill Emi."

"Pardon me?" Father Mateo asked.

"The golden coin," the actor repeated. "The one you found on Emi's body. It belongs to me. I'd like it back."

Father Mateo reached for his purse, but returned his hand to his lap at a glance from Hiro.

"Why would you give a golden coin to the sister of a girl you planned to marry?" Hiro asked.

"Would you admit to having an affair with your future sister-in-law?"

"I would not have an affair with her in the first place," Hiro answered.

"You see?" Yuji said. "I didn't think you would understand. I knew, if I told you the truth, you'd think I killed her."

"Indeed." Hiro paused. "A lie works so much better to prove your innocence."

"What made you decide to confess this now?" Father Mateo asked.

"Chou came to the rehearsal. She told me she revealed the affair to you." Yuji hung his head in shame. "Since you already know the truth, I saw no harm in claiming my golden coin."

"When did you give the coin to Emi?" Hiro asked.

Yuji raised his head. "The coin is mine, and Emi is dead. With respect, sir, the details no longer matter."

"If you want the gold, you will answer my questions," Hiro said. "Otherwise, you are free to leave. I will not entertain a commoner's arrogance."

CHAPTER 45

Yuji raised his hands, as if in surrender. "I simply wondered why it mattered. Sir, I meant no disrespect."

"Adding 'sir' does not transform your rudeness into proper speech." Hiro glared at Yuji. "Answer my questions or leave, but show respect."

Ana returned with a teapot and three cups on a tray. She set them in front of Father Mateo, bowed, and left the room.

Hiro noted the lack of snacks, a clear sign of Ana's disapproval. The housekeeper had no issue serving treats to the prostitutes in Father Mateo's congregation. She didn't mind when the priest invited beggars to the house for tea. But somehow, in the space between the entry and the common room, Ana had judged the actor—and found him wanting.

Father Mateo prepared the tea, pouring water into the pot from the steaming kettle above the hearth. He poured the fragrant liquid into cups and passed the first one to the guest.

Yuji accepted the teacup and inhaled the steam with a slightly curled lip, as if anticipating a foul odor. His lips turned up in surprise, and he inhaled again, more deeply. He gazed at Father Mateo approvingly and sipped the tea.

Hiro wondered what made Yuji decide to claim the coin. Greed was an obvious motive, yet avarice seemed insufficient to justify the risk.

The three men sipped their tea in silence.

Yuji drained his cup and set it gently on the tray.

Father Mateo refilled the actor's tea.

"Help me understand your world." The Jesuit set the teapot down. "In Portugal, a man would never have an affair with his sister-in-law."

Hiro stifled a smile. Father Mateo had grown adept at using his foreign status as a shield for topics Japanese people could never broach directly.

"In most of Japan, an affair like this is also inappropriate," Yuji said, "but actors live by different rules. We must. Otherwise, we could not gain the following, and patronage, required to earn a living."

"Required . . . for those whose talent does not suffice," Hiro added.

Yuji narrowed his eyes a fraction. "Talent alone is never sufficient, even though it should be. Women see an attractive man on the stage and want to know him better. Actors gain no favor by ignoring such desires. Refuse these patrons, and they turn their interest to another.

"An actor, without an audience, is nothing. His flower fades like a blossom that blooms and dies in a single night. Actors' wives must understand. They cannot expect the kind of husband a farmer or a peasant might receive."

"And Chou understands this?" Father Mateo asked.

Yuji sighed. "She is young. But she will learn, in time."

"None of this explains how you gave the golden coin to Emi," Hiro said. "Or why."

"I thought the gold would buy her silence. Our affair lasted only a single night—an indiscretion I regretted as soon as the moment passed."

"At last you admit it openly," Hiro said. "When did you give her the coin?"

"The morning after . . ." Yuji paused. "Two days before she died."

"Two days?" Hiro asked. "We were led to believe your relationship lasted longer."

"She tried to seduce me for weeks, but I refused until I learned she made herself available to men by the river. After that, I saw no reason to deny my own desire. But then, when it was over . . ."

"You desired her no longer," Father Mateo said bitterly. "You despised her. So you gave her a golden coin and sent her away like a common prostitute."

Yuji took another sip of tea. Hiro suspected the actor needed time to construct a plausible lie.

"Excuse me." Father Mateo stood up and left the room through the kitchen door. It seemed an odd moment to use the latrine, but a person couldn't always control that timing.

After the door slid shut behind Father Mateo, Yuji bowed his head. "I apologize for disturbing your afternoon."

Hiro stared at the actor and said nothing.

Yuji fumbled his teacup but recovered it without spilling. He set the cup down carefully before him. "I only came to request the coin. Once I have it, I will leave and bother you no longer."

Hiro did not believe the actor's story about the coin. A man did not reclaim a gift he gave to hide his indiscretions.

"You waste your time and ours," Hiro said. "We do not have the coin."

Yuji hid his dismay behind a smile. "You had it yesterday."

"Satsu wanted it. I believe he planned to throw it in the river."

Yuji's eyes widened in horror. "Throw it in the river? Why?"

"As an offering, to prevent Emi's ghost from wandering on the bank forever."

"Has he done it already?" Yuji asked.

"Does it matter?" Hiro shrugged. "I do not care."

Yuji bowed from a seated position. "I apologize for taking so much of your time. If you will excuse me, I should go."

"I think you should stay. I want to know what you said to Emi on the riverbank the night she died."

Yuji looked nervous.

"Tell me, or tell the magistrate," Hiro said.

"Th-the magistrate doesn't care." Yuji stammered over the words. "He forbade an investigation."

"Would you care to test his interest?" Hiro shifted his balance as if to rise.

"No—all right, I saw her," Yuji said. "I went to the river because I wanted Emi to return the coin. I worried that Chou would see it and misunderstand and get upset.

"I couldn't risk the conversation at home, so I went to the river. Emi was there, talking with a merchant. He was drunk. I stayed near the bridge and waited for him to leave, but he wouldn't go. He lay down on the bank, and Emi sat beside him. A few minutes later, he fell asleep." Yuji smiled. "What sake adds to the will, it removes from the skill."

"Spare me your feeble attempts at humor," Hiro said.

"After the merchant fell asleep, Emi walked down to look at the water. I approached her and asked for the coin, but she refused to give it back." Yuji's eyes filled with tears. "She said she wanted to keep it as a token of our secret love."

Hiro decided that Haru was right about Yuji's acting skills—or lack thereof.

"She said, if I tried to take it, she would scream," the actor continued. "There was a yoriki nearby. I couldn't risk it."

"A yoriki?" Hiro asked. "Not a dōshin?"

"Everyone in the theater district recognizes Yoriki Hosokawa," Yuji said. "I assure you, Emi was alive when I left her. I have no reason to lie to you. I came here only to retrieve my coin."

"For that, you must speak to Satsu."

"You know as well as I that I will never mention it to Satsu." Yuji bowed from the waist. "Please, may I have permission to leave, without you involving the magistrate?"

Hiro stood up. "You may leave. I will show you out."

CHAPTER 46

When Hiro returned to the common room, Father Mateo was kneeling by the hearth with the coin in his hand. He gestured for Hiro to join him.

"Why do you think he wants this coin so badly?" the Jesuit asked. "And do you think the yoriki was really by the river when Emi died?"

"You were listening behind the door?" Hiro glanced toward the kitchen.

Father Mateo nodded. "He wouldn't answer my questions. I thought the conversation might go better if I left."

Hiro stared at the priest, impressed with his cunning.

"You don't have to look so surprised." Father Mateo poured himself another cup of tea. "Yoriki Hosokawa didn't mention seeing Emi by the river the night she died."

Hiro knew what the priest was thinking. "He wouldn't mention it, if he killed her. Unfortunately, that omission does not prove his guilt. He may not have noticed the girl at all. Samurai overlook commoners all the time."

Father Mateo sighed. "Everyone saw everyone else by the riverbank that evening, and everyone has a valid excuse for being there." He laid the coin on the tray beside the teapot. "I do not want to leave Kyoto with Emi's murder unresolved."

"So you have mentioned. More than once." Hiro noted the priest's unusual sorrow. "This killing bothers you more than others. Why?"

"The girl is your cousin," Father Mateo said.

"Which explains why her death should bother me, not why it impacts you so deeply."

193

Father Mateo stared at Hiro for several seconds. "When I saw her body, it reminded me of another—whose death I caused."

"*You?* You killed a girl?"

"I did not kill her," Father Mateo said, "and yet, I am responsible for her death."

In the silence that followed, Hiro longed to ask what happened, but friendship and etiquette barred the question. He realized, yet again, how little he knew about the priest. It struck him as odd that he felt so close to a person whose past he knew essentially nothing about.

"Her name was Isabel," Father Mateo said. "She was my sister."

"You had a sister?" Questions swirled in Hiro's mind like leaves in a whirlpool, though he would never ask them. Friends did not summon the ghosts of the dead for the sake of curiosity.

Father Mateo nodded. "I have not spoken her name aloud in years, though I think of her, and pray for her, every day."

"You need not speak of this," Hiro said. "I apologize for intruding on your privacy."

"No, I want to tell you. Perhaps, then, you will understand why Emi's death impacted me so deeply. That is, unless you would rather I did not speak."

Hiro nodded, knowing Father Mateo would take the gesture as consent.

"In my country, most couples have many children," Father Mateo said, "but God allowed my parents only two. They had given up hope of having any children at all. But then, God answered their prayers—first with me, and, six years later, with Isabel.

"I adored my sister from the moment she was born. When she grew old enough, we played together constantly. She loved to run and explore, like a boy, and though my parents scolded me, I encouraged her wild ways. I protected her. I never believed that she would come to harm. . . ."

Father Mateo clenched his jaw. His hand crept up to the scar on his neck, and he rubbed it absently, lost in memory.

Hiro waited as the silence stretched between them.

Father Mateo's eyes refocused. "On the day I turned fourteen, my father gave me a horse of my own—a fine gray stallion—and told me he had apprenticed me to an acting troupe. All of my childhood dreams were coming true.

"I couldn't wait to ride my horse. I didn't even bother with a saddle. Isabel wanted to ride behind me, but Mother said no, and Isabel cried so hard it broke my heart. Then Father said that she could ride, provided she held onto me tightly and that I held the horse to a walk."

"Your father allowed a woman to ride a horse?" Hiro asked. Father Mateo's reactions to Japanese women had made Hiro think that women in Portugal couldn't do much at all.

"No one could ever say no to Isabel. She had ridden before, on Father's mares, and I was a good enough horseman that my father trusted me to keep her . . . safe." Father Mateo cleared his throat. "As soon as we left the stable, Isabel wanted the horse to go faster. I refused. I didn't know the stallion yet, and Father said to keep him at a walk. Isabel called me a frightened mouse and dared me to make the stallion run. When I refused a second time, she kicked the horse in the ribs as hard as she could."

Father Mateo's eyes grew red. "The stallion bucked. He ran. I couldn't hold him. Isabel fell off. . . ."

Hiro's chest grew tight. To his surprise, his own eyes threatened tears. He regretted forcing Father Mateo to relive such vibrant pain.

The priest continued, "I jumped from the horse and ran to her, but she had broken her neck in the fall. I had no time to go for help. She died there, in my arms." He looked at Hiro in despair. "It was my fault."

"It was not your fault. Her death was an accident."

Father Mateo shook his head. "I should have refused to let her ride."

"Your father gave permission."

Father Mateo looked into the fire. "That does not expunge my guilt."

Hiro sat completely still. No words would ease the pain his friend was feeling. Silent support was the only comfort Hiro had to offer.

Eventually, Father Mateo spoke. "The day she died, and for many days thereafter, I prayed that God would kill me too. Guilt overwhelmed me. I could not bear my father's sadness or my mother's grief. I never joined the theater troupe. I could not summon the strength to hide my sorrow, let alone pretend at joy. I found some small relief at Mass. When I bowed my head to pray I pretended Isabel was there beside me."

"Is that why you became a priest?"

Father Mateo smiled. "A few months after Isabel died, I dreamed I was in church, and when I raised my head she *was* beside me. She took my hand and said, 'Do not worry about me anymore. God wants you to care for others, for the ones who are left behind.'

"I awoke with tears running down my face and the first real peace I had felt since my sister died. God allowed her to speak to me—he called to me through her."

"It was only a dream," Hiro said. "Your god was not in it."

"But he was. He spoke through Isabel. That night I offered him my life, and now I live to serve the ones he loves."

Hiro was not convinced that Father Mateo's god had spoken, but respected his friend enough to keep that opinion to himself.

"You don't believe me." Father Mateo smiled.

"I believe that it happened the way you described it, which makes it true in the only way that matters."

Father Mateo stood up. "If you will excuse me, I am late for afternoon prayer." At the door to his room, he turned back. "Thank you."

"For what?" Hiro asked.

"For being the kind of person I could trust with Isabel's memory. In twenty years, there has not been another."

CHAPTER 47

Hiro picked up the golden coin, which the priest had left behind at the hearth. The leather dangled off his palm. He wished the coin could tell him its secrets, and not only the ones relating to Emi's death. The gold had passed through many hands before arriving in Japan and many more before it ended up on a dead girl's neck.

The coin did not belong to Yuji. Hiro felt certain of that, at least. Actors of his status would not normally get a salary. The spending money they possessed came solely from their patrons' gifts. A man like Yuji wouldn't waste his precious coins on a girl, and if he had, he would not risk his future to recover such a damning token.

Yuji wanted the gold itself.

But why?

Hiro slipped the coin into his sleeve and rose from the hearth. The golden puzzle would have to wait. For now, he had more important problems—specifically, how to smuggle Father Mateo, Ana, and Luis out of Kyoto.

Ana, at least, presented no issue. Commoners needed a travel pass, but guards at the barricades often made exceptions for elderly, cranky women visiting sick relatives in the country.

The Jesuit and Luis would not be so lucky.

Footsteps thumped in the entry, and Luis Álvares stormed into the common room. He looked around and shouted, "Mateo!"

Father Mateo's door slid open. "Has something happened?"

"A message from Ōtsu." Luis raised his hand, revealing a crumpled parchment. "Simão Duarte will reach Kyoto tomorrow afternoon."

Momentary weakness flooded into Hiro's knees. At least the new merchant had not arrived already.

"He wants me to meet him at the gates an hour before sunset and accompany his wagons to my warehouse." Luis waved the message like a miniature flag. "Of all the inconsiderate . . ."

"Out of the question," Hiro said. "You will not meet him."

"Of course not," Luis snapped. "Simão can't order me around like a servant."

"That isn't the issue," Hiro replied. "We will have left the city before he arrives."

Luis turned to Father Mateo. "Is he still on about that shogunate nonsense?" He shook the letter. "Simão explained it all in his message. The shogun needs a second merchant because he needs more weapons to prepare for the coming war. He doesn't understand that a single merchant can handle everything. It's simply a misunderstanding. One which will cost me dearly, but—"

"More dearly than you can imagine," Hiro said.

"Father Vilela has ordered us to leave Kyoto immediately." Father Mateo approached the hearth. "The Church has decided the city isn't safe. We have to go tomorrow, and I want you to close your warehouse and come with us."

"Has everyone taken leave of his senses but me?" Luis turned his face to the kitchen and yelled, "*Ana!* I'm eating supper in my room!"

"We cannot stay in the city," Father Mateo repeated.

"Then go," Luis said, "but leave me out of it. I'm not going anywhere."

The merchant stomped to his room and shut the door behind him with a rattle.

Hiro looked at Father Mateo.

The Jesuit raised a hand. "Not now. Even assuming you're correct about Matsunaga-*san*'s intentions, he won't come after Luis until Simão has settled in. We don't have to figure this out tonight. Tomorrow, I'll send a message to Father Vilela, explaining the situation and letting him know we need more time."

The priest returned to his room and closed the door.

Hiro's chest grew tight, as it always did when he was trapped between bad options. He wished he could obtain some proof of the plot against Luis. Hisahide would not wait to execute his plan, but without evidence Hiro would never persuade the priest—or the merchant—that the situation was now urgent.

The minute Simão reached Kyoto, Luis and Father Mateo were out of time.

The sun had set, which meant that no one could enter Kyoto until morning. However, that didn't necessarily mean the priest and his household were safe tonight.

Hiro went to his room, changed into a dark-colored tunic and matching trousers, and left the house. As he climbed up onto the roof, he yawned.

Tired or not, he wouldn't sleep tonight.

As he watched the street from the ridge of the roof, Hiro pondered the details of Emi's murder. He couldn't dismiss the thought that Satsu wanted more than just the name of his daughter's killer. The coin was connected to the crime, despite the lack of evidence, but Hiro had also begun to doubt the murderer had given the gold to Emi. Yuji and Jiro had no money, and neither Satsu nor Botan had reason to give the girl a gift at all. The yoriki needed gold and wouldn't have left the coin behind, which left only the mysterious man who promised to purchase Emi's place in a teahouse. And, despite what they'd been told, Hiro had seen no evidence such a person even existed—

—at which thought, the mystery unraveled itself completely.

Hiro knew who killed Emi, and why, and the answer—though clearly the proper one—surprised him. Better still, he suspected he could reveal the killer's identity in time to get Father Mateo out of Kyoto before the yoriki's deadline.

He spent the rest of the night reviewing the evidence in his mind, and one by one the pieces fell into place. By the time the eastern sky turned pale blue and gold with the promise of dawn, Hiro knew his answer was correct.

His spirits lifted, buoyed by the fiery glow that preceded the rising sun.

He wished he had time to watch the sun's rebirth, but lives would stand or fall by his timing today, and Hiro would not risk the Jesuit's life for the sake of a sunrise.

He hurried off the roof, barely noting the pleasant smells of dying leaves and wood smoke in the air. Back in his room, he donned his gray kimono and thrust his swords through his favorite obi. If he had to flee Kyoto with nothing but the clothes on his back, at least he would be wearing the ones he liked.

He paused to straighten the samurai knot atop his head and slipped a pair of shuriken into his kimono sleeves. One of the weapons clinked against the golden coin he had left in the hidden pocket the night before.

Hiro walked to the veranda door, slid it open carefully—and startled.

CHAPTER 48

F ather Mateo stood on the veranda, arms crossed and wearing the same expression Hiro's father had worn the day an eight-year-old Hiro tossed a smoke bomb into an occupied latrine.

"I suspected you might try to sneak off without me," Father Mateo said.

"We need to leave today. I thought you'd be packing." Hiro found it odd that he hadn't heard the Jesuit's footsteps or the squeaky timber that alerted him to movement on the porch.

"You solved it, didn't you?" Father Mateo asked. "You know who murdered Emi. Otherwise, you wouldn't be sneaking out alone so early."

"I'm not certain," Hiro said, "but I'll know in an hour. Two at most."

"I'm coming with you." Father Mateo raised a hand, as if to ward off argument. "I spoke with Ana. She will pack the household goods and knows a merchant whose cart we can rent tomorrow. I'll write to Father Vilela when we return and let him know we need another day."

"And if he won't give it?" Hiro asked as he started toward the garden gate.

Father Mateo followed. "What can he do? Expel us from the city?"

As they passed Okazaki Shrine, an enormous crow flew out through the torii, circled over the road, and landed on the shoulder of the white-clad temple maiden standing near the shrine.

Hiro looked at the priestess and suddenly realized she wasn't the woman who normally sold amulets at the entrance.

But she wasn't a stranger, either.

The woman's face scarred Hiro's mind as surely as her hands had marked his shoulder and his inner thigh.

"Neko?" He choked on the name.

He didn't understand how this was possible. She should have been older, by a decade—but Hiro could never forget that face, or the knowing smile that spread across it as he spoke.

Father Mateo looked confused. "Cat? What cat?"

Hiro barely registered the Jesuit's confusion. His heart beat fast, and his shoulder ached with the memory of a pain that cut far deeper than torn flesh and injured bone.

The temple maiden bowed to Father Mateo. "No, sir. *Neko* does mean 'cat,' but in Japan it is also a name." She turned to Hiro. "However, it is not *my* name. I am Mika. Neko is my sister."

As Hiro's thoughts began to clear, he noted subtle differences: the bridge of the nose, and the shape of the woman's ears. Even so . . . "You look just like her."

Mika nodded. "Everyone says that, but for the difference in age, we might be twins."

A memory flashed through Hiro's mind. "I saw you in the street two nights ago, near Father Mateo's home. I did not see your face, but the shape was yours. You weren't alone."

Mika nodded and gestured to the torii.

A pair of boys stepped out from behind the pillars. The skinny one stood as tall as Father Mateo. Hiro recognized him also.

"You set the charge on the bridge," Hiro said.

The skinny boy nodded.

"Ichiro!" Father Mateo exclaimed. "When did you return to Kyoto?"

Hiro looked at the second boy and recognized him as well. Ashikaga Ichiro was the son of a murdered samurai whose killer Hiro and Father Mateo had brought to justice earlier that summer. A cousin

of the late Shogun Ashikaga, Ichiro had fled the city shortly after the
shogun's death.

"Do not use his name," Mika said. "It is dangerous."

"You've been following us for days." Hiro lowered his voice and
looked around. "Is Kazu with you?"

"He's not in the city." Ichiro extended his hand to the crow, which
fluttered its wings and hopped across to the young man's arm. "Hanzo
sent us to you, with a message. You must return to Iga immediately."

Hiro wondered when and where the young samurai had obtained a
crow and trained it to follow him so well. Unfortunately, more pressing
concerns prevented that particular line of questions. "Has Hanzo ter-
minated my assignment to guard the priest?"

He hoped the answer was no, though he couldn't imagine another
reason for the head of the Iga ryu to summon him home.

Mika shook her head. "On the contrary, Hanzo says you must
bring the priest and leave as soon as possible—today, if you can."

The order seemed legitimate, but Hiro found it hard to trust the
girl. She looked too much like the woman who had betrayed him. "If
Hanzo sent you with a message, why did you wait so long to deliver it?"

Ichiro stepped forward to answer. "Hanzo ordered us not to
approach, or reveal ourselves, unless we could speak with you alone.
We tried . . ."

"You were the beggar outside Pontochō." Hiro glanced at the crow.
"The bird attacked the dōshin to protect you."

Ichiro looked at the crow with pride. "He did." He gestured to
the slender boy. "And Roku tried to contact you at Shijō Bridge, but a
yoriki reached you first."

"It looked like you were in trouble," Roku said. "I planted a charge
by the bridge to distract him."

"It worked." Hiro paused, remembering. "I saw the crow in the
Jesuit's garden also."

Ichiro nodded. "I put him there hoping you would approach the
wall, but you stayed too close to the house. I couldn't reveal myself."

"Why make contact now? I'm not alone."

"We've waited too long as it is. We had to risk it." Ichiro stroked the crow. It closed its eyes and ruffled its feathers in response.

"Only the priest is here," Roku added, "and he's supposed to go with you anyway."

Hiro was almost ready to believe them, but not quite. "Why would Hanzo send such an important message with a group of children?"

"A test, to see if we're ready for bigger assignments," Mika said. "If you don't reach Iga in time, we fail."

Father Mateo frowned. "In time for what?"

"Someone tried to kill Hattori Hanzo." The tall boy sounded worried.

"Shut up, Roku," Mika hissed. "Hanzo told us to deliver the message and nothing more."

"Who tried to kill Hanzo?" Hiro asked.

"A traitor," Roku answered, "but he failed."

"The Koga ryu is sending a delegation to Iga to discuss an alliance," Ichiro said. "Hanzo wants two of his best shinobi to observe the negotiations and to protect him—and the visitors—from harm."

"Who's the other bodyguard?" Hiro dreaded the answer because he suspected he already knew it.

Mika smiled. "My sister, Neko."

"Of course." Hiro wondered whether Hanzo remembered the last time his "best shinobi" had seen one another. Neko was covered in Hiro's blood—and Hiro had sworn to avenge the betrayal.

Blood for blood. It was the shinobi way.

Hanzo doubtless expected Hiro to put his personal issues behind him. Hiro wasn't certain he could . . . or that he wanted to.

"Will you go to Iga?" Ichiro sounded hopeful.

Hiro nodded. "We will leave this afternoon."

"Thank you." Ichiro bowed, causing the crow to spread its wings for balance. He looked at the others. "We should go."

Mika and Roku bowed, and all three of them disappeared into Okazaki Shrine.

CHAPTER 49

Hiro turned to Father Mateo. "At least that ends the argument about where to go when we leave Kyoto."

Father Mateo frowned. "There was an argument?"

Hiro resumed his course toward the river.

Father Mateo hurried to catch up. "Hattori Hanzo may lead the Iga ryu, but he has no authority over me."

"Only a dead man refuses an order from Hanzo," Hiro said. "Some refuse because they are dead, and the rest are dead because they refused. Which one are you?"

"I didn't say I wouldn't go. . . ." Father Mateo paused as if distracted by another thought. "How did they enter the city without travel papers?"

"Ichiro and the others?" Hiro asked. "Who says they had no papers? The shogun's seal is easy to forge, for those with the proper training."

Father Mateo didn't answer because they had reached the bridge.

The samurai on guard stepped out to meet them. "Good morning. Business in the city? Or another bowl of noodles?"

"Noodles," Hiro lied, though his stomach wished otherwise.

The guard stepped sideways to let them pass. "Perhaps, one day, you will show me the cart you favor."

Hiro bowed. "I would be honored."

On the opposite side of the river, Hiro turned south on the road that followed the western bank. Father Mateo fell in step without comment.

Sunrise burnished the trees and buildings with an orange glow. Crimson curls of sunshine danced across the river's surface, glinting off the ripples like embroidery on silk.

Hiro inhaled the scents of the city: wood smoke, fish, and here and there the rancid smell of trash. As they passed an alley, the stench of ammonia wafted from night soil buckets awaiting collection. As usual, Kyoto's riot of smells made Hiro long for the mountain air of Iga.

"The Yutoku-za sits east of the river," Father Mateo said, "but we're on the west. Are we going to talk with Jiro?"

Hiro nodded, impressed by the priest's deduction.

"Don't tell me he's guilty after all."

"Not of Emi's murder," Hiro said, "although if I have deduced correctly, he is not entirely innocent either."

By the time they reached Shijō Market, the shops had opened. People thronged the narrow street. Noren fluttered in the breeze as merchants stood before their shops, arranging the displays to best advantage.

Hiro and Father Mateo stopped in front of the expansive store whose noren read "BASHO—BEST RICE IN KYOTO."

"Is that a new noren?" Father Mateo nodded at the indigo banner.

Hiro took a closer look. "It does seem new."

"What happened to the old one?"

Hiro gestured to a line of birds that roosted on the building's eaves. Their tails hung over the entrance to the shop. "Most likely, unwanted embellishments from above."

Father Mateo laughed. "Can't you wash a noren?"

Hiro considered the delicate calligraphy on Basho's sign. "Yes, but extra spots and streaks can change the meaning of the words. Also, merchants consider the noren a symbol of their business. No one wants a stained or faded sign."

Basho's wife, a heavyset woman in dust-covered robes, emerged from the shop. She recognized Hiro and Father Mateo, but didn't look pleased to see them. "Good morning. With apologies, the shop is not yet open. Please return later."

"We don't want rice today," Hiro said. "We have come on other business."

She frowned. "We've barely repaired the damage from the last time 'other business' brought you here."

The floorboards creaked behind her.

"These men had nothing to do with that, Hama." Basho laid a hand on her shoulder. "I will handle the matter from here."

Hama gave her husband a doubtful glance, but bowed and walked away.

Basho stepped forward. The merchant was tall and burly, and his robe had a coating of fine, pale dust. His graying hair was in need of a trim.

He bowed. "May I help you this morning?"

"We have come to speak with Jiro," Hiro said.

"I'm afraid I cannot permit that," Basho replied.

When Hiro didn't respond, the merchant added, "Yoriki Hosokawa said I didn't have to speak with you, and Jiro doesn't either."

"How much did you pay him for that protection?" Hiro asked. "And what are you trying to hide?"

Basho glanced over his shoulder and lowered his voice. "How did you know the yoriki asked for money?"

Hiro didn't answer.

After a moment, Basho continued, "He said he knew about the girl, and if I paid, he'd make the trouble go away—as long as I didn't tell anyone, including you and the priest, what really happened. If I talked, or didn't pay . . . I know it was wrong to pay him, but we would lose everything if the magistrate told the guild about Jiro's loan."

"His loan?" Father Mateo asked. "What loan?"

"The loan he made to the girl." Basho looked confused. "That isn't why you're here?"

"Let me talk with them, Uncle." Jiro appeared behind Basho. "I can set this right."

"The yoriki ordered us not to speak with them," Basho said.

"Hama told me I had to, so they wouldn't cause more trouble." Jiro glanced toward the back of the shop.

Hama stood by the warehouse door, arms crossed and glaring at the men like a witch about to cast a curse.

"The yoriki doesn't want Magistrate Ishimaki learning that he steals from the people he's supposed to protect," Hiro said. "But we know what he's doing."

"That doesn't excuse the loan," Basho replied. "If the guild discovers we made a loan to a woman . . ."

"What loan?" Father Mateo repeated.

"Please?" Jiro asked Basho.

The merchant looked nervous, but nodded. "All right, you can tell them what you know."

"I arranged for Basho to make a loan to Emi, before she died." Jiro looked at the ground as if ashamed.

"He told me the client was a man," Basho added. "I would not have made the loan if I knew the truth before I gave my word."

"Why won't you make a loan to a woman?" Father Mateo asked.

"I cannot," Basho replied. "The guild has rules. A different moneylender has the rights to lend to women in the entertainment wards. By the time I learned the truth, we had the collateral and the payment had been made."

"Collateral?" Father Mateo asked.

Hiro nodded. "A mask, for nō, unless I miss my guess. Do you still have it?"

"Emi stole the mask?" Father Mateo sounded shocked.

"The mask was stolen?" Basho turned on Jiro. "This gets worse and worse! You said she owned it."

Jiro refused to meet his uncle's gaze. "That's what she told me—she said it was an inheritance, the only thing she had left from her father. She wanted to sell it in order to buy her freedom from the teahouse."

"And you believed that story?" Hiro asked. "You told us she had 'finally' found a way to buy her freedom—why not sell the mask before, if she had owned it all along?"

Jiro's shoulders sagged. "She said she didn't want to sell it because it was the only thing she had from her parents, but she had no other choice. The teahouse owner wouldn't let her go unless she paid in gold.

"I didn't think she would lie to me. We loved each other—at least, I thought she loved me too. We planned to use the rest of the money to run away to Edo"—he glanced at Basho—"I'm sorry. I never meant for anyone to get hurt."

Basho nodded. "It doesn't matter now."

Hiro wondered whether Emi truly cared for Jiro or if she had used him. The facts suggested the latter, but in the end Basho was right. It made no difference anymore.

Father Mateo looked at Hiro. "When did you figure out what really happened to the mask?"

"Last night, after Yuji left. He wanted the coin so badly, but I didn't believe his story about giving it to Emi. Also, he had to know that we'd tell Satsu about his claim. Yuji is selfish, and arrogant, but not even he would take a risk like that for the sake of greed alone. There had to be something more he didn't tell us."

"But how did you connect the coin to the mask instead of the murder?" Father Mateo asked. "We had no evidence of that."

"The evidence told us nothing about the coin," Hiro said, "and the killer should have taken it off the body. Everyone with a motive to kill her also wanted, or needed, money. In addition, Satsu kept talking about the coin, and Yuji wanted it badly enough to risk his reputation to obtain it. Again, that suggested the coin had value beyond the price of gold."

"But how did you make the connection between the golden coin and the missing mask?" Father Mateo asked.

Hiro smiled. "Once I realized who killed Emi, I knew the killer was not the source of the coin. The only answer that fit the facts was that Emi stole the mask herself, and the coin was the only way to get it back."

CHAPTER 50

"How could the coin return the mask?" Father Mateo asked. "That makes no sense."

"It does to a samurai," Hiro said. "We often take out loans and use our heirlooms as collateral. Emi couldn't hide the mask at home. She needed somewhere safe to put it while she found a buyer. No place in Kyoto is safer than a moneylender's storehouse."

"But how did Yuji figure it out?" Father Mateo asked. "He didn't even know the mask was missing. And what about Satsu? How much do you think he knew?"

"Satsu lied to us from the beginning," Hiro said. "He already knows who killed his daughter. He may or may not have realized that Yoriki Hosokawa is the one who bribed the Yutoku-za, but he knew the coin—and Emi—were connected to the missing mask. He never wanted us to find the killer. He asked us to investigate because he hoped that we would find the mask."

"Why not tell us that's what he wanted?" Father Mateo asked. "Unless . . . he is involved?"

"That is for Satsu to explain." Hiro turned to Basho. "Do you still have the mask?"

"It's in the warehouse," Jiro said. "I'll get it."

"Just a minute." Basho raised a hand. "The loan was not repaid. The mask is mine."

Hiro withdrew the coin from his sleeve. "I suspect this pays the debt in full."

Basho drew back in surprise, but accepted the coin. He examined it. "This is the same golden coin I gave the girl. I recognize this mark in the side." He looked at Hiro. "But it does not pay the debt in full. I also gave her a handful of silver."

"For that, you must look to Jiro," Hiro said. "I suspect he spent it in Pontochō."

Basho looked appalled. "You kept the silver?"

"She gave it to me," Jiro said. "For helping arrange the loan to buy her freedom."

Hiro decided not to tell Basho the rest of the truth—that Emi had not been an entertainer after all. He saw no point in causing Jiro any further trouble.

Basho's expression wavered between anger and confusion. "Why would you do this? The guild will expel us—*both of us*—for knowingly making a loan on a stolen item."

"I didn't know it was stolen." Jiro's eyes filled with tears. "She said it belonged to her. We planned to sell it and use the money to repay the loan and go to Edo. I'm sorry, Uncle. I never meant for any of this to happen."

"Did you kill her?" Basho asked.

"No!" A tear spilled over Jiro's eyelid and traced a damp line down his cheek. "I loved her. When someone killed her, I panicked. I didn't know what to do."

"That's why you came to see us the morning she died," Father Mateo said.

Jiro nodded and wiped his eyes. "Nobody knew about our plan to run away together. When she died, I panicked. At first, I thought I might have killed her while I was drunk, and just forgotten, but later— after I talked to you—I realized I would not forget a thing like that. Then I was afraid the killer would come for me as well."

"Give us the mask," Hiro said. "We will return it to its owners. After that, I promise you will be safe."

Jiro looked at Basho for permission.

The merchant nodded. "Fine. But you're working off the silver you spent, and quite a bit more besides."

An hour later, Hiro and Father Mateo knocked at the entrance to the Yutoku-za. The Jesuit carried an oblong package wrapped to look like a bag of rice.

"No matter what happens," Hiro whispered, "do not reveal the mask until I tell you."

"Didn't we come to return it?"

"We will," Hiro said, "but only after the killer confesses."

"Satsu killed her, didn't he? He figured out she stole—"

The door swung open. To Hiro's surprise, Haru stood in the entrance. The child bowed. "Good morning. I wasn't expecting you today."

"Is your father at home?" Hiro asked. "We would like to see him."

Before the boy could answer, Satsu appeared behind his son.

Father Mateo reached into his purse and removed a silver coin. "Haru, would you like a bowl of udon?"

The little boy's eyes lit up as he saw the coin.

"What's going on here?" Satsu asked.

Hiro noted the inappropriate tone, but did not object. Their visit endangered the theater troupe, and no one stood nearby to overhear the actor speaking rudely to visitors of samurai rank.

"We have come with important information," Hiro said. "I suggest you let your son have udon while we talk inside."

Haru gave his father a hopeful look. When Satsu nodded, Haru accepted the coin from the priest with a grin and a bow. Halfway out the door, he paused. "You are not coming with me?"

"We have already eaten," Hiro said, to save the Jesuit the lie. "Go and enjoy it."

"I will—and thank you." Haru raced away.

Satsu stepped away from the door. "Please come inside."

He led them through the entry and into the common room. To Hiro's surprise, the room was empty.

"Haru wakes up early," Satsu said, "but adult actors normally do not."

Chou and Nori entered the room from the other side. Each woman carried a tray with a teapot, cups, and bowls of steaming soup and rice.

At the sight of Hiro and Father Mateo, the women lowered their trays and bowed.

Satsu gestured to the door behind them. "Take the food away. We will eat later."

"Actually," Hiro said, "I would prefer if the women stayed. They have a right to hear what we've discovered."

Father Mateo raised a hand as if to run it through his hair, but paused and returned the hand to his side. Hiro noted the priest's restraint. At last, his friend was learning.

Satsu gestured to the hearth. "Would you like to sit down? May we offer you tea?"

Father Mateo knelt by the hearth, but Hiro remained by the door that led to the entrance and the street. He pondered a subtle way to request Yuji's presence. Then he remembered Satsu's lies and decided he didn't care. "Get Yuji."

Satsu began to object, but Hiro raised a hand. "I want him here. Go fetch him. Send a woman, if you wish."

Chou seemed confused. Nori's eyes flew wide, on the edge of panic. Satsu looked at his daughter. "Go find Yuji."

Chou bowed and left the room. A short time later, she returned without her tray. Yuji and his mother, Rika, followed the girl into the room. Both appeared recently woken and quickly dressed.

Yuji frowned at the sight of the visitors.

Hiro gestured toward the hearth. "Sit down."

Satsu took the host's position, next to Father Mateo and facing the door. Nori set her tray at the side of the room and knelt behind her husband, with Chou at her side, while Yuji knelt in front of Chou.

Rika knelt beside her son—the only woman who approached the hearth.

Satsu turned to Hiro, who remained in his position near the door. "I assume you called us here because you know the name of Emi's killer."

"Indeed," Hiro said, "but first, please tell me: when did you realize Emi stole the mask from the Yutoku-za?"

CHAPTER 51

Nori gasped in horror. "No! Emi would never steal from her family!"

"And yet, she did," Hiro said. "If you don't believe me, Yuji can confirm it."

Chou's mouth fell open. Her lower lip trembled.

Satsu gave Yuji a look of disgust. "You knew all along? And said nothing?"

"I don't know what you're talking about." Yuji brushed a lock of hair from his face.

"Please, my daughter was not a thief." Nori bowed her head to the floor. "I beg you, sir, believe me—she would not steal."

"All prostitutes steal," Rika said.

Nori pushed herself to a kneeling position. "Emi was not a prostitute, and she is dead. How can you say such things?" Her eyes turned red and filled with tears.

"She met with men by the river," Rika said, though her voice had softened. "Your denial does not change the truth."

Chou bit her lip and lowered her gaze to the floor. Beside her, Nori raised her hands to hide her face, presumably to cover her emotion.

"Enough." Hiro looked at Satsu. "When did you learn the truth?"

Nori shook her head. Her shoulders trembled, but she made no sound.

Satsu drew a breath and held it, pondering his response. "I did not know for certain," he said at last. "I suspected, but I couldn't prove it. I hoped your investigation would reveal the truth."

"Why not tell us that from the beginning?" Father Mateo asked.

"I gave you the coin," Satsu replied. "I thought it would lead you to the mask."

Hiro heard the ring of truth in Satsu's words, but knew—with frustration—he could not trust the actor's honesty.

"Please understand," Satsu continued, "Emi couldn't have stolen the mask alone. Botan kept it hidden away in his personal chamber. No woman could have entered there and taken a mask without someone noticing. Someone had to help—" He looked at Yuji.

"I didn't help her steal it." Yuji sounded offended. "Someday, the mask will be mine. Why would I steal from the troupe I plan to lead?"

"Because you loved her," Hiro said, "or so you told me yesterday, when you attempted to recover your golden token."

Nori raised her head from her hands and shook it slowly, in disbelief.

Rika glared at her son, dismay and fury written on her face.

"I did not love her," Yuji said emphatically. "She meant nothing to me."

Chou gazed at her hands, as if ignoring the conversation.

"Why did you give her a golden coin if you did not care about her?" Hiro asked.

Chou raised her head. "*You* gave her the coin? You swore you didn't. Why did you lie to me?"

"I didn't lie to you," Yuji protested. "I lied to the samurai and the priest."

"That much is true," Hiro confirmed, "though you went to great lengths to persuade us otherwise."

"You were supposed to love me," Chou insisted. "Not Emi."

"I didn't love her," Yuji said. "It wasn't my fault . . ." He trailed off as if he realized the words were not convincing Chou.

She turned her face away, and her eyes grew red.

Nori's tears began to flow at her daughter's anguish. She turned to Rika. "You call my daughter names, but your son disgraces himself and shames our family by association."

Rika pressed her lips together. For once, she didn't argue.

"I did not have an affair with Emi," Yuji declared. "I didn't love her. This I swear."

"Then why did you confess to all of it yesterday?" Hiro asked.

Chou let out a choking sob and covered her mouth with her hands. Nori laid a comforting hand on her daughter's shoulder.

Satsu rose to his feet. "Did you come to speak the truth or just to throw more kindling on a fire? I no longer care who killed my daughter. She is gone, as is the mask. Neither will return to me. Please go."

Father Mateo stood up and walked to the common room door, but instead of leaving he turned to face the room. "Like Hiro, I regret your distress, but no one is leaving until we have shared the information we came to deliver."

The Jesuit had positioned himself directly in front of the door, blocking the exit.

"I lied." Yuji looked nervous. "I lied about the affair and the coin. I simply wanted the gold."

Chou shook her head, sending a tear down her cheek. "You lied to *me*. Emi told me you gave her the coin."

"That's impossible." Yuji shook his head. "I didn't . . . When did she say that?"

"The night she died." Chou no longer tried to stop her tears. Her nose turned red. "She said she had the coin because of you. That you helped her so she could leave Kyoto. She said you did it because you wanted her instead of me."

Nori's tears increased. She shook her head as if unable to believe what she was hearing.

"I have no money," Yuji said, "and if I did, I wouldn't waste it on Emi. You must believe me. It's the truth. You are the woman I intend to marry."

Chou sniffled and wiped her tears. "I do believe you. And I forgive you. Emi cannot cause us trouble anymore."

"Because you killed her," Hiro said.

Nori gasped. Yuji's eyes flew open in shock, and Rika's mouth fell open.

CHAPTER 52

Only Satsu did not react to Hiro's words.

"Satsu," Nori pleaded, "tell him this cannot be so."

The actor shook his head. "I'm sorry. That, I cannot say."

"But . . . she's your daughter also. Please . . ." Nori reached for her husband, but her hands fell short.

Satsu sighed heavily. "Please proceed with the explanation."

Nori shook her head in protest. She turned pleading eyes on Chou, but her daughter simply looked away.

"Satsu knows Chou killed her sister," Hiro said.

"How?" Rika asked. The others seemed too shocked to say a word.

Satsu nodded. "She is the only killer who would leave the coin behind."

"I came to the same conclusion," Hiro said. "She could not bear to see Emi with a prize that Yuji gave her, but she could not take it off the body, either. Yuji might see it and know what she had done."

Yuji gave Chou a horrified look and scooted away from her on the floor.

Hiro turned his attention to Chou. "The problem is that Emi lied to you. She did not get the coin from Yuji. She received it from a moneylender, as a loan on the stolen mask."

Chou's eyes widened in disbelief. She turned to Yuji. "Is this true?"

Yuji leaned away from her and nodded.

"No," Nori said. "I don't believe you. Chou would never do this thing."

"I trust you can explain how you reached these conclusions?" Rika

217

asked. "With apologies if it seems I doubt your word—I simply wish to know."

"I can explain it, and I will." Hiro continued, "The first clue was the coin. Most people assume a girl like Emi could only receive a coin from a man—specifically, a man with whom she had an illicit relationship. I initially made that same mistake myself. Also, most killers would not leave such a valuable coin on the body. That bothered me from the outset, but I hoped the killer's identity would offer an explanation for that problem.

"I began my investigation with the suspects. Yuji revealed himself at once as a rogue and a liar, but also selfish. He wouldn't have left the coin behind, any more than he would give a woman such an expensive gift. He believes that women owe him favors, not the other way around."

Hiro turned to Satsu. "I suspected you, as well."

"Only a fool would seek investigation of a murder he committed," Satsu said.

"I never eliminate suspects on that basis," Hiro replied. "I have known too many fools. Moreover, your behavior hinted you already knew who murdered Emi. However, I soon realized you did not kill your daughter."

"How?" Satsu asked.

"Again, the coin was the answer," Hiro said. "You initially told us you wanted to find the link between the killer and the coin, but all of our later conversations focused on the coin alone. You refused to accept that Botan might have sold the missing mask. You seemed absolutely certain it was stolen. You also wanted the coin returned, and though you claimed you wanted it for the value of the gold, your focus on it seemed too strong—there had to be something more. Like me, I think you suspected Emi stole the mask and that the gold related to the theft.

"You would not have killed your daughter, even to preserve the family honor, if she held the key to finding the mask."

"But how did you know I suspected her involvement in the theft?" Satsu asked.

"You told us you expected her to run away or leave Kyoto," Hiro said, "and yet, you did not know she met men by the river. She couldn't have run without money, and since you knew she had no job, it stands to reason you assumed she got the coin in return for the mask."

"Please," Nori begged, "this cannot be true. Neither of my daughters would do the terrible things you claim."

She looked around the room for support, but no one met her eyes.

"A samurai threatened to harm the Yutoku-za unless we paid him," Nori said. "He demanded gold, but my father did not have the sum he wanted. He made threats—he must have killed Emi and stolen the mask."

"I know about the samurai." Hiro spoke gently, out of respect for the woman's pain. "The man who threatened your father is a yoriki. He wanted gold to buy a place in the shogun's army. We know, because he threatened others also. He did not know about the coin until after the murder happened, when he overheard us showing it to the magistrate. The man is a thief, but he did not kill your daughter."

"Maybe he didn't see the coin when he killed her." Nori clasped her hands together. "I beg you, do not blame this crime on Chou."

"The coin was part of the murder weapon," Hiro said. "The killer saw it."

"You showed the coin to the magistrate?" Satsu asked. "Did he take it from you?"

"We no longer have it," Hiro affirmed.

Satsu sighed. "Then hope is lost. I never even figured out how Emi stole the mask."

"Yuji can answer that, I believe," Hiro said.

The young man's face turned as red as the coals in the hearth.

"He claimed that Emi seduced him," Hiro continued, "but Emi told Chou a different story—one which Haru heard, and confirmed, so I think it more reliable. Emi wanted to reveal Yuji's lack of character. She did invite his affections, but also claimed there was no affair, despite Yuji's words to the contrary."

"Emi could have lied," Rika said. "Women of poor virtue often do."

"As do actors," Nori added as tears flowed down her face again, "and your son has already confessed to lies."

"Enough," Satsu whispered. "Let the samurai finish."

"I believe that Emi told Chou the truth," Hiro said. "She tricked Yuji into giving her the mask. He could never admit to that, so he allowed you all to believe he had an affair with Emi instead. You could forgive a moral slip, but not complicity in the theft of your greatest treasure."

"Emi was my greatest treasure," Nori said.

Chou gave her mother a wounded look. Everyone else's attention shifted to Yuji.

Satsu scowled. "Is this what happened?"

Yuji folded his arms across his chest. "No—that is, not exactly."

"Feel free to correct my errors," Hiro said.

Yuji glanced at the others as if hoping someone would speak on his behalf.

No one did.

"Chou told me Emi was meeting a man by the river. I didn't believe her, because"—he paused, as if weighing how much of the truth to tell—"Emi always refused my advances and said she didn't want a man at all. But Chou insisted it was true, so one evening, about a week ago, I followed Emi to the river. She met and talked with a man—he looked like a merchant, of all things.

"Afterward I confronted her. She told me her life was not my concern. But when I threatened to tell Satsu what I'd seen, she changed completely. She suggested . . . well, she asked if I still wanted her."

He glanced at Chou. "I told her I did. She said we had to be careful, so no one would see us. She said we should meet at an inn by the river, one of the places that rents its rooms for coppers and asks no questions. She asked me to bring a mask so I could give her a private performance. . . ."

Yuji trailed off as if hoping he wouldn't have to complete the story.

Everyone else in the room looked horrified. Rika shook her head, expression wavering between disgust and fury. Chou's eyes filled with tears that did not fall.

"You agreed to this?" Satsu demanded.

"You were betrothed to Chou!" Rika added.

"Let him finish," Hiro said. "What happened then?"

"The night before she died, I took the mask and met her at the inn," Yuji continued. "I sneaked the special one from Botan's office because no one would notice it missing overnight. Botan only opens the box when he needs the mask for performances, and *Aoi no Ue* doesn't use it."

"How did you manage it?" Satsu asked. "The trunk where he stores that mask is always locked."

"I know where Botan keeps the key." Yuji looked at the hearth and fell silent.

"Keep going." Hiro felt no sympathy for the actor. A man could attempt to conceal his crimes, but if they came to light he had to own them.

"When I reached the inn, Emi had ordered a flask of sake," Yuji said. "The innkeeper kept refilling it, and Emi kept drinking, so I did too. Eventually, I needed to use the latrine. . . .

"When I returned, she was gone, along with the mask. The innkeeper said she had left me a message—a piece of paper that called me a worthless fool. That's when I realized she tricked me. She was only pretending to drink. She wanted to get me drunk so she could steal the mask."

"Why didn't you come straight home and explain what happened?" Satsu asked.

"It would have ruined me! Botan would dismiss me from the troupe, and you would cancel my betrothal."

"Your betrothal to Chou is canceled," Satsu said, "and, I assure you, when he hears this tale, Botan will ensure you never set foot on a stage in Kyoto again."

CHAPTER 53

"Had you told the truth, we might have avoided this tragedy," Satsu said to Yuji. "Now my daughter is dead and the mask is gone, and though you committed neither crime, morally you are responsible for both."

Father Mateo started to speak, but Hiro shook his head. An important part of the story remained to be told.

Chou bowed her face to the ground. "I'm sorry, Father. Emi told me she met Yuji at the inn, and he confirmed it, but I did not know about the mask. They never mentioned it. I did not even know that it was missing."

"Tell us what happened the night Emi died," Hiro said. "And this time, tell the truth."

Chou pushed herself to a sitting position. The tears had left her eyes. "I loved my sister. I did not want to kill her."

Hiro nodded. "I believe you."

"I never cared that Emi was pretty and I am not, or that everyone liked her better than they like me." Chou's determined expression looked out of place on her mild face. "Emi wanted to sing and dance. I wanted a home and a husband. We didn't fight, because we didn't need to. I never wanted Emi's life. She never wanted mine.

"But after Father formally announced my betrothal to Yuji, everything changed. Emi said I was foolish to love him. She said I would be miserable as his wife. I thought she said it because she wanted Yuji for herself. I saw them talking, many times. They stood too close together. Emi denied that she wanted him, but he was always there, beside her. I told her to leave him alone. She called me stupid.

"She said Yuji wasn't worth fighting over." Tears welled up in Chou's eyes. "He was worth it to me."

She sniffled, wiped her eyes, and continued, "Two days before Emi died, she told me she had found a man to help her buy a teahouse. She was meeting him that very night. She stayed out late—much later than normal—and when she returned, she wouldn't tell me where she'd been. A little while later, I saw Yuji sneaking back into the house. I stopped him and asked where he had been, but he wouldn't tell me either. I knew he was the man that Emi meant."

"I never promised to help her buy a teahouse," Yuji protested.

Chou continued as if he hadn't spoken. "The next day Yuji came to me, looking for Emi. I asked if he was with her the night before, and he said yes, but he promised it would never happen again." She turned to Yuji. "You should have told the truth. I would have understood. I would have helped you."

"If I told you about the mask, it would have ruined everything," Yuji said.

Chou wiped the last of her tears away. "Emi was right. You only care about yourself."

"Then what happened?" Hiro asked.

"That afternoon, Emi showed me a golden coin. She said it was proof I couldn't trust Yuji and that he was the reason she had it. I thought she meant he gave it to her. Now, I realize . . . I told her to give it to me, but she refused. Then Mother came in and I had to pretend that nothing was going on." Chou looked at her parents. "I am sorry. I thought, if you knew, you'd make Yuji marry Emi instead of me."

"How could you still want him? He betrayed you," Satsu said.

"Because I love him," Chou insisted. "I thought . . . with her out of the way, he would realize he loved me too.

"That night I followed Emi to the river. I stayed in the shadows. I wanted to see it when Yuji told her it was over. First she met a merchant, and they talked. The man lay down—I think he fell asleep. Emi just sat there, and I got bored, but just as I decided to leave, Yuji came out from under the bridge.

"Emi left the other man and went to Yuji. He took her in his arms, like a lover—"

"That was not an embrace," Yuji interrupted. "I grabbed her in anger. I wanted her to tell me what she did with the sacred mask. She showed me the coin and taunted me. She said the gold was the key, but I would never find the lock it opened."

"So you grabbed her," Hiro said.

"But I did not kill her," Yuji insisted. "I knew, if I did, I would never find the mask."

"What did she do when you grabbed her?" Hiro asked.

"She threatened to scream. She told me there was a yoriki patrolling along the riverbank, as well as the samurai guarding Shijō Bridge. She said if I didn't let her go, she would claim that I attacked her, so I left."

"You left?" Father Mateo echoed.

Yuji looked at the priest. "What else could I do? No one can leave the city at night. I needed a plan to recover the mask. I went home, and Mother can attest I was there the rest of the night."

"My wretched child deserves no favors," Rika said, "but he was here."

Hiro turned to Chou. "What happened after Yuji left?"

"I confronted Emi by the bridge," Chou said. "I asked her why she wanted to steal my husband. Emi claimed I had it wrong, but I knew what I saw! She was lying.

"I looked at the coin around her neck. I'd never felt so angry and betrayed. I grabbed the coin"—Chou pantomimed the action—"I wanted to tear it off and throw it in the river. But Emi grasped my hands, and we struggled. I wrapped the leather thong around my wrist."

Again, she mimed the action.

"Emi put her hands to her throat. I realized I was choking her, but I didn't stop. I couldn't. I felt so angry. I wanted her to hurt, the way that I did when I saw her close to Yuji.

"Emi fell down. My hands were twisted up in the leather, so I fell too, but I didn't let go. . . ."

Chou's words trailed off as the memory flooded through her. She looked at her hands, as if reliving what they had done. "Emi stopped struggling. Her body went limp. I didn't realize ... And then it was over. Her eyes went empty. She didn't breathe. That's when I realized she was dead. I didn't know what to do. If I took the coin, Yuji would see it and know ...

"I dragged her body up the bank and left her with the sleeping man. I hoped the police would blame him for her death. It was wrong, but I was scared." She looked at Yuji. "I thought, with Emi dead, you'd want to marry me again."

Yuji's eyes were wide with horror. Rika and Nori seemed equally stunned.

Satsu stared at his daughter with an expression that slowly hardened into regret.

Hiro did not envy the difficult choice that Satsu had to make.

Nori's whisper broke the silence. "Why?"

"I never meant to hurt her." Chou turned to her mother. "You have to believe me. I had no choice."

"There is always a choice," Satsu said, "until the deed is done. Now, however, the lot is cast and you must answer for your crime."

"My crime?" The glaze in Chou's eyes suggested her mind refused to process the situation fully.

Nori shook her head and whispered, "*No*. I cannot lose them both."

"You killed your sister," Satsu said.

"But it's over." Chou seemed puzzled. "Emi is gone and the mask is also."

"Emi is gone," Hiro said, "but the mask is not."

CHAPTER 54

Hiro gestured to Father Mateo. The Jesuit opened the bag and withdrew the mask.

Satsu's mouth dropped open. "You found it? How?"

"As you suspected, by tracing the coin," Hiro said. "The morning after the theft, Emi left the mask with a moneylender—a relative of the merchant she met by the river—as collateral for a loan. I don't know whether she planned to sell the mask in Kyoto or in Edo, but she knew that no one would look for it in a moneylender's storehouse."

"How did you trace the moneylender?" Satsu asked. "How did you know she hadn't sold the mask?"

"She had no reason to stay in Kyoto once she had the money from the sale," Hiro said, "and a mask like this is worth far more than a single golden coin. Once I knew she didn't get the coin from a suitor, or from Yuji, I realized a moneylender offered the perfect place to hide the mask. The moneylender would keep it safe, and the loan she received— a coin—was fairly easy to conceal."

"Kyoto has dozens of moneylenders," Satsu said. "How did you find the right one?"

"The man Emi met by the river worked for a moneylender." Hiro omitted the clue about Jiro having coins to spend. "I decided to try the logical option first. It proved correct."

Satsu bowed to Hiro, and then to Father Mateo. "May I have the honor of returning the mask to Botan? I will confess that Emi stole it and accept whatever penalty he demands."

Father Mateo handed the mask to Satsu, who accepted it with another bow.

"It is yours to return," Hiro said, "but Yuji should suffer the penalty for the theft."

"I didn't steal it!" Yuji snapped.

Rika's hand flashed out and slapped her son across the face. "Bow down and beg the samurai's forgiveness!"

Speechless, Yuji lowered his face to the floor.

"Your father was too proud of you," Rika continued. "He fostered your talent at the cost of your character. Others accomplished the theft, and the murder, but you set the chain of events in motion. You will accept responsibility for your actions, even if it ends your career. At least it won't put a rope around your neck."

Rika looked at Chou. "Not everyone here will be as fortunate."

Chou shook her head, eyes wide, as Rika's meaning struck her.

"*No!*" Nori threw herself at her husband's feet. "I beg you. No one has to know. We do not have to lose them both for this."

Satsu closed his eyes for a moment, as if steeling himself to speak. "The law is clear. Death is the only penalty for murder. It must be done."

Nori did not raise her face. Her body shook with desperate sobs.

Chou hung her head, accepting her father's judgment. "I only wish I did not have to cause you public shame."

Satsu looked at Hiro with a question in his eyes.

Hiro nodded.

"If you are strong enough," Satsu said, "we do not need to involve the magistrate."

A keening wail rose from Nori, who rocked back and forth as if in pain. Rika moved to Nori's side. Yuji pushed himself to a kneeling position, but kept his gaze on the floor.

"Can a woman commit . . . self-determination?" Father Mateo whispered in Portuguese, substituting the translated word for *seppuku.*

Hiro shook his head. "That ritual is reserved for samurai."

"Then how?" the Jesuit asked.

"A rope and a tree," Hiro answered.

"Suicide is a mortal sin," Father Mateo whispered.

"So is murder," Hiro replied, "if I remember the tenets of your faith."

Father Mateo seemed surprised. "You paid attention?"

"Your house has open rafters." Hiro shrugged. "And voices carry."

"Please excuse us," Satsu said to Hiro. "I must help my daughter do what must be done."

Nori lunged for Chou and sheltered her daughter beneath her body. "Satsu, no. I cannot lose them both. You cannot take her from me."

"Is there no alternative?" Father Mateo asked the actor. "I could speak to the magistrate."

"No!" Nori shrieked. "He will order her hanged in public!"

Satsu turned to the priest, eyes red and glassy with unshed tears. "My wife is correct. Chou's life must answer for her crime. Privacy is the only mercy anyone can offer. That way, the Yutoku-za will not suffer public shame as well."

Chou embraced her mother and stood up, though it took some effort to disentangle herself from Nori's grasp. When she did, the older woman collapsed to the floor.

"I am sorry, Mother," Chou said, "but I have disgraced you enough already. Please forgive me. There is no other choice."

"A day," Nori begged. "Just one more day."

"I would rather do it now." Chou blinked back tears. "Before I lose my nerve."

"May I go too and pray with her?" Father Mateo asked.

"We do not pray to your foreign god." Satsu spoke gently. "Thank you for the sentiment, but it is better if you leave."

Hiro caught the Jesuit's eye. "You cannot help her," he said in Portuguese. "You must not interfere."

Father Mateo seemed on the verge of tears as well, which startled Hiro into silence.

"Please excuse me," Satsu said. "I will walk you out, and then I must go with Chou, to assist. I give you my word, this will be done today."

"Of course." Hiro bowed to Satsu. "Please accept my condolences on your losses."

The actor bowed back more deeply. "Thank you for allowing me to keep this matter private."

"I will stay with Nori," Rika said, "and my worthless son will confess to Botan. I promise he will take responsibility for his actions."

Yuji hung his head like a beaten dog.

Hiro nodded. "We will leave you to your duty."

Satsu escorted Hiro and Father Mateo to the door. When they reached the street, he stepped outside and closed the door behind them.

"I must go and help my daughter," he said, "but first, I wish to apologize. I did not believe you would help me if you knew that Chou was guilty from the start. When did you know I realized she was the killer?"

"When Chou removed the coin from Emi's body, you asked if she was positive that Emi hadn't told her about the coin." Hiro paused. "You didn't ask the expected question—if Chou had seen the coin before—which meant you knew she had."

"Because she used it to murder her sister." Satsu sighed. "Did you know the entire truth from that moment?"

"No," Hiro said. "In fact, I didn't realize the importance of your statement until last night. Without all the evidence, taken together, the words alone would not have solved the crime."

"I regret that we had to meet under such unfortunate circumstances," Satsu said.

"I regret it also," Hiro said. "We are leaving the city this afternoon. Have you any messages for Iga?"

"Please thank your mother for raising an honorable son."

"You should leave the city also," Father Mateo said. "The Miyoshi army is marching on Kyoto."

"I've heard the rumors," Satsu replied, "but for now, I think we will stay. Samurai always need entertainment, and men who wear masks can often survive where those who wear swords cannot." His smile faded. "Please excuse me. I have a daughter to assist . . . and then to mourn."

CHAPTER 55

Hiro and Father Mateo walked home together in heavy silence. Hiro knew the Jesuit disapproved of death by suicide. He wondered if the priest would have preferred Chou die by public hanging, but didn't ask.

Words that could not help were often better left unspoken.

As they reached the bridge at Marutamachi Road, the samurai on duty stepped out to meet them. "Heading home?"

Father Mateo bowed. "I have finished my business."

Hiro sensed finality in the words.

As the samurai moved aside to let them pass, a voice behind them yelled, "Stop those men!"

Hiro turned to see the yoriki approaching.

The guard looked wary. Hiro considered running, but it wouldn't solve the problem. Better to talk their way out of this, if they could.

"Is something wrong?" the samurai asked as Yoriki Hosokawa reached them.

"These men are under arrest," the yoriki said. "They failed to pay a fine."

"The fine is not due until later today." Hiro gestured toward the sun. "We still have several hours."

"The fine is overdue," the yoriki snapped.

Father Mateo turned to the guard. "Please help me. I have committed no crime. This man abuses his power to steal from the innocent."

"How dare you!" Sunlight flashed on the yoriki's sword as it flew toward Father Mateo's neck—and stopped with a clang as Hiro's katana met it in the air.

230

The yoriki froze, stunned by the interference.

"Step aside, ronin!" he demanded.

"No." Hiro didn't lower his sword. "I am saving you the embarrassment of killing a foreign priest and starting a war. Come to the foreigner's home. We will pay you in full."

Hiro felt the pressure on his katana lessen slightly as Yoriki Hosokawa considered the offer. He hoped the yoriki's greed would prevail. The man wanted money badly, and Father Mateo would earn him nothing dead.

Hosokawa lowered his sword. "Fine. But we're going immediately. No tricks."

Hiro sheathed his katana. "A samurai always honors his word."

The guard stepped away with visible relief as Yoriki Hosokawa returned his sword to its sheath as well.

Hiro and Father Mateo walked up the road with the yoriki between them.

The Jesuit leaned forward and looked at Hiro. "Have you got the money?" he asked in Portuguese.

"Speak Japanese!" the yoriki ordered. "None of your foreign trickery."

Hiro didn't answer. He was working out a plan.

They had almost reached the Jesuit's home when the yoriki stopped and demanded, "What's going on here?"

A horse-drawn wagon stood in the road in front of Father Mateo's home. Straw-wrapped sake barrels filled the cart. A man in an artisan's tunic and trousers stood beside the bony horses hitched to the front of the wagon. He turned, and Hiro realized with shock that the man was Ginjiro.

Luis and Ana emerged from the house with woven baskets in their hands.

The yoriki turned to Father Mateo. "You were planning to flee the city!" He reached for his sword.

"Wait!" Hiro raised a hand. "We have the payment in the house, as you demanded. We would never leave without paying you."

Yoriki Hosokawa looked suspicious. "Why is the cart already here?"

"Packing a house takes time," Hiro said. "Please come inside."

"No tricks." The yoriki drew his sword. "The foreigner goes first. Then you. Then me."

Father Mateo walked toward the house. Hiro followed.

"You stay here," the yoriki growled at Ana and Luis as he passed.

"Go to the kitchen and don't look back," Hiro whispered in Portuguese as they entered the common room.

"No foreign talk!" the yoriki snapped. "I told yo—"

The final word became a gurgle as Hiro spun, wakizashi in hand, and opened a gash in the yoriki's throat.

Yoriki Hosokawa dropped his sword and clutched his neck. His eyes went wide with surprise and disbelief.

Crimson blood welled up between his fingers and spilled down across his tunic. The flow pulsed with every beat of his heart. He choked and spat out blood.

Hiro stepped forward and thrust his sword through the yoriki's chest, using an upward angle designed to pierce the lungs and heart.

Yoriki Hosokawa fell to his knees and coughed again. A rivulet of blood dripped off his lips and spattered on the wooden floor.

"I promised you payment in full, and now you have it." Hiro withdrew the sword. "A samurai keeps his word."

Yoriki Hosokawa tried to speak. The effort sent a spray of blood across the floor. He choked and slumped over, dead. Blood drained from his mouth and pooled around his face.

Hiro wiped the blade of his sword on the yoriki's surcoat.

"Hiro," Father Mateo gasped, "what have you done?"

"What I had to." He returned his sword to its sheath.

"Luis has silver. We could have paid him."

"He would have killed you the moment he had it." Hiro looked down at the yoriki's body. "He could not risk you telling Magistrate Ishimaki what he'd done."

"He didn't kill Botan or Jiro," Father Mateo objected.

"Commoners have no access to the magistrate, but Ishimaki would listen to you. He had no intention of letting you live." Hiro shook his head. "The Hosokawa are mostly noble. The clan is better off without him in it."

Luis walked into the room. "We heard shouting." He noticed the body. "And now that's happened. Good thing I arranged for us to leave the city promptly. They would hang you both as murderers by nightfall."

"You arranged...How do you know Ginjiro?" Father Mateo asked.

"I don't, but I know you saved his life. And now he's saving yours. Let's go." Luis turned around and left the house, as if expecting the others to follow.

They did, though Hiro took the time to change his bloodstained clothes for clean ones. As he left his room, he regretted the loss of his favorite gray kimono. While this one was also gray, it was only his second-best.

Outside, Ginjiro let go of the horses' rope and bowed to Hiro. "Please do not tell me what happened here. Some things, it is better not to know. I am glad to help you, but we should hurry. Get into the barrels now."

Ana had already climbed into the cart. She held her basket in one hand and used the other to open a barrel. Clasping the basket tightly against her chest, she climbed inside.

"We have an hour, at most, before they come," Luis said as he reached the cart.

"Before who comes?" Father Mateo asked.

Luis's cheeks flushed angry red. "Simão Duarte arrived this morning, earlier than expected. A few minutes after he reached the warehouse, a pair of samurai showed up and ordered me to go to the shogun's palace. Apparently, the shogun wants to revoke my license and our travel permit."

"He wanted to see you in person for that?" Father Mateo sounded suspicious.

"I didn't believe it either," Luis said, "so I sneaked out the back of the warehouse and ran directly to this man's brewery."

Hiro eyed the merchant's bulging belly and puffy legs. "You ran?"

"I do possess the ability." Luis glared.

Ginjiro climbed into the back of the cart and sealed a lid on the barrel with Ana inside. "Don't worry," he said. "The barrels have concealed holes in the sides to help you breathe."

"Concealed air holes?" Hiro asked.

Ginjiro smiled. "On occasion, I cart more than sake out of the city. Please forgive me, but I cannot tell you more."

CHAPTER 56

G injiro lifted the lid from another barrel. "The merchant told me that Shogun Matsunaga intends to kill you. I have no intention of letting that happen."

Father Mateo looked toward the house. "My Bible . . ."

Luis retrieved a leather-bound tome from his basket and handed it to the priest. "Here, I brought it for you. I have my silver too. The rest we'll replace when we get wherever we're going."

"How did you outrun Hisahide's samurai?" Hiro asked.

"They didn't know I'd left the warehouse." Luis climbed awkwardly into the cart. "I told them I needed time to finalize the ledger so I could pay my final taxes when they took me to the shogun. Simão offered to make them tea. He had no idea I planned to escape out the back—and it serves him right if they blame him for helping. Trying to take my business . . ."

Ginjiro helped Luis into a barrel. It wasn't an easy fit, but they managed.

"You next," Hiro said to Father Mateo.

While the Jesuit climbed into the wagon and concealed himself in a barrel, Hiro looked up and down the street. He didn't see anyone in the road or watching from a doorway.

Hiro jumped into the cart.

Ginjiro indicated an open barrel. "You'll have to use that one. The rest are full of sake, in case the guards at the city gates want to test my wares."

"Thank you for this." Hiro took off his swords and climbed into the barrel. He crouched down, leaving just enough room to stand the swords beside him.

Ginjiro lowered the lid without a word.

Hiro crouched in the dark, stuffy barrel and listened to the cart rumble over the narrow, earthen road. A few minutes later, the wheels creaked to a halt.

They had reached the barricade that led to the Tōkaidō Road and freedom.

Hiro's heart pounded so hard his ears began to ring. He heard the muffled sound of voices, first at a distance but coming closer. The wheels crunched and stopped as the cart inched forward. There must be a line at the gates.

At last, he heard Ginjiro address the guards.

"I'm heading for Ōtsu," Ginjiro said. "Here are my papers."

"This doesn't list the cargo," the guard objected. "It just says 'sake.'"

"The sake shop at Ōtsu has a standing order for as many barrels as I can spare," Ginjiro said.

Footsteps thumped to the back of the cart.

"We should open these up, to make sure he's really carrying sake."

"What else would he have in there?" another voice asked.

"A cartload of spies," the first voice answered.

A flush of adrenaline passed through Hiro's muscles. He wanted to reach for his dagger, but any movement could make the barrel creak or wobble.

"I wouldn't defile my barrels with spies." Ginjiro laughed. "I brew the best sake in Kyoto."

"Smuggling pays better than sake," the voice declared. "Open them now!"

"If you ruin my sake, you'll pay for every drop," Ginjiro said. "I know my rights. My papers are in order."

"Are you threatening me?" the samurai asked.

"He's got a point," the second voice countered. "What kind of idiot puts a spy in a barrel? Anyone could open it to check. Let him go. I'm hungry, and we can't eat until this line gets through the gates."

"Fine," the samurai said, "pass through. But next time, put the number of barrels on the papers, or we're opening every one—and you can pay for the loss yourself, old man."

"Yes, sir," Ginjiro replied. "I humbly apologize for the oversight."

The cart began its journey through the barricade.

Hiro didn't relax until the sounds of the city faded behind them, leaving only the rumbling creak of the cart. But just as he relaxed, his stomach clenched.

In the rush to depart, he had forgotten Gato.

Hiro told himself that cats were resilient. Gato would find a new home. And if not, she hunted well enough to survive alone. Even so, his throat closed up. He tried not to think about Gato's fur or the rumble of her purr beneath his hand. Most people would say she was only a cat, little different than any other, but the pain in Hiro's heart said otherwise.

He would miss her deeply.

Several hours later, the cart stopped moving. Hiro had fallen asleep, but jumped awake when the movement ceased. His muscles ached from hours of confinement. He strained his ears for the sound of guards or commotion, but heard nothing.

"We're safe and alone," Ginjiro said. "I'm opening the barrels."

Cool, fresh air flooded into the barrel as the brewer lifted the lid away. Hiro stretched and pulled himself upright. He climbed out and helped Ginjiro free the others.

The cart sat beside a stand of trees that obscured the road.

"I pulled back here for privacy," Ginjiro said. "We're a couple of miles from Ōtsu. I didn't want to get too close before I let you out."

"We have to walk the rest of the way?" Luis's face grew red. "I left a pair of perfectly good horses back in Kyoto!"

"Better the horses than your head," Father Mateo pointed out.

"You should return to Kyoto," Hiro told Ginjiro. "You don't want Hisahide's guards to catch you on the road."

"I doubt he even knows you've left the city," the brewer said. "Besides, I really do have a standing order at Ōtsu. I simply moved up the delivery date."

"We'll travel separately." Hiro fastened his swords to his obi. "I don't want anyone telling the shogun's samurai we were seen together."

Ginjiro nodded. "Safe travels, Hiro. I don't know why the yoriki and Shogun Matsunaga want you dead, but I am glad they failed."

"For today, at least," Hiro said.

Ginjiro turned the cart around and started up the Tōkaidō. As he pulled away, he called back over his shoulder, "Do not worry about Suke. I'll see that he eats, and even pour him a flask from time to time."

Hiro smiled and waved. For the first time in his life, he wished a samurai could bow to a commoner without dishonor.

As the cart rumbled off, Father Mateo clutched his Bible to his chest. "Thank you for remembering this, Luis."

Hiro thought of his shinobi weapons, hidden in his room, and of the box of drugs and poisons he'd left behind. He didn't care about any of them. He could get replacements at Iga, and he had enough weapons on his person to see them through the journey. Like the priest, there was only one item Hiro truly cared about.

But his had been left behind.

Ana's basket mewed.

Hiro turned to the housekeeper in shock. "Did you bring Gato?"

"Hm. Did you think I'd leave her there to starve?" Ana lifted the lid of the basket, and Gato's tortoiseshell head peeped out, eyes squinting in the sunlight. She mewed and pulled back into the basket as if nervous about her strange surroundings.

"I brought your medicine box as well," Ana said. "In case of need."

Father Mateo looked at the basket. "Did you bring anything of your own?"

Ana drew herself to her greatest height—not much to brag about—and said, "A person of my age and experience has no need for material things."

"Now that we're safe," Luis said as they started up the road on foot, "how will we get to Yokoseura? I have enough silver to rent the horses, but Ana isn't allowed to ride."

It seemed as good a time as any to break the news.

"Only you and Ana are going to Yokoseura," Hiro said. "Father Mateo and I are going to visit my relatives, at Iga."

For a moment, Hiro worried that Luis would try to join them. The merchant wouldn't survive a day in Iga, even if Hanzo granted permission for him to stay.

"Enjoy that," Luis snorted. "When you tire of living like savages, you can join us at Yokoseura."

"I am not going to Yokoseura." Ana glared at Hiro. "Hm. I didn't risk my life to be sent off with Luis like an old kimono. Where Father Mateo goes, I go."

She set her face forward and added, "I've always wanted to go to Iga. They say there are shinobi there, and *kunoichi*"—she glanced at the priest—"that's what they call the ones who are women."

"Yes, I've heard the term," the Jesuit replied.

"Perhaps we will even see one," Ana said.

"You want to see a shinobi?" Hiro glanced at Father Mateo and scowled when he noticed the Jesuit's grin.

"Hm. When I was a little girl, I wanted to become a kunoichi," Ana said. "It wasn't possible, of course, but I'd still like to see one before I close my elderly eyes for good. They wouldn't have to worry about me telling anyone, either. A woman my age knows how to keep a secret."

She turned to Hiro and pushed her basket toward him. "Hold this. I have something in my sandal."

Luis kept walking, unwilling to wait while the housekeeper dealt with her shoe.

Ana gave Hiro a knowing look and bent to examine her foot.

A strange suspicion came over Hiro. He lifted the lid of the basket and swept his hand around the interior. Gato purred and licked his finger. He felt his medicine box, and the cat, and then his fingers struck a padded bag that made a clinking sound, as if it held a selection of metal objects.

Hiro knew at once what it contained.

It wasn't all of the shinobi weapons he left behind, just the ones that fit in the basket without impeding its other cargo, but these weapons had been hidden in the secret compartment beneath the false-bottomed chest in Hiro's room. He wondered when Ana found it, and thereby realized he was shinobi.

He doubted she would tell him, if he asked.

Ana straightened and reached for the basket. "Hm. You can give that back now—unless you intend to carry it to Iga?"

Hiro handed her the basket, and Ana started after Luis, her back as straight and her face as stern as ever.

Father Mateo looked at Hiro. "How are we going to tell her no? I can't believe she wants to go to Iga."

"And go she will." Hiro smiled at the priest. "Don't worry. She knows how to keep a secret."

ACKNOWLEDGMENTS

The list of people I want to thank gets longer with every book I write. Although my name is the one on the cover, this book was by no means a solo effort, and I am grateful to everyone who had a hand in getting both the story and me across the finish line.

To Michael and Christopher—thank you for the constant love, support, and reinforcement that allows me to spend so many hours playing with—and killing—my imaginary friends.

To my incomparable agent, Sandra Bond—thank you for finding this book a home, for all the hours you invest on my behalf, and for your friendship. I am deeply grateful.

To my editor, Dan Mayer—thank you for your considered, thoughtful approach, and for giving Hiro and Father Mateo a home; also, special thanks to Jill Maxick, Jeff Curry, Nicole Sommer-Lecht, Lisa Michalski, Hanna Etu, and everyone else at Seventh Street Books who contributed to making this book not only a reality, but better than I could have made it working on my own.

To Heather, Kerry, Julianne, Chuck, and Amanda—thank you for wielding the +10 Banhammers of Critique and the Scalpels of Peer-Editing Skill with much-needed force and precision.

To the Rocky Mountain Fiction Writers, the organization and each of its members—thank you for being my "herd"—I love you all.

To Paula, Spencer, Robert, Lola, Spencer (III), Gene, Marcie, and Bob—thank you for loving this crazy scribbler and encouraging her to follow her dreams. And to Anna and Matteo—thank you also for lending me your names.

To all of my friends—you know who you are—I wish I had the space to mention every one of you by name. I am truly blessed by your friendship and support.

And last, but certainly not least, to every reader—thank you for sharing this adventure with Hiro, Father Mateo, and me. If you liked this book, or any other, I hope you'll consider telling a friend about it. Your praise and your recommendation are the greatest rewards an author can receive.

CAST OF CHARACTERS
(IN ALPHABETICAL ORDER)

Where present, Japanese characters' surnames precede their given names, in the Japanese style. Western surnames follow the characters' given names, in accordance with Western conventions.

Ana – Father Mateo's housekeeper

Aki – an actor with the Yutoku-za

Basho – a wealthy Kyoto rice merchant

Botan – head of the Yutoku-za, a troupe of actors specializing in *nō* theater

Chou – Satsu's elder daughter; sister to Emi and Haru

Emi – Satsu's younger daughter; sister to Chou and Haru

Father Mateo Ávila de Santos – a Christian priest from Portugal, currently working in Kyoto

Gato – Hiro's cat

Ginjiro – a sake brewer; owner of Ginjiro's brewery

Hama – Basho's wife

Haru – Satsu's son; brother to Chou and Emi

Hattori Hiro – a *shinobi* (ninja) assassin from the Iga *ryu*, hired by an anonymous benefactor to guard Father Mateo; at times, he uses the alias Matsui Hiro

Jiro – Basho's apprentice

Luis Álvares – a Portuguese merchant whose weapon sales finance Father Mateo's work

Magistrate Ishimaki – a judge appointed to oversee justice in Kyoto

Matsunaga Hisahide* – a samurai warlord who seized Kyoto in June 1565

Nori – Satsu's wife

Oda Nobunaga* – a samurai warlord

Ozuru – a shinobi assassin from the Koga *ryu*, on assignment and posing as a carpenter in Kyoto

Rika – Yuji's mother

Satsu – an actor with the Yutoku-za; Nori's husband and father to Chou, Emi, and Haru

Suke – a Buddhist monk who frequents Ginjiro's brewery

Tani – Botan's elder brother

Tomiko – Ginjiro's adult daughter

Yoriki Hosokawa – a *yoriki* (assistant magistrate) in the service of Magistrate Ishimaki

Yuji – an actor with the Yutoku-za

* Designates a character who, though fictionally represented, is based upon a historical figure. [All other characters are entirely fictitious.]

GLOSSARY OF JAPANESE TERMS

D

daimyo: A samurai lord, usually the ruler of a province and/or the head of a samurai clan.

F

futon: A thin padded mattress, small and pliable enough to be folded and stored out of sight during the day.

H

hakama: Loose, pleated pants worn over kimono or beneath a tunic or surcoat.

I

ichibancha: "first picked tea"—tea leaves picked in April or early May, during the first picking of the season. *Ichibancha* is considered the highest quality, and most flavorful, type of tea.

J

jitte: A long wooden or metal nightstick with a forward-pointing hook at the top of the hand grip; carried by *dōshin* as both a weapon and a symbol of office.

K

kami: The Japanese word for "god" or "divine spirit"; used to describe gods, the spirits inhabiting natural objects, and certain natural forces of divine origin.

kanzashi: a type of hairpin worn by women in medieval Japan.

katana: The longer of the two swords worn by a samurai. (The shorter one is the *wakizashi*.)

kimono: Literally, "a thing to wear." A full-length wraparound robe traditionally worn by Japanese people of all ages and genders.

koban: A gold coin that came into widespread use in Japan during the later medieval period.

kunoichi: A female *shinobi*.

kyogen: A traditional form of Japanese theater, featuring comic or satirical plays, which was traditionally performed between *nō* plays. *Kyogen* actors were lower-ranked socially, and within the theater guilds, than actors who performed in *nō*.

M

miso: A traditional Japanese food paste made from fermented soybeans (or, sometimes, rice or barley).

N

nō (sometimes written *nô* or *noh*): A Japanese dramatic form, where the plays (customarily performed by all-male casts wearing masks) retold traditional Japanese stories through stylized recitation, song, and dance.

noren: A traditional Japanese doorway hanging, with a slit cut up the center to permit passage.

O

obi: A wide sash wrapped around the waist to hold a kimono closed, worn by people of all ages and genders.

oe: The large central living space in a Japanese home, which featured a sunken hearth and often served as a combination of kitchen, reception room, and living space.

ōtsuzumi: A hand-held, hourglass-shaped drum; one of the three types of drums used to accompany *nō* drama.

P

Pontochō: One of Kyoto's *hanamachi* (literally, a "flower town"), a district containing geisha houses, teahouses, brothels, restaurants, and similar businesses.

R

ronin: A masterless samurai.

ryu: Literally, "school." *Shinobi* clans used this term as a combination identifier and association name. (Hattori Hiro is a member of the Iga ryu.)

S

sake (also *saké*): An alcoholic beverage made from fermented rice.

-sama: A suffix used to show even higher respect than *-san*.

samurai: A member of the medieval Japanese nobility, the warrior caste that formed the highest-ranking social class.

-san: A suffix used to show respect.

seppuku: A form of Japanese ritual suicide by disembowelment, originally used only by samurai.

shinobi: Literally, "shadowed person." *Shinobi* is the Japanese pronunciation of the characters that many Westerners pronounce "ninja." ("Ninja" is based on a Chinese pronunciation.)

shite: The term for the leading actor in a *nō* drama.

shogun: The military dictator and commander who acted as de facto ruler of medieval Japan.

shogunate: a name for the shogun's government and/or the compound where the shogun lived.

shoji: a sliding door, usually consisting of a wooden frame with oiled paper panels.

shuriken: An easily concealed, palm-sized weapon made of metal and often shaped like a cross or star, which *shinobi* used for throwing or as a hand-held weapon in close combat.

T

tabi: An ankle-length Japanese sock with a separation between the big toe and other toes to facilitate the use of sandals and other traditional Japanese footwear.

tanto: A fixed-blade dagger with a single or double-edged blade measuring six to twelve inches (15-30 cm) in length.

tatami: A traditional Japanese mat-style floor covering made in standard sizes, with the length measuring precisely twice its width. *Tatami* usually contained a straw core covered with grass or rushes.

tokonoma: A decorative alcove or recessed space set into the wall of a Japanese room. The *tokonoma* typically held a piece of art, a flower arrangement, or a hanging scroll.

torii: A traditional, stylized Japanese gate most commonly found at the entrance to Shinto shrines.

U

udon: A type of thick wheat flour noodle, often served hot in soup or broth.

umeboshi: Pickled plums; a favorite Japanese snack that dates to medieval times.

W

waki: The term for a supporting actor in a *nō* drama.

wakizashi: The shorter of the two swords worn by a samurai. (The longer one is the *katana*.)

For additional cultural information, expanded definitions, and author's notes, visit http://www.susanspann.com

ABOUT THE AUTHOR

Susan Spann** is the author of three previous novels in the Shinobi Mystery series: *Claws of the Cat*, *Blade of the Samurai*, and *Flask of the Drunken Master*. She has a degree in Asian studies and a lifelong love of Japanese history and culture. When not writing or practicing law, she raises seahorses and rare corals in her marine aquarium.